MW01088186

Dare to be Wicked.

The Daring Daughters Book 1

By Emma V. Leech

Published by Emma V. Leech.

Copyright (c) Emma V. Leech 2021

Editing Services: Magpie Literary Services

Cover Art: Victoria Cooper

ISBN No: 978-2-492133-24-4

Other Works by Emma V. Leech

Daring Daughters

Daring Daughters Series

Girls Who Dare

Girls Who Dare Series

Rogues & Gentlemen

Rogues & Gentlemen Series

The Regency Romance Mysteries

The Regency Romance Mysteries Series

The French Vampire Legend

The French Vampire Legend Series

The French Fae Legend

The French Fae Legend Series

Stand Alone
The Book Lover (a paranormal novella)
The Girl is Not for Christmas (Regency Romance)

Audio Books

Don't have time to read but still need your romance fix? The wait is over…

By popular demand, get many of your favourite Emma V Leech Regency Romance books on audio as performed by the incomparable Philip Battley and Gerard Marzilli. Several titles available and more added each month!

Find them at your favourite audiobook retailer!

Acknowledgements

Thanks, of course, to my wonderful editor Kezia Cole with Magpie Literary Services

To Victoria Cooper for all your hard work, amazing artwork and above all your unending patience!!! Thank you so much. You are amazing!

To my BFF, PA, personal cheerleader and bringer of chocolate, Varsi Appel, for moral support, confidence boosting and for reading my work more times than I have. I love you loads!

A huge thank you to all of Emma's Book Club members! You guys are the best!

I'm always so happy to hear from you so do email or message me :)

emmavleech@orange.fr

To my husband Pat and my family ... For always being proud of me.

Table of Contents

Family Trees

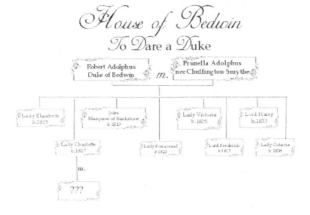

House of Bedwin
To Dare a Duke

Robert Adolphus Duke of Bedwin	*m.* Prunella Adolphus nee Chuffington-Smythe

- Lady Elizabeth b.1815
- Jules Marquess of Blackstone b.1819
- Lady Charlotte b.1817
- Lady Rosamund b.1823
- Lady Victoria b.1825
- Lord Frederick b.1827
- Lord Harry b.1833
- Lady Octavia b.1838

Lady Charlotte b.1817
m.
???

House of Hunt
To Steal a Kiss

Nathaniel Hunt	*m.* Alice Hunt nee Dowding

- Leo Hunt b.1815
- Arabella "Bella" b.1820

House of Cavendish
To Break the Rules

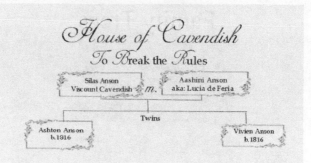

| Silas Anson
Viscount Cavendish | m. | Aashini Anson
aka: Lucia de Feria |

Twins

| Ashton Anson
b.1816 | | Vivien Anson
b.1816 |

House of Trevick
To Follow her Heart

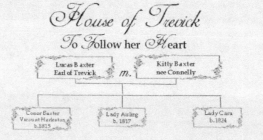

| Lucas Baxter
Earl of Trevick | m. | Kitty Baxter
nee Connelly |

| Conor Baxter
Viscount Harleston
b.1815 | Lady Aisling
b. 1817 | Lady Cara
b.1824 |

House of St Clair
To Wager with Love

| Jasper Cadogan
Earl of St Clair | *m.* | Harriet Cadogan
nee Stanhope |

Cassius Cadogan
Viscount Oakley
b.1815

House of Cadogan
To Dance with a Devil

| Jerome Cadogan | *m.* | Bonnie Cadogan
nee Campbell |

Twins

| Greer Cadogan
b.1817 | Elspeth Cadogan
b.1817 | Alana Cadogan
b.1825 |

House of Morven
To Winter at Wildsyde

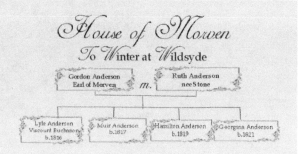

Gordon Anderson
Earl of Morven

m.

Ruth Anderson
nee Stone

Lyle Anderson
Viscount Buchanon
b.1816

Muir Anderson
b.1817

Hamilton Anderson
b.1819

Georgina Anderson
b.1821

House of de Beauvoir
To Experiment with Desire

Inigo de Beauvoir

m.

Minerva de Beauvoir
nee Butler

Hartley de Beauvoir
(adopted at Age 6)
b.1809

Kathleen de Beauvoir
(adopted at birth)
b.1824

House of Rothborn
To Bed the Baron

| Solo Weston Baron of Rothborn | m. | Jemima Weston nee Fernside |

| Larkin Weston b.1816 | Grace Weston b.1821 |

House of Knight
To Ride with the Knight

| Gabriel Knight | m. | Lady Helena Knight nee Adolphus |

| Florence Knight b.1817 | Evie Knight b.1822 | Felix Knight b.1824 | Emmaline Knight b.1826 |

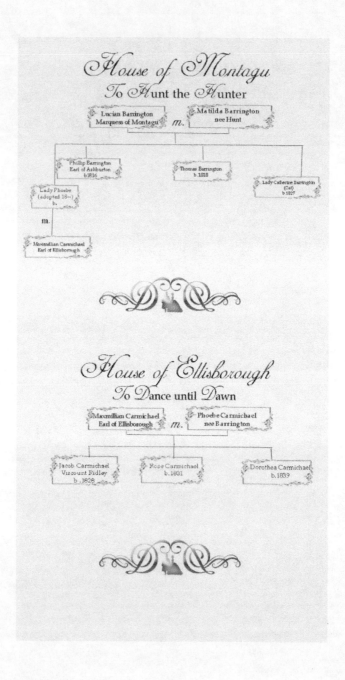

House of Montagu
To Hunt the Hunter

Lucian Barrington
Marquess of Montagu *m.* Matilda Barrington
nee Hunt

Phillip Barrington
Earl of Ashburton
b.1816

Thomas Barrington
b.1818

Lady Catherine Barrington
(Cat)
b.1827

Lady Phoebe
(adopted 18--)
b.

m.

Maximillian Carmichael
Earl of Ellisborough

House of Ellisborough
To Dance until Dawn

Maxmillian Carmichael
Earl of Ellisborough *m.* Phoebe Carmichael
nee Barrington

Jacob Carmichael
Viscount Fidley
b.1828

Rose Carmichael
b.1831

Dorothea Carmichael
b.1839

Chapter 1

It is so unfair!

Why does everyone else get to see the coronation of the new queen but me? I promised to be good and not fidget, and I'm certain my brothers were bored to tears. I cannot wait to be a grown-up like Eliza and Lottie. At least they will tell me all about it when we're all at Holbrook. Pip and Tom probably fell asleep.

—Excerpt of an entry to the diary of Lady Catherine 'Cat' Barrington, youngest daughter of the Marquess and Marchioness of Montagu.

28ᵗʰ June 1838, Beverwyck, London.

"Oh, my feet hurt!" Lottie wailed as Eliza dragged her up the steps to the front door. "I'll never dance again."

"If only you'd never speak again," Eliza muttered. After a tedious carriage ride home, the excitement of their long day had given way to exhaustion, and her legendary patience was unravelling with speed.

"If *only* you'd not lost my favourite hair clasp."

"I apologised for that," Eliza said calmly and with admirable restraint in the circumstances, forcing herself not to snap. Lottie was tired and irritable, that was all. "I shall replace it."

Lord, but her feet hurt! Her head too, and she longed for the sanctuary of her own room and her comfortable bed. Not that she would have missed the coronation of the young Queen Victoria for anything, though if anyone involved had possessed the slightest idea of how the ceremony ought to have proceeded, Eliza was quite certain the thing could have been done in little more than an hour. The *five* hours it had taken had been interminable and fraught with anxiety, as no one had seemed to know what was going on. There were already mutterings about 'yet another botched coronation.' Not a murmur of complaint had passed her lips, however. Whilst her parents had been invited, her father had paid a staggering twenty guineas apiece for the three tickets to admit his eldest children. In his view, such an historic event was not to be missed. Despite her aching head and feet, not to mention her posterior, Eliza was grateful to have been a part of it, even if moments of utter chaos had punctuated all the pomp and ceremony.

Farce had almost become tragedy as poor Lord Rolles—who was eighty if he was a day—fell down as he attempted a flight of stairs. Miraculously he'd been unhurt, but only the actions of the queen, who had kindly moved towards him to stop him making another attempt, had saved him from further harm and humiliation.

"I wasn't the one complaining about being squashed just because I fell asleep."

Eliza sighed. Lottie was still harping on, seemingly determined to wear out Eliza's temper. Lottie was the only person capable of ever undermining Eliza's unflappable calm, but somehow, she accomplished it with remarkable ease.

"You drooled on my shoulder," Eliza said tartly.

Lottie blushed, glared at her, and opened her mouth to retaliate.

"Oh, do stop bickering, children," their brother Jules protested, though at nineteen he was younger than Eliza by four years and Lottie by two. "Honestly, it makes a fellow's head hurt to be in your company for five minutes together, let alone a day like today. Mama, make them stop."

"*Children*?" Lottie retorted. "I believe you were the one who kept demanding to know when you could go home."

"Yes, yes. It has been a trying day," their mama said, her tone soothing and not quite in line with the pointed look she sent them all. "We are all tired and quarrelsome, so why do we not hold our tongues long enough to shed our hats and coats and go to bed?"

"Oh, but Mama, I'm starving!"

Jules snorted and opened his mouth to make some comment about Lottie's capacity to eat at any moment of the day or night, before catching his mother's glacial look and changing his mind.

"I shall have a tray sent to your room, dear."

Lottie favoured her brother with a smirk before smiling prettily at her mother. "Thank you, Mama."

"If you could remain silent for the time it takes you all to reach your own rooms, I should be enormously grateful," their father remarked, the amusement in his green eyes quite taking the sting out of the reprimand.

Age had not softened the Duke of Bedwin's harsh, if handsome, countenance, nor his uncompromising profile, which was the sort that might put one in mind of villains and dark deeds. Though his thick black hair was greying, he was hale and hearty and a force to be reckoned with. Unless, of course, you were their mama. One look from her and he turned to mush. Eliza smiled to herself.

"Of course, Papa," she said.

"Angel," he murmured fondly as Lottie huffed.

"You never call me angel," she grumbled, handing her hat and gloves over to a footman as their butler, young Jenkins, greeted them.

"I wonder why that could be," Papa said with a lift of one dark eyebrow. He laughed at her disgruntled expression and bent to kiss her cheek. "Go to bed, my dearest hoyden. I shall send you hot chocolate and cake. Does that soothe your temper?"

Lottie grinned at him and cast her cloak at an amused looking footman.

"Of course!" she said and danced up the stairs as if she hadn't been about to collapse from fatigue just seconds earlier.

Eliza watched her go and sighed. If only the promise of chocolate and cake could give her such a burst of energy. She was ready to drop.

"You did very well today, Eliza, I was proud of you—of all of you," her father amended, resting his hand on Jules's shoulder as he watched Lottie disappear along the upstairs landing.

Jules yawned, smothering it behind his hand. "Well, I'm dashed glad, as I've never been so bored in all my life. I hope to God the queen has a good long reign in her, for I've no desire to endure that performance again any time soon. G'night, Sir, Mama."

"Don't forget we must leave for Holbrook before midmorning," Mama warned him as he climbed the stairs.

There was an audible groan of protest, but Jules kept moving, disappearing in the same direction as his sister.

"Well, goodnight—" Eliza began, only to give a gasp of alarm. "Mama!"

Her father moved fast, catching her mother about the waist just before she fell,

"Oh!" Mama raised a hand to her head, her countenance pale. "Oh, dear."

"Prue, darling, what is it?" the duke demanded, stricken.

Eliza's mother gave them both a rueful expression. "Well, it is a little early to tell yet, but my money is on another girl, around the end of November, if I know anything."

"Mama!"

"Prue! B-But we said… we agreed… no more," her father exclaimed.

Mama snorted and returned an arch look. "Don't look at me like that. I hardly did it all by myself."

"*Mama*," Eliza said faintly, smothering her mouth with her hand and trying hard not to laugh.

Her poor father looked as if he needed a drink.

"Seven!" he said, as if he could argue her into changing her mind about it. "Deuce take it, you impossible creature, we agreed seven was quite enough."

Mama shrugged and leaned into the duke, her blue eyes soft with adoration. "But eight is such a nice round number. We shall call her Octavia."

Papa sighed and leaned down to kiss her.

"Darling," he said helplessly.

Mama's maid appeared at the top of the stairs and the duchess smiled up at her. "Perfect timing, Sally."

The woman hurried down to her mistress and gave her an arm to lean on.

The duke stared after her. "Prue, are you quite—"

"Fit as a fiddle! Just a little tired so don't start fretting over me, Robert, darling. I will be perfectly fine," the duchess said with a blithe smile. "Like shelling peas," she added with a wave of her hand and a snort of laughter as she made her way up the stairs.

"Shelling peas? Oh, good God, that woman…." her father said.

He stood, misty-eyed, watching her go—too shocked to move, Eliza suspected.

"Go to bed, Papa," Eliza urged him.

"She's not as young as she once was," he said, his voice taut with strain.

"No, but she really is fit and strong, and far too stubborn to allow anything to disturb her plans for the future. She will be fine, Papa. I'm certain of it."

He nodded, a little of the tension leaving his shoulders.

"She will," he said, with the determined air of a duke whose word was law. "She will."

"Come along," Eliza said, threading her arm through his. She caught sight of the butler, who had discreetly made himself scarce during Mama's little revelation. "Jenkins, I think perhaps Mama would like some chocolate too."

"At once, Lady Elizabeth. And yourself?" he asked, a knowing look in his eyes.

Eliza smiled. Well, why not? "Yes, please."

Young Jenkins—so called to avoid confusion, for he was the son of their last butler—moved briskly to do her bidding. She smiled at her father and walked beside him up the stairs. He said nothing more until they were halfway up.

"You must be excited to see Cassius tomorrow?"

Eliza glanced at him, unable to hide the little flush of colour she felt heating her face.

"I am," she said softly.

Her father fell silent and she got the unnerving sensation he was about to say something she wouldn't like.

"There's no need to rush into anything. You do know that? You're young yet, and he's been away a long time now. You might not suit anymore. So… you should wait and get to know him better."

"We've known each other all our lives, Papa, it's hardly a rush," she said, laughing, but her laughter died as she caught his expression.

"Yes, but…."

"*But*? Good heavens, surely you approve the match?" Eliza studied her father's face, alarmed by the concern in his eyes. Whatever did he look so anxious about?

"Of course," he said, patting her hand. "But he's been gone for two whole years. People change, feelings change, and…."

Eliza's heart thudded with apprehension. *He might not love you anymore.* The words remained unsaid, but she heard them all the same. No. That was silly. Cassius was loyal to a fault, they'd loved each other all their lives, and their lovely future was all laid out for them. It had been for years. He was to help her begin her charitable organisation. They were going to change the world and make it a better place together.

Admittedly, Cassius was only a viscount. To accomplish everything she hoped for, a duke would have been so much better, but… but he was her dearest friend, and she loved him. Surely Papa could have no objections?

"He's your friend, Eliza, your dearest friend."

"Yes," she said simply as he echoed her thoughts, perplexed.

They had reached the top of the stairs. Her father turned and took her hands. "Darling, friendship is certainly not a terrible basis for a good marriage, far from it, but… but it may not be enough.

Just don't go making any rash decisions. There is time yet. Promise me."

Eliza nodded jerkily, unbalanced by this whole conversation. She would marry Cassius. That had always been their plan. They'd never said it in so many words, but they both understood it. He'd told her these years in France would be enough to quiet his desire for travel and adventure and then he'd be ready to settle down. He was coming home from France to propose to her. Everyone knew that. They did.

Didn't they?

Lottie stared blankly out of the carriage window. She had slept heavily but not well, and her eyes were gritty and hot. The carriage was stuffy, too, and little Harry fidgeted between her and Eliza. Lottie didn't mind travelling as a rule, in fact she enjoyed it and never complained about uncomfortable carriages and long journeys. Today though she just wanted to scream at the coachman to stop and let her get out. As Mama was tired and out of sorts, her parents were travelling in their own carriage, so Lottie and Eliza were crammed in with their siblings. Understandably Jules had opted to ride for most of the journey. Like Harry, he hated being confined in a carriage for any length of time.

"Do keep still, Harry, dear," Eliza said, tucking one of her brother's dark curls behind his ear.

"I want to get out," the boy said, pouting and folding his arms. Sitting still for above two minutes together was torture of the worst kind for the child.

"I know, but we can't, not yet. And you must be pleased we are going to Holbrook. Cat will be there."

"Cat? Oh!" the boy said, brightening at once at the name of his favourite person.

Ten-year-old Lady Catherine was beloved by all, a cheeky, cheerful, beautiful child, and youngest daughter of the Marquess and Marchioness of Montagu.

"Do you suppose her brothers have changed their plans?" Ozzie asked wistfully.

Lottie looked to their siblings on the opposite bench. Rosamund, Victoria, and Frederick—or Ozzie, Torie, and Fred, as they were known by the family—regarded her with hopeful expressions.

"No, Pip and Tom have gone to stay at Mitcham Priory."

Ozzie huffed and glowered out of the window, and Lottie smiled. She knew just how the child felt. It was awful when your favourite people were far away from you. Not that the Priory was that far; it was easy enough to visit if they wished to. Being close to your favourite people was not always a blessing, though. Sometimes it was utter misery.

Stop it, she chided herself. She ought to be happy for Eliza. Eliza was good and kind and never said anything rash. She never lost her temper, unlike Lottie. Lottie was not good and kind, either. She couldn't be, or she would not be so angry, so horribly, wildly jealous. Only it wasn't fair. Cassius had left before she'd been able to make him see what was right in front of him. Was she really the only one who could see Cassius and Eliza were all wrong for each other? They were friends, yes—the best of friends, and that ought never change—but… oh, but there was no passion, no desire, no love, not of the sort Lottie wanted, the sort she saw between her parents, or between Montagu and his Marchioness.

The world still feared Montagu. Indeed, he *was* intimidating, but the way he looked at his wife… good lord, it made Lottie blush to think of it! And they were ancient, nearly fifty at least. If they still felt that way after all these years, what must it have been like when they were young? Goodness, it was a wonder they hadn't gone up in flames.

Something that Cassius refused to identify as relief unfurled in his chest. "So you forbid me to propose to her?"

Had that been a hopeful tone? Surely not.

His mother's eyes grew sharp behind her spectacles, studying him.

"Of course not," she said at once. "You are a man grown and *your* decisions are just that, but decisions have consequences, Cassius, and not just for you. I love Eliza as dearly as if she were my own child and, if I were confident you would be happy together, I would not murmur the least objection."

"But you are not confident." Cassius turned and frowned down at his father's desk, tracing a finger over an ink stain that marred the polished wood.

"Neither are you."

That was the trouble with his mother, Cassius reflected gloomily. She was a dashed sight too perceptive for a fellow's comfort and she never minced her words. He said nothing, unable to contradict her, his stomach churning with an acidic brew of guilt and anxiety.

"She's expecting me to propose to her. She's been waiting all this time. How can I—?"

"How can you marry a woman to whom your heart is not fully engaged? That would be horribly unfair to you both."

"I don't know that it isn't," Cassius replied, frustrated now. "It always used to be, but...."

But what? But he'd fallen out of love with her? No, he did not think that was it. Not exactly, for he loved Eliza just as he always had, but... *but,* damn it.

"But it's been two long years. Years in which you have changed dramatically, I can see that much with my own eyes. You've become a man, you've seen something of the world.

Childish visions of what you wanted for the future now jostle with reality, and it has shaken your resolve."

Cassius nodded, wretched. He had longed to see Eliza for months now, to tell her about everything he had seen and done, yet the closer he had got to home, the heavier the burden of his future had grown. The weight of it had sparked a thread of resentment towards his dearest friend, for which he had no explanation and for which he felt himself to be an utter brute. He promised her he would be ready to settle down on his return, a promise he now saw had been beyond foolish. His two years away had not settled his desire for travel but increased it. He'd met so many interesting people who'd told him stories of far off lands that he longed to explore. Eliza was no adventurer. She did not dream of far off places. As a child she had never quite understood the make believe games her sister Lottie had created of travelling through a foreign land, searching for lost treasure. Eliza had always been a little perplexed by the idea, though she had joined in gamely enough in the end. No, Eliza had plans for her future, grand ambitions which he had admired and encouraged, but they all began at home.

"What do I do?" he asked helplessly. "I cannot hurt her, cannot disappoint her."

His mother pushed her spectacles up her nose, set her book aside, and got to her feet before moving towards him. Her expression was grave but full of warmth as she took his hands in hers and gave a little squeeze.

"You need not do anything, not yet. Take pleasure in seeing your friend again, talk to her of everything you've done and let these weeks unfold as they will. You are among friends and family. There is time, Cassius. Maybe you will realise it was merely cold feet and she is the one you want above all others, and you may propose with a happy heart, or it may be that she too will be relieved. You are not the only one who has changed during your time apart."

Cassius nodded and let out a slow breath. He had been out with his father when Eliza and her family had arrived, and the ladies had immediately gone to change out of their travelling clothes.

"Prue has gone for a lie down, but I suggested a walk about the gardens to Bedwin and the girls." his mother said. "I always prefer to stretch my legs after a carriage journey, and it will give you a chance to introduce the friends you brought with you in an informal setting. I imagine they all will be awaiting us by now, so we had best not delay."

"It will be good to see everyone again," he said, offering his arm. "The children must have grown up so much."

"They have indeed. Fred is becoming a fine young man, and Harry quite a handful. Rosamund and Victoria promise to be every bit as lovely as their sisters, naturally."

Cassius guided his mother out onto the terrace where their guests awaited, seated beneath a shady awning. A tea tray was set out with jugs of lemonade and plates of cakes and biscuits displayed prettily among cut glass bowls of sweet peas and roses. The duke, who had been leaning against the balustrade, straightened and smiled warmly as they approached.

"Harriet, your hospitality is as wonderful as always. We so look forward to our visits to Holbrook."

"And we to having you all here. Jasper will join us shortly, and he is very much looking forward to seeing you again."

Bedwin nodded his approval and turned to Cassius. "Well, young man, your travels appear to have agreed with you. How good to see you, and looking so well."

"I am well, sir, and it is a pleasure to be home and in such excellent company."

Movement to the duke's left caught Cassius's attention, and he turned his head to discover Eliza smiling at him. She was as neat as a new pin, her presence as calm and reassuring, as dearly familiar as the scent of rain on an English summer day.

"It is good to have you home, Cassius," she said softly.

All at once his anxieties fell away, replaced by the simple pleasure of seeing his friend. They had been playmates since they were little more than months old, and no amount of fallings out and childish bickering had ever impacted on a relationship that had steadied them both through the ups and downs of their lives.

"Eliza." Cassius put out his hands to her and Eliza took them. He looked down for a moment, seeing her slender fingers engulfed by his much larger hands, her skin ivory white against his golden tan. She wore a pretty muslin gown with a small, printed pattern, and a cap of white tulle and lace and ribbons hid most of her glossy dark hair. When he met her gaze, her green eyes lit with pleasure. "It is good to see you again."

She smiled a wide, radiant smile that made him grin.

"Ah, and here is Lottie, late as usual," Bedwin said with a chuckle.

Cassius turned his head to greet Eliza's naughty little sister. Two years Eliza's junior, she had driven Eliza to distraction when they were younger, always pleading to be a part of their secrets and their games, but Cassius had always liked her and enjoyed her mad schemes. Most of the trouble they'd been caught in as children had been of Lottie's devising.

"Lottie," he began, but whatever he'd been about to say he could not fathom as his gaze settled on her and his breath caught in his throat.

He could not breathe, could not think. Time froze as a creature exploded onto the terrace, so vivacious and vibrant that everyone else seemed to be a paper cut out. She burst out of the doors in a flurry of skirts and petticoats, everything about her alive, everything in motion, running to him with every expression of joy. Before he could speak or react, she had flung her arms about his neck and Cassius was enveloped in softness and a frothy excess of femininity. Acres of lace and silk and rustling petticoats foamed about his legs like a gentle sea, and instinctively his hands went to her waist and… oh. what a waist. She was slender and yet curvaceous in all the right places, her hips flaring and… and her breasts pressing against his chest. Desire slammed into him, hot and fierce and totally unexpected, wrong-footing him so he did not know what to do, what to say. The scent of her rose about him, delicate and yet maddening. The barely there perfume of jasmine tinged with something green, something fresh and spring-like, and—*oh God*—the scent of a woman, not a child, not a girl, a *woman.*

Who in the blazes was this creature and what had she done with Lottie, the little girl with scabby knees, and arms and legs like sticks? Where was that girl with freckles and an infectious laugh that made him laugh too, no matter how blue devilled he was?

"Cassius!" she cried, such delight in that one word it was as though he'd given her the most splendid gift imaginable. "Oh, how we've missed you! How wretched of you to have been gone for so very long, and you hardly ever wrote to us. What have you been doing all this time? Have you had all the adventures you'd hoped for? Are you a marvellous artist now? Are you the talk of France? Did you go to Paris and have lots of scandalous love affairs?"

"*Lottie,*" her father protested. "Calm yourself, child. Put the poor man down and don't be so impertinent, you wretched creature. You might remember you are a young lady. However is the poor man to answer a single question if you keep adding another before he can draw a breath?"

"Sorry," Lottie said, chastened, colour flushing her cheeks.

To his regret, she unwound her arms from his neck and took a step back. He hated the look of mortification in her eyes and wanted to take it away, but she carried on, quieter now.

"I'm so sorry, Cassius. I did not mean to embarrass you. I got carried away. Only it's so wonderful to have you home again."

Cassius stared at her. His heart was thudding too hard behind his ribs and he felt giddy and disorientated, as if he'd been hit with a brick. The world had changed around him. This new version of it looked the same but was not the same at all, and neither was he.

"That's all right," Cassius said, finding his tongue at last, which appeared to have been temporarily nailed down. Good God, what had happened in the time he'd been away? Was this… this *goddess* truly Lottie, the girl he'd known all his life, the girl he'd helped teach to ride and laughed with and pulled out of more muddy puddles than he could count? When had she transformed from the gawky, awkward little scrap of mischief he'd known into… into….

His heart gave a definitive and uncomfortable thud behind his ribs, and Cassius knew without a doubt that he was in a world of trouble.

Nicolas Alexandre Demarteau leaned against the wall, regarding his half-brother, Louis César de Montluc, the Comte de Villen, with amusement.

"*Arrêtez*," Louis said, catching his eye in the mirror.

Nicolas snorted, aware that Louis hated being observed when he was getting ready. His valet, a precise Englishman by the name of Elton, fussed about like an aggravating bluebottle, adjusting here and there and brushing invisible fluff from his master's exquisite person. Elton took his work seriously, and why not? The man considered himself an artist, and if an artist were to show his work to advantage, he needed the very best canvas available.

Blessed with thick dark hair, the looks and physique of a young god and those startling blue eyes, Louis César de Montluc was most certainly that.

"If you have quite finished primping?"

"*Oui*," Louis replied, giving an impatient click of his tongue.

"English, Louis," Nic reprimanded him.

For that he was rewarded with an arctic glare.

"I am quite finished. Thank you for your patience, Nicolas. A pity you did not take five minutes longer on your own toilette or, indeed, five minutes." Louis flicked an elegant finger at Nic's cravat and sighed. "*Quelle horreur.*"

Nic batted his hand away. "Come along, we did not come 'ere for the fun of it."

"*H*ere," Louis corrected him with a smirk.

Nic glowered with irritation. "As you say, brother. We did not come *h*ere for our *h*ealth."

Louis's eyebrows quirked. "Really? I thought that was precisely why we'd come."

"Very well, if you need me to remind you what this is all for. We have come so you may woo the eligible Lady Elizabeth Adolphus and marry the girl as soon as may be and take your rightful place in society."

Louis snorted, a flash of some dark emotion glinting in his eyes.

"My rightful place," he said in disgust.

"It *is* your right," Nic said, angry now. "And after everything we've done, I'll not let you mess it up now. Your blood is as pure as the duke's, and don't you forget it."

"I am unlikely to do so, when my very own guard dog growls the truth of it at me whenever I am in danger of enjoying myself," Louis said with a wry smile. "Come along then, Nic, let us play nicely with the ladies and gentlemen, and do try not to bite anyone."

Nic favoured his brother with a smile that showed too much of his teeth, and Louis laughed as he opened the door and walked out.

They made their way down the stairs and were greeted by the butler who led them through the building. Nic tried not to stare about him like some country bumpkin, but he had never seen a house as vast, as lavish, or as ancient as Holbrook. Not in daylight, at least. Creeping about in the dead of night was a more familiar experience.

The brothers had accumulated a vast fortune between them in Paris, and Louis César had made a name for himself in society. Not an *entirely* respectable one, but marriage to the right girl would do a great deal to smooth his way, to bring him acceptance among the higher echelons of society where he ought to be welcomed with open arms. They had been working to that end, despite the rumours about their past and the suspicion that still clung to them, and then that damned letter had arrived, threatening to ruin everything. They had decided they would do well to leave Paris. After all, English society was far more rigid, more demanding of respectability. If they could triumph here, no one would ever look down their noses at Louis César again.

Nic could not say the same for himself, having committed the heinous crime of illegitimacy—as if he had a choice in the matter—but he cared nothing for that. People could look down at him to their hearts' content if his brother and their illustrious bloodline were secured for generations to come. So here they were, having befriended Viscount Oakley during his time in France, and having heard much of the house party his parents gave each year. The Marquess of Montagu would be here, and they had met his daughter some years ago in circumstances the marquess would certainly wish to keep quiet. Not that they would tell tales, but it was a connection they had every intention of using to the full. Most important, though, was the information pertaining to the Duke and Duchess of Bedwin, and more specifically their lovely daughters.

The two eldest girls were of age, and Nic had wondered if Cassius had any interest in either of them. He had told Nic and Louis at some length of their beauty and accomplishments, but he only ever spoke of them with the affectionate tones of a proud older brother. Nic hoped that was the case, at least, for the viscount had become a good friend, and it would grieve them both to hurt him by interfering with any romantic plans he may have. Indeed, Nic had been enchanted by his stories of the two sisters, especially by the description of Eliza. From what Cassius said, and the little pencil sketch he'd done to illustrate, Nic had imagined her as some angelic vision of goodness. She seemed to him to embody every charm and quality that a man could wish for in a wife. She would be perfect for Louis. Impeccable lineage, good-natured, kind and gentle... the perfect wife, and a good mother. How could Louis fail to be happy with such a sweet creature at his side? Especially if she was as lovely as Cassius had indicated.

The butler guided them out onto a sunny terrace and Nic was struck at once by how quintessentially English and charming it was. A far cry from the life they had lived in France.

These past years, Louis had been forced to distance himself from the world they had created at Rouge et Noir—the most exclusive and infamous club in Paris—but Nic had lived it to the full. A life filled with wickedness and vice, and a world apart from this picture of the perfect English summer day, from the pretty china tea set, and the table laid with mouth-watering cakes and biscuits, to the crystal bowls filled with sweet peas and roses and... and... *her.*

A young woman sat at the table, a cup and saucer in hand. Her head was tilted towards Cassius, the ghost of a smile hovering at her lips. Her posture was upright, her expression serene, the perfect English rose. Nic's heart gave a most uncharacteristic thud in his chest. Longing rose inside him like a tide and no matter how he forced it down, it swelled inside him, pushing at his ribs. *Non, Non. Dieu ayez pitié, s'il vous plaît pas cela.* Oh no. Oh, no, no. For God's sake. It was utterly ridiculous....

Cassius stood to greet them, and introductions were made around Nic, greetings and exchanges of names. He moved through it in a daze, waiting for the moment he discovered her name, though he knew it already, knew with some sick sense of inevitability that the universe was laughing at his expense.

"And these lovely creatures you must know already, for I have told you so much about them."

"Lady Elizabeth," Nic said, hearing his voice as if someone else had spoken, unable to tear his gaze from the embodiment of his wildest dreams. Her name escaped him before he could stop it and before he could hide the unguarded look he felt sure must be in his eyes.

"Yes!" Cassius said, grinning. "You see, Eliza? Your fame travels before you."

The young woman blushed and raised her gaze to Nic, revealing thickly lashed eyes the colour of absinthe and likely as dangerous.

"I am most pleased to meet you, sir," she said.

Oh, mon Dieu.

Chapter 3

Dear diary,

It is so lovely to be back at Holbrook. All the Adolphus family are here. I do like Fred very much, for we are about the same age and he never treats me like he thinks me a silly girl, and little Harry is so funny. He adores me – naturally – and it is wonderful to be among friends. I do hope Lady Helena and Gabriel come too, though Papa says there is some urgent problem with the laying of their railway line, and they may need to postpone their visit. I hope not, for I was looking forward to seeing Florence, Evie and Felix, and – I suppose – Emmeline too, for she is my best friend. Even if she is an insufferable know-it-all.

Today we met some friends of Cassius. A Mr Demarteau and his brother, who is a Count. The Comte de Villen. Isn't it a marvellous name? Like a wicked seducer in a Gothic novel. He looks wicked too. No man that handsome can be entirely good. I do hope not anyway, for I want there to be some excitement over the holidays. There must be a romance, perhaps a scandal too. Nothing truly horrid, only the exciting kind where everything works out in the end. Mama says I must not read Mrs Radcliffe again until I am older, for I am precocious and will turn out to be a dreadful creature and go to the devil if she does not keep me in hand. I think she is teasing me.

Everyone believes Cassius will ask Eliza to marry him, but I don't think Eliza wants to. At least, if she does, she ought not to have blushed so when she was introduced to Mr Demarteau. Lottie though, my word, if she doesn't have a care and stop gazing at Cassius like he's the last cream cake in the entire world, everyone will know she's in love with him. Everyone but him, likely, for my sister Phoebe says men are remarkably slow to notice such things.

I cannot wait to grow up and fall in love. I hope that it will be romantic and exciting and something we can tell our children like the duchess wrote Mama and Papa's story in The Eagle and the Lamb. They think I have not read it but I have. It is all very well reading about it in books, though, but to live it… Well, I am certainly too young, even I know that, so I must content myself with watching everyone else. I shall tell you everything too, of course. Fear not.

Oh, what a summer it will be!

—Excerpt of an entry to the diary of Lady Catherine 'Cat' Barrington, youngest daughter of the Marquess and Marchioness of Montagu.

30th June 1838, Holbrook House, Sussex.

Lottie made her way down to the breakfast parlour, relieved to discover she was among the first to rise. Usually Eliza beat her to it, but her sister had been in a strange mood last night, oddly distracted. At dinner, Lottie had found she'd had to repeat the same question three times before she could gain a sensible answer, which was most unlike Eliza. Apparently she'd had a headache. If Eliza admitted she had a headache, that likely meant she had the most appalling megrim, for the woman would never utter a word that would cause anyone else any trouble or discomfort. She was far too good. It was a little sickening sometimes.

"Oh, Cassius!" Lottie exclaimed with delight, immediately cursing herself for making such a fuss about finding him alone at the breakfast table. Of course he'd be here. He lived here, did he not?

For a moment he stilled, giving her a look she could not decipher. Most likely he was wishing her to the devil, for she would spoil his quiet breakfast. He'd looked to be deep in thought as she'd come in, after all, and now she was so giddy with nerves she would not be able to stop herself from babbling. Mama always said she had tongue enough for two sets of teeth when she was anxious. Besides, Cassius must prefer Eliza's quiet calm to Lottie's chaos if they were to marry. Eliza had always spent the time they were all together trying to evade her sister. It had been most unfair, too, for she'd only wanted their company. Well, *his* company.

He stood as she entered, smiling politely. "Good morning, Lottie. This is an unexpected pleasure. What are you doing up so early?"

"Oh, well, the sun came streaming through the window this morning and I simply could not stay in bed when it was such a beautiful day. There is so much I want to do, and I cannot decide what to do first. Which of course means I shall drift about doing nothing at all and driving everyone quite mad while I demand to know what they are doing, and can I join in?" Lottie snapped her mouth shut, aware she had done precisely as she feared, and let her wretched tongue run away with her. She shot Cassius a nervous glance to see if he looked annoyed, but there was an arrested expression on his face she could not read. Probably he was stunned at quite how irritating she could be in such a short space of time.

She flashed him a grateful smile as he pulled out the chair beside him and made a promise to herself to keep her blasted mouth shut. He settled back to his breakfast and, once he was occupied, Lottie glanced at him from beneath her eyelashes. Her heart squeezed in her chest. Good Lord, it was so unfair that a man be as beautiful as that. It hurt to look at him. What chance did a girl have when a fellow went about looking like that? It should be made law that he carry a warning sign about his neck advising impressionable young ladies to keep their distance.

Why had her mother not kept them apart? She was usually such a sensible woman. Had she failed to notice her friend's son had become a temptation beyond bearing? Beauty like that was dangerous. It had to be.

Her gaze drifted back to him. The sun that streamed into the bright room glinted on his blond hair and highlighted a strong, square jaw. He had a little cleft in his chin, and those beautiful eyes were thickly lashed and—*oh, those magnificent shoulders.*

She sighed.

Well, he could hardly be surprised if one fell in love with him, could he? *Would* he be surprised, she wondered? Would he care? Or would he laugh and think her a silly little chit? The idea made her cheeks heat. No doubt she appeared naïve and gauche compared to all the girls he'd met on his travels. She knew he'd spent time in Paris, after all, and she could only imagine how the sophisticated French women had reacted to his masculine beauty. No doubt they'd have climbed over each other to get to him. She pushed the thought away as jealousy stirred.

"It is a lovely day," Cassius said, breaking into her thoughts. "And I expect Mother has made plans to entertain you all, so you need not fear being bored. She is quite adept at telling you what it is you wish to do. Strangely, she is usually correct, too."

"I like your mama," Lottie said, making a valiant effort to stop swooning and sighing and eat something. It wasn't easy. Determinedly, she reached for a fresh bread roll and concentrated on the conversation. "She's always been very kind and welcoming to us, though she's awfully intimidating. I'm sure she thinks me an utter ninny."

Cassius laughed, a deep rich sound that so delighted her she dropped the roll and it bounced off her plate and onto the floor. "Oh, drat!"

A footman leapt forward and swept the roll up before offering Lottie another. *Oh, elegantly done, Lottie dear.* She cringed, not daring to meet Cassius's eye. No wonder he wanted to marry Eliza. *She* would never do something so horribly embarrassing as juggle her breakfast. Still, at least her perfect sister had not been here to see it. Small mercies.

"She really doesn't."

Lottie looked up, a little perplexed.

"My mother doesn't think you a ninny."

"Well, a good job she was not here this morning, or she'd likely change her mind," Lottie said with a bright smile, though her stomach was tight. What was she playing at? She ought to have run in the other direction the moment she found Cassius here alone. As if she hadn't made a spectacle enough of herself yesterday when she's seen him for the first time. Not that she'd meant to. Lottie had meant to show him how she'd grown into an elegant young lady like her sister, well-mannered and sophisticated, but her heart had other ideas. The moment she'd seen him she'd wanted to burst with joy, and it had all escaped her, bubbling up in an embarrassing show of adoration that Cassius had clearly found excruciatingly embarrassing. She'd put him so far out of countenance he'd been dumbstruck, and he had barely met her eye ever since. No doubt that was why Eliza had been so distant and out of sorts last night, too. Why would she not be when her own sister made such a fool of herself over the man *she* intended to marry? The idea made Lottie's stomach twist.

"Lottie?"

She blinked, realising too late she'd been staring miserably at her plate without saying a word.

"What's wrong?" he asked.

She turned to Cassius, finding her heart swell at the concern in his eyes, at the soft tone of his voice. His eyes were the oddest shade. Turquoise, like his father's. They were so beautiful it made her ache inside, and his voice… She sighed again, knowing she was ridiculous, but his voice was deep and rumbled deliciously. It made her shiver, helpless with longing. Was she going mad? It seemed like a kind of madness, to want him with such ferocity. She had loved Cassius before he'd left with a childish passion for his sense of adventure, his irrepressible laughter, and his kindness. Now though that love had a new element, a passionate desire to touch him, to feel his hands upon her that made her all on edge, as if she really was losing her mind. The temptation to get up and throw herself into his lap, to wrap her arms about him and demand he kiss her was so tantalising she feared she might do it. She wondered what he would do if she did, what he would say if she confessed all, if she told him she loved him, hopelessly and desperately, and that she feared something in her would wither and die if she must watch him marry Eliza. She must go away once they were wed. Perhaps she would go to France, but no, she would be bound to visit all the places he had been and wonder what he had thought of it, and if he had painted it, and if the sunlight had been the exact same shade of gold and… and good God, she was revolting.

"Lottie?"

"Nothing!" she said, sending him a blinding smile of such force she was surprised her jaw didn't crack. "I'm just not used to being up so bright and early. It's a shock to the system."

Cassius gave a slightly nervous laugh and Lottie tried to swallow her misery and mortification by stuffing her mouth full of bread and butter. She could not taste it. Her throat was so tight she could barely swallow. The bread promptly got stuck and she was compelled to take a large gulp of tea to force it down.

"Good morning."

Lottie looked up to see her sister enter the room. Oh, just what she needed.

Eliza was perfect as usual and made Lottie feel too fussy in her bright blue gown with white ribbons and lace. Today, Eliza wore an understated morning dress of fawn silk with bishop sleeves that narrowed at her slender wrists. It was simply cut and exquisite, quite different from Lottie's frills and lace and bows, but she adored pretty things and could never resist a ruffle. Now, Lottie felt childish, whilst Eliza looked as effortlessly beautiful as always, though Lottie well knew it would have taken her an age to achieve the tumble of thick dark curls that framed her lovely face. She experienced a stab of unwelcome jealousy and the bite of bread roll felt like a lump of lead, cold and heavy. She pushed her plate away, the rest of the roll uneaten.

"Are you sure you are quite well?"

Cassius's voice was low and filled with concern. Lottie turned to find him watching her and hated herself for stealing his attention when he ought to be fussing over Eliza.

"Yes, of course. Just not terribly hungry," she said, forcing a smile to her lips. Misery rose inside her, smothering her until she wanted to sink into the floor.

Eliza had barely sat down when the rest of the family tumbled in, with all the attendant noise and chaos that the Adolphus brood generally brought with them. Mama rounded up Harry, who was filling his plate with plum cake, and had a word with Fred before he could stuff down every last sausage, and the room filled with merry chatter, for which Lottie was vastly grateful. As everyone found their places a shadow cast over the room and she looked up to see the towering figure of Mr Demarteau filling the doorway. He was large indeed, and did not look like a nobleman, but then she remembered being told that Nicolas Alexandre Demarteau was the beautiful Comte's illegitimate half-brother. The two men seemed very close, with Demarteau hovering about his younger brother like a guardian protector. Certainly his expression was daunting, and those black eyes… Lottie shivered, and then followed his fierce gaze to discover it had settled on Eliza. There was a place still beside her, but Demarteau looked at it, frowned, and turned away, choosing to sit instead on the far side of the table next to their little brother Harry. Lottie glanced back to see if Eliza had noticed and saw a dull red flush on her sister's cheeks. A surge of anger burst inside her to see Eliza so mortified. No man would ever choose to sit next to a child instead of beside a beautiful woman unless he meant to slight her. How dare the man act so, and why? Eliza was exquisite and her manners were perfection, so she could not possibly have offended him.

"Lottie. Lottie, whatever is wrong? Are you quite certain you are well?"

Lottie turned again to discover Cassius staring at her in alarm, his gaze settling on her hand which seemed to have clamped itself around the butter knife so hard her knuckles were white. She dropped it with a clatter, which made Eliza wince.

"Sorry, no, I… I seem to have something of a headache. Do excuse me, I think I shall take a walk," she said in a rush, and hurried from the room before she could do or say anything to make herself even more ridiculous.

"Wait!"

Lottie paused just outside the door to see Eliza had followed her.

"May I come too? I'm afraid my headache is no better this morning either. I expect the excitement of the coronation and travelling yesterday has caught up with us both."

"Of course, and yes, I'm certain that's it," Lottie agreed, hardly in a position to tell her sister the truth.

"You do look peaky," Eliza said with a frown of concern, laying the back of her hand to Lottie's forehead. "You're not coming down with something?"

Lottie's heart ached at the worry in Eliza's voice. If only her sister wasn't such a good person, perhaps then she would not feel like such a wicked creature for loving the man Eliza wished to marry and wanting him for herself. But Eliza *was* good, and so Lottie must be wicked, for she did love him, and want him, and whatever was she to do? She felt she would run mad before very much longer and they were to be here for three whole weeks. The season was yet in full swing and Lottie had suggested she remain in London, staying with her Aunt Helena and Uncle Gabe, as business was keeping her uncle in town, but Mama had been adamant. They had endured endless parties and social events since April and she thought Lottie looked worn to a thread. Little did her mama know it was nothing to do with dancing till all hours and going to bed closer to dawn than dusk, but the sleepless nights spent thinking of Cassius and everything she was about to lose. Not that you could lose something that was never yours to begin with.

They both gave a sigh of relief once they were out of doors. It was warm already and promised to be a glorious day.

Lottie glanced at her sister, noting the tense line between her eyebrows. Eliza looked back at her. "You saw, didn't you?"

Lottie nodded. "Whyever did he do it?"

Eliza let out a breath. "Oh, thank heavens. You mean to say you don't know either? I was terrified I'd made some obvious *faux pas* and offended him without even realising it."

Lottie snorted at the idea. "Don't be such a silly goose. As if you could. You've never offended anyone in your entire life!"

Eliza stared her at in disbelief.

"Oh, well, I'm different. We're sisters, we're bound to bicker, and you know I enjoy a good argument and you will provoke me by being so... so...."

"What?" Eliza demanded, her tone one of indignation.

"Bloody perfect!

"Lottie!" Eliza exclaimed in shock.

"*See*?" Lottie said triumphantly. "Even Mama swears when she's terribly cross."

Eliza huffed. "Well, why did he do it, then? He practically gave me the cut direct and yet yesterday, when he first saw me, I...."

"You what?"

Eliza shook her head, frowning. "Oh, I don't know. I'm being foolish and reading too much into it, I'm sure."

"Well, it *was* odd."

"What was odd?" piped up a little voice.

"Oh, good morning, Cat," Lottie said, holding out her hand to the little girl.

Cat took it, falling into step with them. "Do you mean Mr Demarteau?"

"Oh, good lord, did everyone see?" Eliza demanded in horror.

Cat shook her head. "Oh, no. Everyone else was too hungry, but I'd had breakfast hours ago. I only came back to see Fred and tell him to meet me in the stables once he was done. If he can move after eating so many sausages, that is."

"He does like sausages," Lottie said with a fond smile.

"I think you must remind him."

"Of sausages?" Lottie asked, frowning.

"What? Oh, no," Cat said, shaking her head. "Of someone he loved."

"Who did Fred love?" Eliza asked in alarm.

"Not Fred!" Cat sent them an expression of pure exasperation. "Mr Demarteau. I think he must have loved someone who looked like you. Perhaps she died in the reign of terror. She might have been an aristocrat and had her head cut off, and he's still pining for her."

"My goodness, child, what an imagination you have," Eliza said, laughing even though her hand went to her throat. "The revolution was over forty years ago. Just how old do you think he is?"

"Quite old," Cat admitted.

Lottie spluttered. "Darling, he can be no more than thirty-five at the very most."

"That *is* quite old," the girl protested, which sent them both off into peals of laughter.

"Oh, I'm so glad you came, Cat," Eliza said with a sigh. "I feel so much better."

Chapter 4

Dear diary,

I am certain there is something going on.

Eliza wishes to speak to Cassius alone, but he is avoiding her and Lottie is as jittery as a cat on hot coals whenever Cassius is around. Eliza can't keep her eyes from Mr Demarteau and Mr Demarteau will leave a room the moment she enters. Meanwhile, everyone can see that Eliza has caught the comte's eye and he intends to court her.

Oh, this will be vastly entertaining. Better even than Mrs Radcliffe!

—Excerpt of an entry to the diary of Lady Catherine 'Cat' Barrington, youngest daughter of the Marquess and Marchioness of Montagu.

30ᵗʰ June 1838, Holbrook House, Sussex.

"So, this is where you are hiding."

Cassius looked up, an unwelcome flush of heat making a slow crawl up his neck. Eliza was framed in the doorway of the summerhouse, her trim figure backlit by the bright afternoon sunlight outside. Her words made something hot and uncomfortable squirm in his belly, for although she was teasing him without a hint of reproach, he had indeed been hiding from her.

"Mother has given me leave to use the summerhouse as my studio," he said, gesturing to the chaos of packing boxes filled with paints and art materials, and the stacks of canvases he had brought back from France piled against the walls.

"It makes a perfect studio," she observed with a nod, looking about her with interest.

"Yes, the big windows make it wonderfully light and the view over the lake is one I shall never tire of. It is away from the house, too, and free of distractions."

"Oh," she said, hesitating on the threshold. "I—"

"Oh no!" Cassius said in a rush. "I never meant you. You could never be a distraction to me, Eliza. Er... I mean...."

What the hell *did* he mean? He wondered as Eliza stared at him with a puzzled expression. Except he had been distracted from everything since the moment Lottie had burst onto the terrace and back into his life. He'd been able to think of nothing else but the vivacity he'd seen in her eyes, her obvious joy in seeing him, and... and he could not help but wonder....

Eliza gave him a kind smile. "It must be strange to be home after your adventures. No doubt it will take you a week or so to settle back to it after the excitement of everything you've seen and done."

Cassius let out a breath and picked up one of the small earthenware jars he stored his paints in to keep them fresh. How typical of Eliza to remove any tension, to put him at his ease. It was what he liked most about her, how easy she was to be with, how she smoothed away the wrinkles in life with a soft word, and a kind gesture. It was gift few people possessed.

"Yes. I admit I'm all at sixes and sevens. I seem unable to settle to anything, even painting, so I thought I would arrange the studio."

"And perhaps arrange your disordered mind at the same time," Eliza said with a twinkle in her eyes.

Cassius laughed. "Quite so."

He watched her as she moved about the studio, touching the bristly tops of paintbrushes stuffed in a jar and inspecting bottles of walnut oil.

"Cassius," she said, the way she spoke his name clearly the prelude to something significant.

His stomach tightened.

"Oh, here you are!"

Lottie appeared in the doorway and Cassius jolted in shock. The sun caught the gold of her hair, shimmering around the edges, giving her the appearance of an angel with a halo of light glowing about her. Heat rushed over him, memories of the Lottie he had known for so long crashing into the vision before him. Mischievous Lottie, causing havoc and making him laugh, teasing him and playing tricks coalesced into this mystical vision that he wanted to paint, wanted to touch, wanted to do bad, bad things with. Longing rose inside him, the force of it knocking the air from his lungs. Cassius dropped the jar.

It hit the floor with a crash and the dozen or so pig's bladders stored inside burst on impact. Cobalt blue and crimson lake burst against cadmium yellow and viridian, chrome orange and lead white. A rainbow of colour splattered everything from his boots and the empty fireplace to the hem of Eliza's gown.

"Oh!" she said in consternation, jumping back too late to avoid the patter of ruinous oil paint against the delicate fawn silk of her gown.

"Eliza!" Cassius exclaimed, mortified. "My God, I'm so sorry, I... Damnation, I'm a bloody fool!"

Eliza looked up at him in shock. "It's only a little paint, Cassius."

"But it's ruined," he said, his throat tightening. "It's quite ruined."

"It's just a gown, Cassius. I have many more, and my maid is a marvel, you know. No doubt she'll have some clever method of having it cleaned or a way to disguise the damage. There's no harm done."

Cassius watched as Eliza hurried away to repair the damage to her gown, too aware he had not been speaking of the dress at all. He would ruin everything, damage a friendship that had lasted their whole lives if he gave into this overwhelming desire for her sister. Cassius looked up to see Lottie dithering just inside the door, wringing her hands together.

"It's my fault, isn't it?" she said miserably.

"What?" he asked in alarm, wondering if his feelings were so bloody obvious.

"I erupted in on you like... like an explosion and..." She gave an unhappy huff of laughter and gestured at the mess of colour on the ground. "I always leave a trail of destruction, though, don't I? You must remember that much about me. I was always forcing myself upon you both, spoiling your games."

Cassius did not remember her spoiling anything. Now he thought about it he realised she had made everything more exciting, finding adventure when Eliza would have stayed closer to home. He looked down at the paint for he could not look at her. Each bladder was about the side of a walnut and every one had detonated to create a starburst of paint. He stared down, finding a smile tugging at his mouth as he saw the pattern it had created: a joyous, vibrant blaze of colour against the dull background of the floor beneath. It was too perfect an analogy for the dazzling creature before him and the effect she'd had on the world about her.

"I think it's beautiful."

Lottie shook her head, clearly feeling wretched. "You are just being kind. It's a dreadful mess."

"No. Look."

He held out his hand to her, gesturing for her to come closer. She did, and his breath caught as she placed her fingers upon his.

"See how the yellow has burst over the green and blue, and those little speckles of red and the white over there, like stars."

Lottie gave a soft laugh of delight and the sound thrilled inside of him. It lit him up, catching at his heart, making him feel lighter, making him feel nothing was impossible.

"Fireworks!" she said, turning to stare at him, her great blue eyes alight with pleasure.

"Fireworks," he repeated, unaccountably breathless, staring at her as something similar burst in his chest, little blasts of sensation lighting him up inside because she was near him, gazing at him like he had hung the moon. She liked him. Well, he knew she had always admired him, in an awestruck, girlish way. Was... Was this the same, or was it...?

She looked away suddenly and withdrew her hand from his grasp. The distance between them grew as she moved back, heading towards the door. He wanted to follow her.

"Still, it is the most awful mess," she said. "You should punish me by making me clear it up myself. My mother would, I assure you."

"I think I shall leave it as it is and let it dry, and then I shall always remember you."

Not that there was anything in the world capable of making him forget her, or the way she had made his entire world ignite into the most extravagant carnival of colours he could imagine. Had it been only yesterday? And yet she had always been there. He had just not taken the time to notice. Lottie had always been in his life, making him laugh, entertaining him with her joyous nature and her nose for mischief. She was the one who had dragged him and Eliza on escapades, and she was the one who had forced Eliza to think of adventures of her own in a bid to escape her.

"Yes, you may remember me and the dreadful mess I make of everything," she retorted, with such bitterness that his breath caught.

"Lottie, I didn't mean—"

"I should go."

She ran out in a flurry of skirts, but Cassius thought he'd heard her voice quaver, heard something fragile and hopeless in her words that he could not bear.

"*Lottie!*"

He went to go after her but could not walk through the paint so had to step back and around, squeezing past packing crates, and by the time he got to the door, she was out of sight.

Lottie caught up with her sister, dragging her by the arm. "You must get to Agatha before the paint dries, she might have a chance then."

"Lottie, you know as well I do there will be no cleaning oil paint from this silk. I just didn't want Cassius to fret about it. He looked so mortified, the poor man."

"Yes, and it was all my fault."

Lottie felt sick. She had been wild with jealousy when she'd realised her sister was inside the studio, alone with Cassius. Though she had not meant to eavesdrop, she had heard the way Eliza had said his name, recognised her tone, and knew she was building up to broach a delicate topic. Lottie knew Eliza had wanted to discuss their betrothal and she had reacted without thinking, wanting only to delay the inevitable. She may as well fling herself in the path of an oncoming train in the hope of stopping it for all the difference it would make. Eliza and Cassius had been on this road for too many years and everyone knew it. If she got involved, if she tried to interfere, she would shame herself, expose herself for the horrid, jealous creature she was and give everyone a disgust of her, especially Eliza and Cassius. It was unthinkable. She would lose her sister and the man she loved and be left alone, with nothing and no one.

Oh, she was going to weep. No. No, she must not.

"It wasn't your fault either, you silly goose," Eliza said with a laugh, taking her arm.

Lottie swallowed hard and forced her voice not to tremble. "Of course it was. I made him jump."

"Nonsense, the pot was slippery with oil, like everything else in the room," she added, holding up her gloves which bore greasy marks on the fingertips.

"Oh, there you are, girls. Good heavens, Eliza, what have you been doing?"

The sisters looked up as their mother accosted them, staring in dismay at Eliza's ruined gown.

"A little accident with some paint, Mama."

Their mother glanced at Lottie.

"Yes, it was my fault," Lottie said gloomily. There, even her mama knew any disaster was more than likely her doing, even if she never reproached her for it. She was a walking accident just waiting for a place to happen, generally when there would be the most devastation possible.

"Well, never mind, accidents happen. Do you know, I've lost *two* pairs of gloves since we arrived, and I cannot fathom where the devil they've gone to? Sally is dreadfully cross with me."

She held out her inky fingers and they both laughed. Their darling mama was a writer of some renown, and her fingers were generally ink-stained. She tried to hide them with gloves but, as she could not write with gloves on and the urge to jot down an idea would come over her at the oddest moment, she would take out her notebook and shed her gloves accordingly. They turned up in the most peculiar places. As children, their favourite bedtime story had been one their mother had written about a pair of gloves separated by accident, and the adventures they had endured before they were once again reunited. She seemed convinced they had a life of their own. As a child, Lottie had believed it too.

"Anyway, do run along and get changed. The comte has asked if he might escort you on a walk to the village."

"Me?" Eliza asked in surprise.

"No, child, I meant to address Harry… of course you! Whyever not? He's an eligible gentleman, and a stunningly beautiful specimen too, if I'm any judge."

"Mama!" they said in unison.

The duchess smirked at them. "Girls, I am not in my dotage yet, and I have eyes in my head. Besides, a fellow like that is hard to miss."

"But isn't he a little… scandalous?" Eliza said.

Lottie regarded the rising colour in her sister's cheeks and realised she was nervous.

"Oh, pish." Mama waved a hand in irritation. "So was your father. You must decide for yourself what kind of man he is, and it is only a walk. Matilda and Harriet and I will chaperone, so it is quite unexceptional. I'm certain Cassius would not have brought people to his home if he believed any ill of them. Lottie, you may come too and keep his brother company. Now, I believe he *is* rather scandalous, but I shall keep a close eye so there is nothing to worry about."

"Come along, Eliza. It will be fun," Lottie urged, refusing to consider her own motivation for getting her sister to spend time with a man who was not Cassius.

Eliza shrugged. "Very well. I shall get changed and be down directly."

Chapter 5

Dearest Harriet,

You must be so happy to have Cassius back home with you again. At this exact moment I could certainly wish my children in France for there is never a moment's peace in the castle. I do not mean it, of course, but I should be pleased if they could keep their tempers in check for above five minutes together. Four such headstrong young people make the castle appear far too small to hold us all. Lyall and Georgina especially enjoy rattling the old walls, bellowing back and forth at each other. I am more than tempted to take up the offers I have had from many of the Peculiar Ladies and send the lot of them away in different directions. Of course, the moment I do so, I shall regret it and miss them all horribly.

— *Excerpt of a letter to Harriet Cadogan, Countess St Clair from her good friend Ruth Anderson, Countess of Morven.*

30th June 1838, Holbrook Village, Sussex.

"I'm afraid you will find the village quaint and rather dull after your time in Paris," Lottie said, looking up at the forbidding features of the man walking beside her as they approached the cluster of buildings huddled about the village green.

"Why would you think so?"

Lottie hesitated, somewhat daunted by the intimidating Nicolas Alexandre Demarteau. His thick eyebrows drew together as he looked down at her and, though she had never considered herself a hen-hearted creature, she found she was not altogether comfortable in his presence.

"Well, let me see… over there are a baker's and a butcher's shop, a chandler, a blacksmith and, just out of sight around the corner, you will find a haberdashery." At his blank expression she hurried to explain. "That is a place where you may buy fabric and small items such as buttons and ribbon and thread. There is the pub, but I imagine it's not terribly exciting for a man who runs a club such as Rouge et Noir."

He cast a curious glance in her direction. "What do you know of Rouge et Noir?"

"Oh, a great deal," Lottie said at once, and then blushed as those dark eyebrows rose. "I mean… that is… Well, Phoebe— Lady Ellisborough—has told us much about it. She so enjoyed her time in Paris, and her description of Rouge et Noir quite captivated us all. I believe she has ambitions to play cards with you again."

Mr Demarteau smirked. "I believe it is my brother she wishes to challenge, not I."

As he spoke, his gaze slid to his brother who was walking a little ahead of them with Eliza. Eliza had her hand on the comte's arm and was looking up at him and laughing at something he said. They made a perfectly dazzling couple. Mr Demarteau's gaze lingered on them for a moment as his eyes darkened with some strong emotion, and his jaw grew tight. Lottie felt her heart skip. Oh, goodness. The man truly had taken her sister in dislike, but she could not imagine how sweet Eliza could have offended him, and in such a short space of time. Unless Cat really was onto something and she reminded him of someone who had broken his heart.

She pondered this for a moment before asking, "Do you hope to find yourself an English wife while you are here, Mr Demarteau?"

His head snapped around so fast, and the look in his eyes was so outraged, that Lottie was quite taken aback.

"I do not," he said, or perhaps *growled* better described the way he uttered the words.

Lottie swallowed and then felt a surge of anger towards the man. How dare he glower at her sister so? Was he so deluded he thought Eliza not good enough to marry his brother? Louis César de Montluc might well be a comte, but Eliza was the eldest daughter of a duke.

"They make a splendid pair, don't they?" she said, studying his face for a reaction. "I am so lucky to have a sister like Eliza. Everyone loves her, you know. She is the sweetest, kindest, most wonderful woman in the world. She will make the perfect wife for some lucky man, for she never says the wrong thing and is always concerned with everyone else's comfort above her own. She quite puts me to shame, as I am not nearly so accomplished either. She sews beautifully and speaks French and Italian, her piano playing is quite the best I've ever heard, and she has the sweetest singing voice. Oh, and she adores children, and they her, naturally. I know she wishes for a family as large as our own. Of course she could have *anyone* she chose. She had so many offers of marriage this last season I've quite lost track. Did you know both a duke *and* a marquess offered for her? But Mama told her she need not rush to make any decisions yet."

Lottie frowned. Instead of easing whatever ridiculous concerns the man might harbour about her sister's worth, her words only seemed to make matters worse. The arm beneath her hand had become rigid with tension.

"Mr Demarteau—" Lottie began, deciding the only way to deal with this was to face it head on.

"If you would excuse me, Lady Charlotte," he said, before she could say another word. He gave her a stiff bow and strode off into the village alone.

"Well!" she exclaimed, staring after him in stunned shock.

Never in her life had she met with such rude behaviour, not even when she'd deserved it.

"Lottie, whatever did you say to the man?"

Lottie turned back to see her mama walking arm-in-arm with Harriet and Matilda.

"Nothing, Mama, I swear it. I was only telling him how wonderful Eliza was and he strode off in a fury."

"How odd," Matilda said, watching the man's figure disappear into the village. "Do you have any idea why?"

"No." Lottie bit her lip, wondering if she ought to confess her suspicions. "I... I know it seems ridiculous, but I think he dislikes Eliza, or at least that he believes she is not good enough for his brother."

This elicited a predictable burst of exclamations from all three women.

"Whatever makes you think so?" her mother demanded.

Lottie shrugged. "Only that he glowers at her so, and whenever she comes into a room, he walks out of it. It is as though he cannot bear to be around her."

"Is that so?" Matilda murmured with interest.

"Well," her mother said with a sniff. "*He* may not like her, but his brother seems to have every intention of paying court."

Lottie looked back at her in surprise. "Goodness. Did he say so?"

She frowned, wanting to ask why her mother was allowing it when everyone knew Eliza was to marry Cassius. The wicked little voice in her head that she disliked so much murmured though, reminding her that it did not matter *why*, only that if Eliza married someone else, Cassius would be free.

"He did not say he wished to court her, not in so many words. Not yet, at least, but his intention was clear enough. He has gone out of his way to make himself agreeable to both myself and your papa, and a man like that does nothing without good reason. I know Phoebe liked both him and Mr Demarteau very much when she was in Paris with Max, and formed a very good opinion of them both. She is an excellent judge of character, too, or I should never have allowed the comte within a mile of Eliza."

"According to Cassius, Mr Demarteau is very protective of his brother," Harriet said, her tone thoughtful. "The comte's title is an old and distinguished one, but the family lost everything during the war. As I understand it, the comte had a difficult childhood and I believe the two brothers have gained something of a reputation with the rapacious manner in which they have turned their fortunes around, and of course, with the ownership of that scandalous club of theirs. A match with a woman of exceptional breeding like Eliza would be just what the comte needs to find acceptance in society again."

"If that is so, why does Mr Demarteau look at her with such ferocity?" Lottie demanded.

"Why indeed?" Matilda asked, a curious glint in her eyes.

Lottie huffed and stalked off towards the shops.

"I will find out eventually," she promised.

After perusing the shops and purchasing some new gloves for her mother, Lottie ambled back outside to the village green. It was a lovely setting, with ducks dabbling about around a small pond. The church bells chimed the hour and the low murmur of chatter drifted from the open door of The King's Head. As the morning wore on, the day grew hotter, and Lottie found a shady spot beneath a large chestnut tree to sit and wait for the others to appear. She'd not seen Eliza and the comte at all, but she knew Mama would keep an eye on them so did not fret over it. Instead, she closed her eyes and leaned back against the tree trunk, wondering what on earth she was to do. The future seemed to be a bleak place, filled with jealousy and resentment towards her sister, which was totally undeserved. After all, it was not Eliza's fault that she'd been born first, that she had been the one to be such a friend to Cassius, so much so that they would marry because of it. Lottie gave a dejected sigh.

"Lord, is it so bad, lovely Lottie?"

Her eyes flew open and she gasped at the elegant young man standing before her.

"Ashton!" she squealed, scrambling to her feet and flinging her arms about his neck.

Ashton laughed, protesting as she knocked his hat to the ground in her exuberance. "Leave off, Lottie. Good God, but you're a hoyden. You'll have the entire village gabbing about us if you don't have a care, and I've barely been here a minute."

Lottie let him go and stepped back again as he bent to retrieve his hat, brushing the dust off it.

"Sorry, Ash," she said, still beaming at him. "Oh, it is so good to see you, but where is Vivien?" Ashton was rarely seen without his twin sister, the two of them nigh on inseparable.

"Taking a nap," he said with a snort. "She had me up talking until all hours last night with some bee in her bonnet but, unlike me, she has no stamina."

"Are your parents here?"

"No. They may come later but they were promised to attend some party or other. Dull affair, I think. Duty rather than pleasure. Mama was not pleased."

Lottie smiled. Ash's parents, Aashini and Silas Anson—Lord and Lady Cavendish—were rather scandalous and great fun, and Lottie always enjoyed seeing them. Ash and his sister were dear friends, though, so she could hardly be disappointed.

"So, what were you sighing about so dramatically?" Ash asked her.

He regarded her with interest and Lottie returned his scrutiny. She wondered why she had not fallen madly in love with him instead. He was handsome: tall and lithe, with golden skin that spoke of his mother's Indian heritage, and hair as black as a raven's wing. His eyes were his father's, a dark indigo that seemed to Lottie to see directly into her brain, for he was one of the most perceptive people she'd ever known. Some among the *ton* might refuse to accept his mother, but no one could deny that Aashini was still one of the most beautiful women in the country, except for perhaps her daughter, Vivien. Though Aashini's father had been an earl, she'd been born out of wedlock to an Indian mother, and there had been quite a scandal when she'd married Viscount Cavendish. Ash and his twin sister had decided at a young age that they may as well enjoy their notoriety, and were generally up to their necks in one scrape or another.

"Well?" Ash pressed, clearly unwilling to let it go. "Why is the sunniest person I know sitting in the shade like some wilting flower, and sighing as if her heart is broken?"

"Perhaps it is," Lottie said, meaning it only as a teasing comment and looking quickly away from Ash as she realised there had been too much feeling behind the words.

"Lottie?" Ash caught her hand, forcing her to turn and look at him.

Lottie swallowed, suddenly desperate to unburden herself to someone. A glance over his shoulder showed Eliza and the rest of their little entourage walking towards them.

"Not here," she said, taking his arm.

They hurried away, walking back towards Holbrook at quite a pace until Lottie glanced back and assured herself everyone was out of sight.

"What kind of trouble have you fallen into, minx?" Ash asked her, though with such a gentle tone she knew she would find no judgement from him.

"Oh, Ash, the worst kind," she lamented, shaking her head. "I'm such a fool, but I promise you I didn't do it on purpose. Is it even possible to fall in love on purpose?"

"I've no idea, but who is it you've fallen for, and why do you look so wretched about it? Do I need to draw someone's cork? For I shall, if he's hurt you."

Lottie gave a mirthless laugh and shook her head. "No, no. Nothing like that. The only person behaving badly is me, I'm afraid. He doesn't love me. I don't even think he knows I exist… well, unless I'm causing havoc and making things explode in his face."

She sighed again and then caught sight of Ash's face, noting the fact he was struggling manfully not to laugh.

"It's not funny," she exclaimed, huffing at him.

"No," he said, his voice strained, his lips twitching. "Only that's why we love you. Making things explode and causing havoc is what you do best, Lottie dear."

"I know!" she wailed, throwing her hands in the air. "But this time I shan't just be making a nuisance of myself I would be ruining *everything*. I… I… Oh, Ash, I'm in love with Cassius."

Ash stopped in his tracks, gaped at her for a long moment and then let out a breath. He reached for her hand, placed it carefully on his arm, and they walked on again.

"Who else knows?" he asked.

"No one," Lottie said in a small voice. She glanced up at him, wondering if he hated her now. "Do you despise me?"

Ash stared at her. "Why the…. Of course not, you ridiculous creature. I'm just wondering how on earth I never saw it before. If I had, I should have helped you."

"Helped me?" It was Lottie's turn to stop dead now and Ash huffed, glancing back to see the others were drawing nearer.

"Come along," he urged. "And yes, why would I not help you? Cassius is one of my closest friends, and you know I adore Eliza, but—"

"But?" Lottie said, knowing she was a bad person to hope what the next words out of his mouth would be.

"But I don't think they're suited. Eliza is too quiet for him. Everyone knows Cassius longs to travel and poor Eliza would hate that."

"Oh, Ash!" She flung herself at him again and Ash made an exasperated sound.

"Good Lord, woman. Must you manhandle me so? You'll ruin my cravat."

"What the devil is going on?"

Lottie jolted with alarm and they both turned to see Cassius had walked around the corner whilst they were occupied. He stood, glaring at them. Lottie gave a squeak of alarm and went to move away but to her shock, Ash held onto her, his hands at her waist.

"Well met, Cassius, old man. Lottie here was just telling me how pleased she was to see me."

Lottie glanced at Ash to see a wicked look glinting in his blue eyes. She pushed at his chest and he let her go this time, though he did not look away from Cassius.

"Was she?" Cassius asked, his tone neutral. "Well, perhaps less exuberance in public, Charlotte. You know how gossip spreads around the village."

Charlotte? She gaped at him in shock. No one ever called her Charlotte. Certainly not Cassius, and what the devil was he looking so prim about?

"I thought you were painting?" she said, aware she sounded defensive now.

Cassius shrugged. "I heard Ash had arrived and was in the village. I thought I'd come and meet him."

"My, I am popular today. You must be careful, the pair of you, such attention will go to my head."

"I'm fairly certain there's no more room," Cassius grumbled.

"Well, can I help it if I'm beloved by all?" Ash held out his hands as if to draw their attention to his general magnificence.

"You are looking splendid," Lottie said, as she was very much in charity with him, and because it was nothing but the truth. "That waistcoat is very—"

"Vulgar," Cassius observed, his blond eyebrows drawing together in consternation as he regarded the admittedly eye catching bright yellow waistcoat with black embroidery. "Really, Ash, whatever were you thinking?"

"Only that if I was to get the least bit of attention from Lottie here, I had better wear something that made her notice me."

Ash winked at her and Lottie could only gape at him in astonishment. Was he flirting? With *her*? What was going on?

Cassius clearly had no idea either as he gave Ash another frowning look of displeasure, and they made the rest of the walk home in silence.

Chapter 6

Dear diary,

I think it is time to reveal my ace — as my sister Phoebe would say.

I cannot wait!

—Excerpt of an entry to the diary of Lady Catherine 'Cat' Barrington, youngest daughter of the Marquess and Marchioness of Montagu.

30th June 1838, Holbrook House, Sussex.

"I'm stuffed," Rosamund complained, flopping down in a chair in Eliza's room, as Victoria arranged the draughts board on a low table, carefully putting each counter in place.

"You sound like a Christmas goose," Lottie observed, at which Torie gave a cackle of laughter.

"Young ladies are never stuffed, Ozzie," Eliza reproved her, though there was a thread of amusement in her words.

"No, but geese are, and Rosamund is a silly goose," Torie snickered.

Ozzie huffed at her younger sister, who responded in character by sticking out her tongue.

"Why are you all in my room, anyway?" Eliza demanded. "Isn't it time you were in bed?"

"Oh, don't be such a stick in the mud. Why must you always be so good and follow the rules?" Ozzie demanded of her big sister. "Besides, Cat told us to be here, remember? She has a surprise for us."

Eliza pursed her lips but said nothing.

"Well, why didn't she show us downstairs?" Lottie asked, smothering a yawn.

It was far from late, but she had not slept well, and she'd been up early too. Not to mention how tiring it was attempting not to feel jealous of her sister, and then feeling guilty for failing miserably. She was tying herself in knots pretending to be happy, pretending to be pleased for Eliza, for how popular she was, how lovely she was, how bloody, damned perfect.

Oh, she was a horrible person.

"Because it's only for girls."

They all looked at Victoria, who glanced up from the draughts board. "Well, that's what she said."

Lottie sighed and watched as Eliza took the dozens of pins from her hair, the thick, dark coils unwinding to form a shimmering mahogany curtain across her back.

"How was the comte?" Lottie asked her, hardly daring to hope that the man might have captured her sister's affections.

"Entertaining and devilishly charming," Eliza said, meeting Lottie's eye via the looking glass. "I can only imagine what a reputation he must have back in France."

"Oh, a terrible one," Ozzie said, her eyes wide with delight. "I overheard the servants talking this morning when they were clearing the table, and they said—"

"Ozzie," Eliza said, shaking her head. "You know how Mama feels about listening to gossip, and eavesdropping too."

Lottie felt an immediate rush of shame for having done the exact same thing earlier that morning. To compensate, she decided to save Ozzie from their sister's gentle scolding.

"Well, she did listen, so we may as well know what they say now."

Eliza sighed but held her tongue, turning back to the mirror.

Ozzie grinned. "Only that he's had a great many mistresses, and that two women duelled over him."

"No!" Eliza and Lottie said in unison as Eliza swung back around on the stool.

"Oh, I thought you didn't want to hear the gossip, Eliza dear," Ozzie said, batting her eyelids at her big sister and looking as if butter wouldn't melt in her mouth.

"Wretch," Eliza muttered. "Tell me everything."

"Well, there's not much more to tell. I only heard a bit of it, but apparently two married ladies fell wildly in love with him, but he chose one over the other. The one he spurned went quite mad and challenged his lady to a duel, which was accepted. According to the gossip, he discovered what was going on and put a stop to it before anyone was hurt, for the spurned lover was a crack shot."

"Oh, what nonsense," Eliza said, laughing. "It sounds like one of Mama's stories."

"You don't believe it?" Lottie asked in surprise.

"Of course not. It's just tittle-tattle."

"Oh, I don't know. I would fight a duel for him. He's dreadfully handsome. Mind you, his brother looks dreadfully wicked too, so either would do," Torie said with a dreamy smile.

"*Victoria!*"

This time both Eliza and Lottie exclaimed, discomforted to hear their thirteen-year-old sister speak so. Like Lottie, Torie had something of a wild streak and needed little encouragement for mischief.

"Well, they would," Torie said sulkily, turning her attention back to the draughts board.

A soft knock on the door had Eliza jumping up to answer it.

"I found this pretty creature," said a lilting voice from the corridor. "Is it yours?"

Lottie heard her sister laugh.

"I suppose it must be. Do come in."

She turned to see Ashton's twin, Vivien, come in with Cat, who was holding a large hat box.

"Whatever have you got there, Cat?" Ozzie demanded.

"Oh, but you know Vivien, she was with us at dinner," Cat said with a saucy grin.

Vivien laughed and clipped her around the ear. "Horrid girl. We want to know what is in the box."

"A surprise," Cat said, looking utterly gleeful. "But you must all sit down in a circle and then I shall reveal it."

Not wanting to spoil the girl's fun, and far too intrigued to quibble, they did as they were asked. Cat got Torie to push the draughts board over to one side and solemnly placed the hat box down as though it contained something precious and fragile.

"Well…." Cat said, pausing for dramatic effect. Honestly, the girl was so theatrical she ought to be on the stage. "We all know the story of the Peculiar Ladies, don't we?"

Everyone rolled their eyes.

The story of the Peculiar Ladies was legend among their families. A group of mismatched women, the shy, the unmarriageable, and the odd girls who found themselves among the wallflowers at every ball, season after season. They had come together to join a book club of sorts, though they never seemed to spend a great deal of time discussing books. To seal their friendships they had all gone through a rite of passage, to take a dare from a hat, hoping in some small way to take control of their own lives. Those dares had brought love and adventure, not to mention a fair bit of scandal, and had cemented friendships that had endured through thick and thin.

They all stared at Cat as she grinned at them, and then took the lid off the box with a flourish.

"Ta-da!"

"Oh!" Eliza exclaimed, getting to her feet. "Is… Is that…?"

"Yes!" Cat was jumping up and down now. "It's the hat. The exact same hat, and you'll never guess what!"

"What?" Lottie asked with a peculiar sensation stirring in her belly.

"It's still full of dares!"

Everyone stared at each other, wide-eyed.

"Well?" Cat demanded. "What are you waiting for?"

"I'll take one!" Torie said, scrambling to her feet.

"No, you will not!" Lottie and Eliza said in unison and then burst out laughing.

"You can't take a dare before you've come out, silly," Cat said, though there was sympathy in her eyes.

Lottie didn't doubt Cat was itching to take one herself.

Eliza was staring at the hat with concern, as if it contained something that might bite.

"Do you think we ought?" she said doubtfully.

"Whyever not?" Lottie demanded. "Goodness! Mama did it. We'd not be here if she hadn't."

Eliza chewed at her lip, clearly unconvinced.

Lottie sighed and turned to Vivien. "You'll do it, won't you?"

A slow smile curved over the young woman's mouth and Lottie felt her breath catch. Good heavens, but she was lovely.

"I believe I will."

Cat gave a little yip of excitement and hurried forward.

"Oh, no. Me first!" Lottie said, waving her hand in the air. If anyone needed this, she did.

Anything to distract herself from the wretched situation in which she had found herself. Perhaps, if she took a dare, she would find someone else to fall in love with, or get herself tied up in such a scandal she'd not have time to pine over Cassius. Anything was preferable to pining, surely?

"Oh, Lottie, really?" Eliza said.

"Yes. Really."

Cat held the hat out in front of her and Lottie took a breath before plunging her hand in. The little bits of paper were yellowed with age and the hat smelled musty, but Lottie's heart was beating hard and fast as the contents rustled around her fingers. With closed eyes, she snatched at a slip of paper and pulled it free.

"What does it say?" Cat squealed with excitement as everyone else echoed the sentiment.

Lottie swallowed hard and carefully opened the paper, which seemed at risk of disintegrating at any moment. She squinted at the writing, brown and blurred with age. It was almost illegible, faded, and rubbed away in the places the paper had been folded.

"I… I can't quite make it out. It says 'dare…' What does that word say, Vivien?"

Vivien took the paper from her and stared at it, holding it this way and that. "Wicket, witches... wicked! Dare to be *wicked.*"

"Oh, no," Eliza said in horror. "It can't say that. Give it here."

She peered at the writing, her frown deepening. "Well, it does look like that but... but it can't be. The dares were all specific things to do. Dance in a garden at midnight, say something outrageous to a handsome man...."

"Bet something you don't wish to lose," Vivien said with a grin.

They all giggled, having heard one of the most scandalous of the stories and still finding it hard to believe that Cassius's mama, Harriet—of all people—had been caught with the Earl of St Clair in the summerhouse. They had been forced to marry, not that either of them had wanted to do anything else. The Earl of St Clair was still a magnificent looking man, and his son had certainly inherited his good looks. Lottie couldn't blame Harriet in the least. Indeed, she could only envy her good fortune.

"Perhaps we ought to write new ones?" Eliza mused.

Lottie gave a snort. "If we do, you're not having a go. You've not got a daring bone in your body."

"Yes, I do!" Eliza retorted. "I *do!*"

Lottie snatched up the hat and held it out to her sister. "Go on then, prove it."

Eliza hesitated. "There's no point, they're illegible."

"It's clear enough. My dare is to be wicked," Lottie said, something wicked indeed stirring to life inside her and making her reckless.

"Oh, no, Lottie, you can't. What does that even mean?"

Eliza pinched her mouth closed at whatever she saw in Lottie's eyes and huffed.

"Very well then," she said, putting her chin up.

Lottie grinned and thrust the hat towards her again.

With a nervous intake of breath, Eliza dipped a trembling hand into the paper slips.

"Oh, dear," she said, and pulled out a dare.

Cassius leaned against the window of the summerhouse, staring out at the darkness beyond. A thin sickle moon cut the sky, like a tear in black velvet, the dark water of lake glinting here and there beneath. His insides were in a knot, probably not helped in the least by the bottle of cognac he'd snuck out of the house and was currently keeping company with.

Blasted Ashton had flirted shamelessly all evening. Not just with Lottie, to be fair; Eliza got her fair share of attention too. In fact, Ash and Louis César had been vying for the title of 'most charming' all blasted evening, damn their eyes. The only person who'd looked more revolted than he had was Louis's brother. Nic had excused himself as early as he could without looking abominably rude, and Cassius had seen him sneaking out in the direction of the pub. He could hardly blame the man.

Cassius had assumed the duke would put his foot down and tell them not to make such cakes of themselves over his daughters. He hadn't. Instead he'd looked on in with an amused glint in his eyes and didn't appear to have the least notion of murdering anyone. It was a terrible disappointment.

He sighed and stared up at the sliver of moon. There was no escaping the truth. He loved Eliza, but as a friend, not as he would hope to feel for a wife. He could not marry her. The world was calling to him, begging him to come and discover it. He'd seen such a tiny corner and he was already restless, desperate for more. Yet that kind of nomadic life would make Eliza miserable, just as spending the rest of his days in England would make him. It would be as unfair to her as it was to him. She was a beautiful, wonderful woman who deserved no less than adoration from her husband, and he could not give her that. He lifted the bottle of cognac to his lips and took another swig. The sooner he told her so, the better. It wasn't as if she would be angry with him. No, Eliza would be kind and understanding, and ensure he felt no anxiety for having let her down… which was far, far worse than her being angry with him.

Bloody hell.

Chapter 7

Louis César,
I received your letter at last. It took some time
to reach me as I was in the South of France
when you departed, and missed all the
excitement. I admit I was surprised by your
flight from Paris. I assume there is a woman
involved in there somewhere, and the tale
delicate enough that you would not give any
details to your old friend in writing. Not
another jealous lady threatening to shoot your
lover, or you, I hope? Was it you at the heart of
it this time, or shall Nic take the blame?

A little bird tells me you have been made
welcome by the Earl of St Clair, and that you
have your sights on marrying a duke's
daughter. I commend you on your choices.
Bedwin would be a powerful ally and silence the
wagging tongues that persist in turning over
the details of your past. I wonder if he would
recognise me after all these years. Perhaps I
should quit Paris too, and consider showing my
face to polite society again? I am bored enough
to consider it might be entertaining. Now that
<u>would</u> give them something to talk about.

—Excerpt of letter to Louis César de Montluc, Comte de Villen, signed... Wolf.

1st July 1838, The Summerhouse, Holbrook, Sussex.

Cassius groaned and clutched at his head.

"Bloody hell," he muttered, blinking against the dazzling light pouring through the studio windows. He squinted as the door open and did his best to focus on the blurry figure that had stepped inside.

"I thought as much," his father said.

"Oh, please, Pa, don't scold, I promise you I'm being punished enough."

"As if I would?" his sire retorted, holding a basket aloft. "I bring coffee."

"Thank God. You are the very best of fathers, sir," Cassius murmured, collapsing back into the chair and rubbing his temples.

The earl nodded and began unpacking the basket. "This is true, so I shan't bother to pretend modesty."

"Did Mother send you?"

"No need. I observed last night how utterly blue devilled you were, not to mention the fact that you clearly wanted to poke Ashton's pretty eyes out with a sharp stick."

"Damnation. Was it that obvious?"

His father glanced back with a wry smile and Cassius groaned and closed his eyes.

"Have you spoken to Eliza yet?"

Cassius peeled his eyes open again to see his father holding out a mug of coffee for him. He took it, curling his hands about the mug and taking a tentative sip. It was hot and strong and heavily dosed with sugar.

"No."

His father said nothing for a moment, returning to pour out his own mug of coffee before picking up a chair and moving it closer. He sat down and sipped his drink, regarding his son with a benign expression that was nonetheless capable of making Cassius feel like a rat.

"I'm going to," Cassius said, his stomach twisting itself back into a Gordian knot. "I swear I will, only… only she'll be so kind and understanding and honestly I'd far rather she shouted at me and told me I was a heartless brute. I'm sure I deserve it."

The earl smiled, such sympathy in his eyes Cassius felt worse than ever. "No, you don't. You both had a lovely vision of what the future could be, but you were children, and the idea did not grow with you. You made each other no promises, and your heart cannot be manipulated into loving someone you feel you *ought* to love. It is not your fault you've fallen in love with her sister, either, though I admit that is dashed awkward, and does rather complicate matters."

Cassius gaped at him.

"Oh, come on. It was obvious. What other reason could you have for wanting to murder one of your closest friends? I admit Ashton's waistcoat was somewhat challenging, but I don't believe it was outrageous enough to provoke such violent emotion as I saw in your eyes at dinner."

"Did anyone else notice?" he demanded, feeling wretched now.

His father shrugged. "I've no idea, but I did, and others will, and eventually Eliza will figure it out. Though I have a suspicion she might not be as heartbroken as you suspect."

Cassius sat up straighter. "Why do you say that?"

"Haven't you seen the way she watches your friend, Mr Demarteau? She seems rather fascinated, though I'm not honestly certain if she is interested or merely horrified by how rude he is to her."

"Nic?" Cassius said in horror. "Oh, good God, no. He's... he's... and Eliza is—"

"Good heavens, you've gone as white as a sheet, Cass. I admit he's a surly fellow, but I quite like him, and I assumed he was someone you trusted. Tell me, you'd not have brought him here if he was beyond the pale?"

Cassius shook his head, uncertain of what to say. "Nic is a decent fellow underneath the glowering exterior, honourable in his own way and a good friend, but... but the life he's lead in Paris, Father. He's *not* the kind of fellow Eliza would wish to marry. He's hardly good *ton*. Not that I care, but Eliza...."

His father shrugged and got to his feet. He smiled down at Cassius and rested his hand on his shoulder for a moment. "Women surprise you, Cass, and perhaps you don't know Eliza as well as you think you do. Either way, that is her affair, not yours. Speak to her, though, and do it soon. Perhaps she will be as relieved as you."

Cassius nodded.

"I will," he promised. "You've my word on it."

Once he'd drunk his coffee, Cassius considered going back to the house to clean up, but everyone would be at breakfast and he wasn't ready to see anyone just yet. Instead he took himself off for a swim in the lake, hoping that a bracing dip in cold water would clear his head and make him better able to face Eliza.

He swam for a good half hour, feeling calmer with every minute that passed. By the time he got out, he was feeling rather less as if he was going to climb the steps to Tyburn and more as though he needed to have a serious discussion with a dear friend.

He'd do it this afternoon, he decided. Perhaps he could invite Eliza to go for a walk with him, and—

"Cassius?"

Cassius jolted at the sound of the feminine voice, suddenly very aware of the fact that he'd been swimming in only his small clothes, which became all but transparent once wet.

"Christ, Lottie!" he exclaimed, covering his dignity as best he could with his hands and searching wildly about for his clothes.

"Goodness, Cassius, you have… *filled out.*"

Lottie was staring at him in rapt fascination, her cheeks a little pink, but her eyes upon him, frank and full of admiration.

Despite feeling utterly ridiculous, Cassius discovered he was shallow enough to experience a rush of pride at her words, more so at the look in her eyes as her gaze travelled down his chest to his belly, and then lower before moving back up again. The slow, scrolling inspection of his person made heat erupt beneath his skin and desire surge in his blood. Hell and damnation, this situation would get awkward indeed if he didn't nip it in the bud at once.

"Where the devil are my clothes?" he muttered, scowling at the ground. He knew he'd left them here somewhere.

"Oh, you mean these?" Lottie stepped daintily to one side to reveal a neat pile of his belongings, which her voluminous skirts had hidden.

"You little devil, you did that on purpose. I never folded them."

She shrugged, unrepentant. "Well, you'd scattered them hither and yon, anything could have happened to them. Why, someone might even have stolen them."

Lottie gave him a wide-eyed glance and pretended to gasp in shock at the idea.

"Don't even think about it," he warned her.

They stared at each other for a long moment and then Cassius lunged. Lottie squealed and snatched up his clothes, running away from him. She crowed with laughter as he raced after her, through the trees, back towards the summerhouse. Thank God they were out of sight of the house from here. Suddenly Cassius was transported back in time, to memories of chasing Lottie about the grounds after she'd purposely said or done something outrageous to provoke him.

"Ask me nicely and maybe I'll give them back," she shouted, dancing out of his reach.

"Give them back or you'll regret it, you little minx," Cassius warned her, trying to grab at the trouser leg dangling from the pile in her arms but she dodged out of reach.

"But why would I do that?" she asked, as her heated expression roved over him like a caress. "It's such a pretty view."

Cassius felt his breath catch and he ground to a halt. His chest was heaving, but he suspected it was less from the effort of chasing her and more because she'd outright admitted she wanted to look at him, that she liked looking at him… that she desired him.

"Do you like what you see, Lottie?" he asked, aware of the change in his voice.

She stilled, standing in the dappled light beneath the branches of an oak tree. The pink that had flushed her cheeks deepened, and she drew in a sharp breath. There was a pause that felt significant, during which Cassius was aware of the blood rushing in his veins, the thud of his heart in his ears.

"I always have," she said, the admission somewhat breathless as she met his gaze, something at once vulnerable and defiant glittering in her eyes. "You just never saw me, Cassius."

His heart ached at the truth of that, at the regret he heard in her voice.

"I see you," he said. "I see you clearly now, Lottie."

"Do you?" she whispered.

He nodded.

She licked her lips and the desire to close the distance between them and kiss her was so tantalising his skin prickled with the need to do it. Eliza deserved better than that, though, and so did Lottie.

"You'd best give me my clothes back," he said, willing her to do it this time. The way she was looking at him was giving his less civilised self some dreadful ideas, which he was far too tempted to give into.

"Spoilsport," she said, but she was smiling at him, such a look in her eyes Cassius felt certain she would not deny him a kiss if he chose to steal one.

Behave, he instructed himself, struggling to hold still and not reach for her as she came closer. Lottie bent down, placing his clothes on the ground before him.

"There you are, then. I'll wait for you in the summerhouse," she said, before turning and hurrying away.

"So you have three suitors?" Vivien said once breakfast was over.

She had followed Eliza, who had escaped with a book, intending to sit on the terrace in the sun until her sister was located. They were supposed to be riding out to Bodiam village for a picnic, but Lottie had disappeared.

"Three?" Eliza set her book down to regard Vivien, who sat beside her. She looked exquisite in a simple white muslin gown embroidered all over with rosebuds. "Whatever do you mean?"

Vivien tsked at her and shook her head, glossy black ringlets bouncing around her face. "Now, now, don't be coy, Eliza. Everyone can see the Comte de Villen is paying you special attention, not to mention everyone telling me you are practically engaged to Cassius."

Eliza frowned down at her book. The comte had been very attentive, that much was true. Cassius, however, had barely spoken to her. Before he'd left France, he'd written often, telling her how much he was looking forward to seeing her again, how much he had to tell her, and he was now playing least in sight. It was strange and out of character and… and she did not know what to make of it. Had she done something, said something, to make him wish to avoid her? Could she have offended him? Perhaps just as she had offended Mr Demarteau, for she could not understand why the man glared at her so and avoided her. She must have said or done something to make him cut her so obviously.

"Eliza, are you listening to me?"

"What? Oh, I do beg your pardon, Viv. No, I was wool gathering, and please don't tell me that Ashton is my third suitor for I shall laugh in your face. I do not know what he was playing at last night, but it was very clearly a game of some description."

A game that had made Cassius very angry. Indeed, he'd given every appearance of being jealous that Ashton was showing her such attention, but if that was so, why—? Oh, good Lord, she was going around in circles.

"Of course not. My brother's motives are his own and generally as clear as mud, though I shall discover them, naturally. He cannot keep a secret from me. I did not count him your suitor, though."

Eliza looked up, frowning at her friend. "Then I don't have the slightest notion who you are speaking of."

She stared blankly into Viv's blue eyes, and gaped as one elegantly arched black eyebrow lifted.

Eliza gaped at her. "You cannot possibly be suggesting that Mr Demarteau is interested in pursuing me?"

"Whyever not?"

"Good heavens, the man cannot bear to be in the same room as me. Since we were introduced, he has hardly spoken to me once above a grunt in reply to a direct question and, on the one occasion I tried to engage him in conversation, he practically cut me dead."

"Exactly!" Vivien said, clapping her hands together in delight.

"Your brain does not work the same way mine does, my darling Viv," Eliza said, shaking her head.

"Her brain is a twisty thing designed to outwit us lesser mortals, Eliza. It is best you accept that now."

Eliza looked up to see Ashton had come to join them.

"I believe you may be right," she said, laughing.

"Of course I am. I am always right. It is a curse I must bear. I do it manfully, as you can see," he added, smirking at her.

"Indeed you do," Eliza replied, deadpan. "We are all deeply impressed."

"Speak for yourself," his sister retorted.

Ashton flashed a dazzling grin and sat down beside them. "Are we all ready, then? I thought we were riding out somewhere?"

"Yes, but Lottie has disappeared, and no one can find her," Eliza said with a huff. "Perhaps I should look for her too. I thought she must have gone for a walk and would be back by now. I suppose she might have gone down to the summerhouse to find Cassius. He wasn't at breakfast either, and—"

"No need," Ash said, pushing to his feet at once. "I'll go."

"Oh," Eliza said, a little startled by the force of his declaration. "Well, that's very kind of you, Ash, but—"

"No trouble at all," Ash said briskly, giving her no further chance to protest as he strode off towards the gardens.

Cassius dressed hurriedly and made his way back to the summerhouse. Lottie was there as she'd promised, waiting for him. She was inspecting the canvases stacked up against the walls of the building. He waited, his heart thudding nervously, wondering what she would make of his work. Though she must have been aware of his presence, she did not hurry, lingering on a painting of women working in a field.

"These are marvellous, Cass. You truly are an artist."

He let out a breath, only in the moment realising how important her opinion had been.

"There is something exciting happening in France, in art," he said, suddenly bursting with the desire to tell her, to explain. "It is a rejection of all the old men of the art world and the lies they tell by idealising and perfecting that which was never ideal nor perfect. It is a desire to paint the truth, Lottie, to paint life as it is, even if it is not always pretty, not always as we might wish to believe it."

Lottie looked again at the painting of the women and he saw what she saw: dirty hands and soiled clothes, backbreaking work under an unforgiving sun that baked the earth dry, the women sweaty and worn out. He felt anxiety lance through him, a fear that she might not see the beauty in such a rural scene. It was far from glamorous, after all. Eliza understood his desire to see the world as it was. It was one of the reasons he had believed they were so well suited, for she had never shied away from the realities in life like some of her station. Eliza wanted to make the world a better place for those who had nothing, and Cassius wanted those who had everything to confront the truth.

"It is honest," Lottie said at last. "An honest representation of what you saw. It is not an imagined depiction of an historical event, in no way contrived. You are making no comment on what it means, nor guiding the viewer to think as you do. It simply is."

His breath caught, an exclamation of delighted surprise in his throat that she had understood, accepted so easily what men were arguing about in heated exchanges all over Europe.

"I can feel the heat of the sun," she said, staring at his painting as though he had opened a window between worlds. "I can smell the parched earth and imagine how hot and tired they are, how their backs must ache. It is a marvel, Cassius... and this one of the lavender fields! Oh, I wish I had seen them with you for they look to be glorious. Was the perfume lovely?"

"It was," he said, too stunned to say more. He could only watch her with his heart swelling in his chest, touched more than he could say by her enthusiasm, her excitement at what he had achieved, her delight in everything she saw. She flicked through canvas after canvas, exclaiming over each one and Cassius was so enraptured by her he did not think to stop her before she reached those hidden at the back.

"Oh," she said, staring down at a nude painting of a woman reclining on a day bed.

She looked up, meeting his eyes.

"She's very beautiful."

He wanted to tell her the truth, that there was no one on earth he found as beautiful as she was, but he was not free to do so yet. Damnation, why had he left this ridiculous situation and not dealt with it at once?

"Was she your lover?"

Cassius hesitated, a beat too long by all accounts.

She smiled and turned back to the painting. "I shall take that as a yes. Well, she looks to have been well pleased by the experience, the lucky girl."

"Lottie!" he said, his voice rough, stunned by the words that had reached inside him and lit a fuse that threatened to burn too hot and fierce. "Lottie, I...."

He didn't know what it was he wanted to say, but he stepped closer, so close the scent of her reached him. It was faint and feminine, that hint of jasmine and something fresh and tantalising that made his chest tight with longing.

Lottie looked up at him and he was caught, held fast in eyes of such blue he was transported back to the Mediterranean.

"Lottie," he said again, dazed now, drunk on her proximity, foolish with desire.

"Cassius." She breathed as much as said his name and he moved a fraction closer, drawn as if tugged by some invisible string but she looked away, breaking the spell.

"You must paint me," she said, her voice a little too loud, the colour in her cheeks telling him she was as aware of the tension simmering between them as he was. "Exactly as I am. Warts and all," she added, glancing back at him with a twinkle in her eyes.

"No one will believe I paint the truth if I come close to capturing you. They shall think me a romantic, for nothing could ever be so lovely."

She opened her mouth, her blush rising, and he was torn between wanting to kiss her and the desire to capture that exact shade of rose pink.

"There is no need to flatter me," she said, but the words were breathless. "You must paint me as I am, as you see me. Will you?"

Sunlight slanted through the window, gilding the elegant curve of her neck, highlighting the straight little nose and burnishing her hair so it shone like old gold.

"Yes," he said, helpless to do otherwise.

"Cassius!"

They leapt apart, and though they had only been talking, their reaction proclaimed them guilty of some heinous crime. Cassius turned around to see Ashton glaring at him.

"Damn you, Cassius. Everyone is waiting for you two and you're damned lucky I thought to come and find you both. What would your mama say if she found you alone down here, Lottie, or your *sister*?"

Cassius turned back to see Lottie blanch at the idea.

"I had better go," she said, hurrying to the door. "Thank you, Ash."

She touched his sleeve as she passed, and Ashton sighed, his expression softening.

"You're welcome. I just don't want to see you hurt, love. You know that."

Lottie nodded and cast Cassius a guilty glance before she hurried away.

"Bloody hell," Ashton swore, the moment Lottie was out of earshot. "You're playing with fire, Cass."

"We were talking," Cassius retorted. "Nothing more. I was explaining about my work and—"

"And that's why you both leapt two feet in the air when I came in, was it? You could cut the atmosphere with a knife, you pillock."

Cassius bristled, irritated. "What's up, Ash? Are you jealous? I suppose I shouldn't be surprised after the way you were pouring the butter boat over her last night."

"To provoke you into sorting this situation out, you stupid devil. My God, it's like watching a carriage accident. You know it's going to happen and there's not a damned thing you can do about it."

"It's not that bad," Cassius said, waving away the comment like an annoying insect. "I shall speak to Eliza this afternoon and sort things out with her."

"Be sure that you do. She's our friend, Cass. I won't have her upset or embarrassed."

"She's *my* friend!" Cassius retorted, stung. "I've not said anything *because* I can't bear to see her hurt. I feel wretched about the whole blasted situation. It was absurd of us to believe I could go away for two years and come back as if nothing had happened, but we did believe it, which is no fault of mine."

Ash let out a breath and patted Cassius on the shoulder. "I know that. I would just hate for the two of you to lose that friendship. I know she means the world to you. I'm just anxious on your behalf. I would hate to see you upset too, you know."

Cassius snorted. "If that were true you'd never have worn that waistcoat. Good God, Ash, what is *wrong* with you?"

Ash looked down at the offending article and stroked it lovingly. "Very few men could get away with wearing such a thing, I'll have you know."

"There are so many responses to that statement I hardly know which to choose," Cassius muttered. "But I suspect those few men are probably confined to Bedlam, driven there by that lurid pattern."

Ash shrugged, regarding his reflection in one of the windows and considering the geometric pattern in red black and gold that was making Cassius feel quite giddy.

"I like it," he said, before turning back to Cassius. "And a man standing in a rumpled shirt which looks like he slept in it, and who hasn't bathed or shaved, really ought not have any opinion on matters sartorial. You look an utter wreck, Cass."

Cassius looked down at himself and rubbed a hand over his bristly chin.

"A fair point," he conceded. "Come on, then, you can escort me back to the house. Just walk ahead of me, will you? That way I can't see your waistcoat."

"Idiot," Ash grumbled, but led him out of the door.

Chapter 8

Dear Phoebe,

I hope this letter finds you all well. As you know we are staying with the St Clair's for some weeks ahead of the grand ball they give each summer. Will you be coming? I do hope to see you.

We have the company of Louis César de Montluc, Comte de Villen and his brother Mr Demarteau. Of course we all remember your stories about meeting them in Paris at their infamous club. I admit they are everything you indicated. What do you know of them, though? The comte has made no secret of his desire to court me, and he is indeed very charming. His brother, however, is rude and surly and… utterly fascinating. I must know more about him, and why on earth he has taken me in such dislike. Before you protest, I must tell you that he truly has, and I am not the only person to have remarked it. I assure you I am not the kind of woman who expects to be universally adored, but he seems unable to bear being in the same room as I. It is vexing and frustrating not to understand what it is that makes him revile me. So please, Phoebe, tell me everything you know.

—Excerpt of letter to The Right Hon'ble
Phoebe Carmichael, The Countess of
Ellisborough, from Lady Elizabeth
Adolphus.

1st July 1838, on the way to Bodiam Castle, Robertsbridge.

"Lottie, have you heard a word I've said?"

"What?"

Lottie turned to see her sister riding beside her, exasperation written all over her face.

"Whatever is the matter?" Eliza demanded. "You've been in such a strange mood of late, and now you can hardly concentrate for two minutes together. I've asked you twice where you were this morning, and I still don't have an answer."

A knot of anxiety settled in Lottie's throat and she tried to swallow past it to no avail.

"I went for a walk," she said, feeling like the worst, wickedest creature in the world. What kind of woman flirted with the man who was supposed to be marrying her sister?

"Lottie."

Lottie turned, filled with shame to see the concern in Eliza's green eyes.

"Won't you tell me what's troubling you, love?"

"It's nothing. Just a headache is all," Lottie lied, before urging her horse into a canter, desperate to put distance between her and Eliza. To her frustration Eliza only followed her, so she slowed again, turning to see that Louis César, his brother, and the Anson twins, Ash and Vivien, were close behind them.

"What do you think of Louis César now?" she asked Eliza, still desperately hoping her sister might have begun a passion for any man who wasn't Cassius.

Eliza smiled, which made Lottie's heart leap with hope.

"He's very charming, funny, and I suspect a great deal more intelligent that he wishes anyone to know. I asked to play him at cards, but he won't," she admitted. "He must know what Phoebe told us about her trip to Paris and how easily he beat her, and everyone knows how clever Phoebe is at cards."

"He wants to marry you," Lottie said, watching for her sister's reaction, but Eliza only laughed.

"Of course he does. I'm the daughter of a duke, with a large dowry," she said, with only a trace of bitterness.

"I'm sure that's not the only reason."

Eliza shrugged. "He needs a respectable match to establish his family name back in society. There is some scandal there, I'm sure, and not just the infamous club he runs with his brother. Not that I can get his brother to speak more than two words to me. Oh, wait, he did say, 'yes, Lady Elizabeth,' when I asked him if the hat I'd picked up was his. I swear I almost swooned at his condescending to speak to me at all."

Lottie felt her eyebrows raise at the repressed fury in Eliza's voice. Her sister never lost her temper with anyone. She could say no more, though, as suddenly the brothers were beside them, with Ash and Vivien close behind. Louis César flashed Eliza a dazzling smile and winked at her.

"Race you to that big oak on the far side of the field," he challenged, before urging his horse forward without waiting for her to accept.

"Oh!" Eliza exclaimed, and then laughed, springing her own mount to pursue him.

Lottie watched the two of them, admiring the picture they made in the sunshine. Eliza was on excellent form today. Her pale blue riding gown hugged her lush curves and her dark glossy curls bounced as she rode. She turned to demand of Mr Demarteau why he was so damned rude to her sister, only to see the look in his eyes as he too watched her and his brother gallop across the fields.

Oh, goodness.

Lottie gasped, never having seen such naked longing in her life.

Demarteau turned his head to see her staring at him in shock and his expression changed in an instant, locked down, cold and remote. It was such a startling change, she wondered if perhaps she had imagined the yearning she'd seen. He turned away and spurred his horse on, following his brother.

"You saw it too, didn't you?"

Lottie turned to see Vivien, her eyes alight with triumph.

"Saw what?" Lottie asked, uncertain now what she had seen.

"Demarteau. He wants Eliza. It's eating him up inside to see her with his brother."

"But… But why does he not…?"

Vivien rolled her eyes and reached to soothe her horse, a highly strung creature who'd taken exception to a patch of jaunty ox-eye daisies and was dancing sideways. "He's illegitimate, Lottie, and his brother needs to marry her to establish himself back in society. You've seen how he stands guard over the fellow, like he's some kind of guardian angel."

Lottie snorted. "He's the least angelic man I've ever seen in my life, but I take your point. You think he's being noble."

Vivien shrugged. "Likely he doesn't think he has a chance anyway, and he resents the fact. That's why he's being so appalling to poor Eliza. He assumes she would look down her pretty nose at him before she gave him a chance."

"Oh, but Eliza would never...!" Lottie exclaimed.

"No, but he doesn't know that, does he? He'll think she's the same as every cut-glass beauty of the nobility. You know how some would react if a man like that even dared meet their eyes, the precious darlings."

Lottie snorted, knowing exactly what she meant. They'd been lucky indeed with their parents. Although her father was a duke, and very aware of the respect due his title, he was neither pompous nor priggish and, if he ever acted the least bit high in the instep, their far more prosaic mama brought him down to earth with a bump. She had never allowed her children airs and graces, and detested snobbery.

Indeed, Aunt Helena had married a self-made man who had been born in the workhouse. The family knew Papa had not been pleased about the match and tried to break them apart, but when it became clear Helena and Gabriel Knight were truly in love, he'd relented. Mr Knight was not considered good *ton*, but he was so wealthy no one could ignore him. So, whilst their parents would never encourage the man, and would certainly not look upon a match between one of their daughters with a man like Demarteau with any enthusiasm, they would not treat him with anything less than respect and courtesy. Vivien was correct all the same: Mr Demarteau did not know that.

"Come on, let's catch them up," Vivien said. She turned to look over her shoulder, discovering her brother dawdling some distance back, his head tipped back to enjoy the sun. "Ash, you slug, come along or we shall leave you behind."

Ash sighed and gathered his reins, and soon they were all galloping across the fields, and Lottie's spirit's lifted. The sun was shining, the countryside ablaze with colour, and she was with her friends. She must enjoy this and pray she would do nothing to cause a rift between them all.

Cassius caught up with his friends just as they settled down to their picnic. Once he'd washed and shaved, his headache had abated enough to ride out after them. They sat in the shade of a copse of trees beside the moat that surrounded the magnificent Bodiam Castle. Swallows dipped low over the water, while birdsong and the distant whickering of the horses made a restful backdrop as he sat down on the blanket beside Ash and Vivien, as far from Lottie as he could get. The temptation to watch her was hard to resist, though, especially as the picture she made had him longing to paint her. Her copious riding skirts were arranged in swathes of pink, and the military style frogging in dark green emphasised her trim waist and the swell of her breasts. Her ride here had been enough to dislodge some of her hairpins, and the neat arrangement was somewhat dishevelled, thick golden curls tumbling to her shoulders. When combined with the flush of colour from the warm afternoon, it gave her the appearance of having been disarranged in a wild embrace. Cassius felt his mouth grow dry.

The sound of Eliza's laughter caught his attention, and he forced his gaze away, instead observing his friend with Louis César. He wasn't sure how he felt about the two of them, and the fact that Louis was obviously flirting with her. Not that he could begrudge either of them. Louis did not know of his understanding with Eliza, and he had been so obviously avoiding her he could hardly blame her for not rebuffing a man like the handsome and wealthy Comte de Villen. Louis César was a friend, and someone he respected and liked, but Cassius had heard rumours that the brothers were dangerous. He had always dismissed such stories, having seen nothing in their manner to give him cause for alarm. Louis was beautiful and bound to be the cause of resentment and therefore gossip. Both he and Demarteau were older than the rest of their group, though, with Nic in his early thirties, and they carried a world-weary air of men who had seen and done everything there was. Could he trust Louis to be the husband Eliza deserved? His reputation would suggest not, but Cassius was hardly in a position to warn Eliza off. He must speak with her today, no matter what. His attention turned back to the conversation.

"But how does anyone go about having a love affair in England?" Louis César complained, his expression one of bewilderment. "It is impossible to be alone with a young lady for even a moment. They are constantly chaperoned, and never from beneath the eyes of their diligent mamas. It is most vexing."

Vivien laughed at his consternation, though her scathing tone indicated she did not disagree in the least. "Indeed, it is not like in our parents' day, which I am told they railed against hard enough. The rules of proper conduct have become ridiculously rigorous. If the thing is done correctly, one must be a perfect young lady and marry a man without ever having a private conversation with him, let alone stealing a kiss—my word, no! —for only a wicked woman would think of doing such a shameless thing. If you are lucky, you might touch her hand when you help her from her carriage, which is quite enough to make the poor creature swoon."

Her brother gave a low chuckle and shook his head. "But, then, comte, you have the rare good fortune that the duchess is a revolutionary."

Vivien laughed at her brother and nodded.

"Our scandalous Mama too and all the Peculiar Ladies, Ash, let us be fair," she said, plucking a grape from the bunch she held and popping it in her mouth.

"*Mon Dieu*," Louis César replied with every expression of alarm as his hand went to his throat. "Should I fear that I will lose my head?"

"Of course," Lottie replied, sharing a glance with Vivien that Cassius could not read. "Everyone loses their heads over Eliza."

"Not forgetting the incomparable Miss Anson and your lovely self, *bien sûr*," the comte added, with such a charming smile that Cassius felt just a little less friendly towards him.

"Oh no," Lottie said with a laugh. "Not me! I'm far too uncomfortable a character for polite society. I'm too outspoken and ruffle everyone's feathers by saying or doing the wrong thing. Mama fears I am a scandal waiting to happen. Eliza, by comparison, is far cleverer, and makes them believe she's a sweet little dimwit so they're not afraid of her, and thus she gets away with murder."

"Lottie!" Eliza exclaimed in amused outrage. "You make me sound positively Machiavellian."

Lottie frowned and shook her head. "Not at all. It is what clever women are reduced to: pretending ignorance so that we do not alarm society. I would do it too if I were able, but I do not have half your brain, and you know my wretched mouth always runs away with me. You have the patience of a saint, Eliza, and well you know it."

"Keep chattering such nonsense about me and I shall prove you wrong, wretch," Eliza said, stealing a grape from the bunch Vivien held and lancing it at her sister.

Lottie laughed as it bounced off her nose. "Oh, I say. Good shot, Eliza."

"Is it truly an act?"

Everyone stilled and the convivial atmosphere dissipated as Mr Demarteau spoke, for until now he'd been silent. His voice was deep, his French accent touching the words and softening them, though his tone was anything but soft. The fact that he had directly addressed Eliza held everyone spellbound.

"I beg your pardon?" Eliza replied, stiffening, her demeanour at once several degrees cooler.

Demarteau's eyes glinted with something dark and fierce and he leaned towards Eliza as he spoke, his voice lowering. "The appearance of a perfect English lady with pretty manners and a sweet temperament. Is it truly who you are, or is it an act as your sister implies?"

"That is not at all what I meant," Lottie said, her colour rising at the implication she had revealed her sister was deceitful when she was only doing what all women must to survive society's strictures.

"I believe Mr Demarteau knows that, Lottie, dear," Eliza said with a tight smile. "He only wishes to poke me with a stick and see if I bite."

"And will you?"

There was an intensity to the demand that Cassius did not like.

"Nic," he said, his tone sharp. "I have told you what manner of woman Lady Elizabeth is, and that she is my dearest friend. I do not believe you need any further explanation than the proof of what is in front of you."

Demarteau dragged his gaze from Eliza to Cassius and inclined his head.

"Quite right, Cassius. Forgive me." He turned back to Eliza, his face unreadable. "*Mille excuses.* Forgive me, my lady, my manners are not fit for your company. I shall remove myself from it."

He got up and left, and Cassius turned back to Eliza to see her cheeks were blazing and her eyes glittering, but her chin was up, her back straight as she watched him stride away.

"Eliza," he began, but Louis César had reached for her hand.

"Forgive him, Eliza," he said softly. "I do not know why he acts so, but my brother has not been himself of late. I will speak to him."

"There's really no need to trouble yourself. I shall disregard it," Eliza said, waving the whole incident away as if it were nothing, though her voice was not entirely steady.

"Nonetheless," Louis said, and got to his feet, following his brother towards the path that led to the castle.

"Well," Vivien said, her eyes alight with mischief as she looked at Lottie. "That *was* enlightening."

"Diverting, certainly," Eliza said, with a brittle tone Cassius did not recognise as belonging to his friend. "I think I shall stretch my legs. I need to work up an appetite before I do justice to this splendid picnic."

She got to her feet, brushing down her skirts, and Cassius knew he must speak to her, at the very least to ensure she was not too upset by Nic's odd behaviour. Louis César was right, the man was not himself.

"I'll come with you," he said, relieved when Eliza gave him a grateful smile and nodded.

"Thank you, Cassius, I should like that."

Eliza hardly knew what she felt as she walked beside the moat, doing a circuit of the castle to calm her jittering heart. The nerve of the man! He did not speak a blasted word to her and when he finally opened his mouth he... he.... Well, she hardly knew how to describe it. For it had not just been his words–which seemed to demand she reveal that she was not the nice, well-mannered lady everyone knew her to be, but some kind of she-devil beneath the civilised exterior–it had been the look he gave her, the sensation of being the entire focus of those dark, dark eyes, and the ferocity of his attention. It was like being cornered by something wild and beautiful, afraid the wrong move might see you bloody with a savage bite, but not wanting to turn away from a creature so rare and powerful. She wondered now if she had been correct to react with such hauteur and anger, if indeed he had been deliberately intent on provoking and embarrassing her, or if there had been a serious question there. If so, her honest answer was that she did not know. She had become uncertain of who she was and what she wanted. For so long she had believed it had been Cassius and a life with him, her dearest friend. Now, though, Cassius was avoiding her, and Mr Demarteau made her wonder….

"Are you well, Eliza?"

Eliza forced her thoughts from the aggravating Mr Demarteau to the man beside her. She looked up at the handsome face of her dearest friend, the man she thought she had loved above all others and gave a sigh of relief. She did love him. Cassius was kind and familiar and he would never provoke her or ask such unnerving questions.

"I am all the better for your company," she said, slipping her arm through his. It was so reminiscent of their lives before he'd gone away that she felt a swell of nostalgia. "Isn't this lovely? Just like old times."

He did not answer, and she glanced up at him.

"Yes," he said hurriedly, smiling. "Very much like old times."

Eliza frowned, disquiet niggling at her. He did not seem entirely at ease in her company and, now that her temper was settling, she remembered he had been avoiding her. Honestly, she felt as if everyone knew something she did not. What with Vivien and Lottie sharing conspiratorial glances, Mr Demarteau's strange behaviour, and Cassius avoiding her, she was getting a tad paranoid. All at once her legendary patience deserted her and she turned to face Cassius.

"Tell me," she said, wondering why her heart was thudding so wildly.

"Tell you what?" he asked, such alarm in his eyes she wondered what she might discover.

"Well, why don't we start with why you have been avoiding me? I have a dozen letters all professing how eager you were to see me and tell me of everything you've done, and you've barely spoken a dozen words to me since you got home. For a man who implied he would ask me to marry him when he returned from his travels, that would seem a little odd, do you not think?"

There, she'd said it. She stared at him, waiting for him to give her some perfectly reasonable explanation and deny that there was a problem at all. Cassius would tell her nothing had changed, and she could get engaged to him and forget about this unsettling, bothersome feeling that she was living someone else's life.

"I…." he began and then cleared his throat. He reached for her hands, clasping them in his own. "Eliza, I've behaved badly and I must beg your forgiveness, only… only, you truly are my dearest friend in the world, and I cannot bear the thought of hurting you, and so… and so I have been a coward, and—"

"You don't wish to marry me."

Eliza stared at him in shock as she saw the truth in his eyes, heard what he was clumsily trying to tell her. He didn't want her. He'd gone away and fallen out of love with her and not been able to face telling her the truth.

She drew in a sharp breath, remembering her father's words, remembering comments other people had made, and the truth made humiliation burn down her neck.

"Everyone knows, don't they?" she said, suddenly finding her corset was too tightly laced. She pressed a hand to her ribcage, still able to feel her heart careening about beneath the busk and several layers of fabric. "Everyone but me."

"No, Eliza," he protested, shaking his head. "That's not true."

"Do your parents know?" she demanded.

He hesitated and she knew she was right.

"What about Ash and Vivien?" She gasped at the guilt she saw flare in his eyes. "Oh… Oh, my word. I should have realised, should have seen, but I never did see anything until it was staring me in the face, did I? I have no imagination, just as you always said. You always complained about it did you not? Lud, what a fool I must look."

"*No*! No, Eliza, never that," Cassius exclaimed, holding her hand tighter, but she snatched it away, unable to bear his touch. She was adrift, uncertain of what she should to do. All the things in her life she had believed to be certainties now appeared to have been built on sand, and her neat world had shifted beneath her feet.

"Leave me alone," she said, appalled to discover she was going to cry. She wasn't even certain why. Hadn't she been questioning if Cassius was right for her, if he was really what she wanted? But it had all happened at once and she could not bear that everyone had known what she had not. How blind she had been.

"Eliza, don't go. I… Oh, God, love, I'm so sorry. I should have told you at once, but—"

"Yes," she said, holding onto her dignity by a thread. "Yes, you should."

"Please understand…."

"No. No, I don't wish to understand. Not yet. I will, I'm sure, but at this moment I want to be very angry, Cassius. So do me the very great favour of going away and *leaving me be*."

She almost got the furious words out, but then her voice quavered, and so she picked up the heavy skirts of her riding habit and ran.

Chapter 9

Dear Aunt Helena,

How I wish you were here. I sorely need some advice. I am so angry and confused, but I am afraid I'm angry with the wrong person and for the wrong reasons. My world is being turned upside down, and it frightens me. I do not know what to do, or even what I want.

I know Uncle Gabe's work is keeping you from Holbrook, but I do hope you will come soon.

— *Excerpt of a letter to Lady Helena Knight from Lady Elizabeth Adolphus.*

1st July 1838, Bodiam Castle, Robertsbridge.

Lottie hurried over to Eliza as she saw her storming towards the horses.

"Eliza, what is it? Whatever is wrong?"

"Nothing," Eliza said, which was patently untrue. "Help me mount, would you?"

Lottie gaped, wondering how on earth to do that.

"But you can't just leave!"

"Watch me," Eliza retorted, such fury glinting in her eyes Lottie was taken aback.

Eliza never lost her temper. Not ever. *She* did, but not Eliza; she was too sweet-natured, too calm, too—

"Are you just going to watch, or are you going to help me?"

Lottie started, staring at Eliza in alarm. "If… If you really want me to, but Eliza, you must tell me—"

"Cassius doesn't want to marry me, and it appears everyone knew it but me."

Lottie swallowed as Eliza's furious green gaze settled on her, and the bitter laugh that followed made her heart hurt.

"*Et tu, Brute?*" Eliza said, shaking her head.

The flush that burned Lottie's cheeks was fuelled by guilt and misery, and she wanted nothing more than to curl up and die of shame. "Oh, Eliza, I—"

"Don't." Her sister held up a hand in warning. "Just… not now. We'll speak later, I promise, but at this moment if I cannot get away and be on my own, I feel I might well do something rash. *Please,* Lottie. Help me."

Lottie nodded, for how could she not? She hated herself, hated that Eliza had been hurt, and humiliated—at least in her own eyes—and hated that she might have played a part in Cassius's change of heart. How could she ever admit her feelings for him now, when Eliza was so obviously in pain?

They manoeuvred Eliza's horse to stand beside a tree trunk, and Lottie helped her with her heavy skirts as she mounted.

"Shall I come…?" she began, disliking Eliza riding off alone in such an emotional state.

Eliza shot her sister such a look that Lottie swallowed the words.

"You'll take care, then?" she asked tentatively.

Eliza's expression softened and she reached down to grasp Lottie's hand. "Don't fret, love. I shan't do anything foolish. I shall go straight home and have a good cry, and by the time you get back I shall be quite myself again."

Lottie nodded, a lump in her throat, but there was something in her sister's expression that made Lottie believe she might never be quite the same again.

By the time Lottie got back to the picnic, she found only Cassius and the twins awaiting her. It was clear that Cassius had told them of his conversation with Eliza. He looked up at her, such agony in his expression she could not remonstrate with him for whatever he had said to hurt her so. Sometimes the truth was painful enough, no matter how carefully you were given the words. Lottie knew Cassius would not have hurt Eliza for the world, any more than she would, and she swallowed down a truth of her own. She could not admit her feelings for Cassius all the while Eliza was reeling from the shock of losing him. Perhaps not for some time after that. She met his eyes, silently understanding that he had come to the same conclusion.

"Well, that did not go as expected," Vivien said, and Lottie found herself relieved at her friend's often tactless nature.

"No," she said quietly.

"Is she all right?" Viv asked, concern in her eyes.

"Should I go after her?" Ash asked, moving to get up.

"No!" Lottie said in a rush, shaking her head. "No. She wants to be by herself for a while. I'm afraid she feels she's been rather made a fool of, because she was the last to know."

Ash sent Cassius a caustic look of irritation, and Cassius blanched.

"I know, I know," he said, running a hand through his hair. "If cutting out my bloody heart would help, I'd do it. It was the only reason I delayed but... but you were all right. I should have told her as soon as I could, and now... Oh, God, Lottie, she hates me."

Lottie shook her head. "Don't be silly. She could never hate you, and she'll realise it was for the best once she calms down. You were never suited in that way. That is the only reason everyone guessed so easily, and I know she'll see that once she can think about it calmly."

Cassius nodded but looked so utterly wretched, she wished she could comfort him, but that was not possible. Not now. Now she would have to stay well away from him, or risk losing her sister for good.

They all turned as Louis César walked back to them alone with no sign of his brother. He frowned to see that Eliza was not with them.

"Where is Lady Elizabeth?" he asked.

"She's gone back to the house," Cassius replied, his tone brittle.

"Ah," said Louis César with a wry smile. "That is a coincidence."

Eliza rode hard, urging her horse on. Bitter tears stung her eyes as the wind whipped at her face and she only wanted to ride faster, farther. She was never reckless, never did anything with abandon, and suddenly she was suffocating with the desire to do something wild. Lottie and Cassius had always complained about her lack of imagination, and she knew her forthright mother looked upon her as though she was a strange cuckoo in the nest. Mama was, after all, a novelist with a marvellous imagination, and a forthright nature, but Eliza had always preferred reality and not attracting notice. As the eldest child of a duke and duchess, she was under constant scrutiny from the *ton*, and she found the idea she might do or say anything to cause her parents embarrassment excruciating. Why, she did not know, for they would never be hard on her and would always take her side. Until recently, the rules had made her feel safe, sheltered from the storm, but now it seemed she *was* the storm, raging against the bars of a cage she had not realised she resented so bitterly. She would not go home, she decided, not yet. Instead she took a path that would lead her to the ruins of Bayham Abbey. It was a romantic Gothic ruin over an hour's ride away, but she loved it there and she needed the freedom.

Movement to her right made her turn her head, and her breath caught at the sight of Mr Demarteau. His powerful horse galloped beside her lighter beast with ease, eating up the terrain as though it flew. She met Demarteau's eyes, for once seeing nothing resembling that aloof, judgemental expression to which she had grown used. Instead, his eyes were full of understanding, full of the same desire to escape. He made a sharp sound of encouragement to his horse, who put on a burst of speed. Her own mount's ears went back, and her horse sprang forward with the desire to follow its companion. Eliza let out a burst of surprised laughter, her heart lifting, and gave the creature its head.

"Where on earth have you been?" Lottie demanded, running to Eliza as she entered the house.

Their picnic had been short-lived after Eliza and Demarteau had gone, with no one much in the mood to enjoy themselves. Lottie had rushed directly to Eliza's room only to discover she had not yet returned. She had worried herself sick the past hour and was on the point of setting up a search party to look for her when Eliza strode into the house.

She was flushed and dishevelled, with a strange glitter in her eyes Lottie had never seen before.

"Riding," Eliza said calmly, handing her hat and gloves to a footman. "I needed to clear my head."

She moved towards the stairs, certainly looking far more self-possessed than she had when she'd left the picnic.

Lottie hurried after her. "Are you quite well? Did anything happen? Did you see Mr Demarteau?"

"Who?" Eliza cast a careless glance back at her. "Oh, him. Yes, we passed each other. I believe he is still out riding."

Lottie frowned, disliking Eliza's calm tone for reasons she could not quite put her finger on.

"He said nothing else to upset you?"

"No. Really, Lottie, do stop fussing about me. I need to wash and change before dinner, and so do you," she added, giving Lottie the benefit of a critical glance.

Lottie felt her temper prick. "Eliza, you left us in an emotional state and said you were coming home for a good cry. I expected to find you weeping in your room."

Eliza shrugged. "Well, I changed my mind. After all, there is nothing to weep about, is there? Cassius does not wish to marry me, and I realise now that he is quite correct, we would not have suited. Papa tried to tell me as much before we came here, but I did not listen. Well, I am listening now, and I realise he was right. He must be, for everyone else could see it too."

"And that's it? The man you believed you were in love with has broken things off and you feel nothing?" Lottie did not know why she was so annoyed by her sister's words, but she was. If Cassius had broken things off with her, she would be wild with anguish, beyond consoling, and this ice-cold demeanour Eliza had adopted was unsettling and out of character.

"Would you prefer to see me prostrate with grief?" Eliza demanded, turning on her.

"No, of course not! Only—"

"Only it is what you expect of me, because that's how young ladies behave in such circumstances? Or were you expecting me to be kind and pretend my humiliation is of no matter, to make everyone feel better by assuring them Cassius is still my friend and there are no hard feelings?"

Lottie hesitated, realising that was exactly what she had expected. She had assumed Eliza would cry in private and then make everything all right by assuring Cassius they were still friends, and everything could go on as before—even if it wasn't true. That was what Eliza did: she smoothed wrinkles, she made everyone welcome and at ease, she was patient with insufferable relatives and people who had no manners. Now, Lottie saw that same sister give a snort of amusement.

"Well, perhaps I will, but I warn you, Lottie, I'm tired of doing what everyone expects of me. I'm tired of being the perfect young lady. You were quite right, after all. It *was* an act, not really who I am. Mr Demarteau saw through it, did he not? It is no wonder he despises me. He must think me a dreadful fraud, and I cannot say I blame him."

"*Eliza!*" Lottie exclaimed, truly startled now. "How can you say so? It isn't the least bit true. You are my sister and I know you better than I know myself. Yes, you hold your tongue when I would say something shocking, but that is because you are kind and patient."

"Is it?" Eliza demanded. "Or is it because I have not the courage to say what I think? Honestly, Lottie, I do not know myself, but I think perhaps it is time I found out. Now, if you'll excuse me, I must change, or I shall be late for dinner."

Lottie watched as Eliza hurried off to her own room. She dithered in the corridor, uncertain of what to do. Footsteps behind her made her turn and her heart leapt as she saw Cassius. To her chagrin, tears sprang to her eyes and she swallowed hard.

"Lottie," Cassius said, his expression dull, wretchedness in every line of his posture. "I've made such a mess of everything."

Lottie felt a sob rise in her throat, and more than anything she wanted to run to him, to throw herself into his arms and find comfort there, but she could not. Her sister was hurt, no matter how coolly she might claim otherwise, and Lottie could not deepen her betrayal by running into the embrace of the man who had rejected her. Instead, she shook her head and ran to her own room.

Cassius endured dinner, there was no other word for it. Eliza appeared to be quite recovered and in high spirits, flirting with Louis César and laughing with Ash and Vivien, who seemed happy to encourage her. She wore a white satin robe that sat low on her shoulders and highlighted her dark hair and green eyes. Indeed, she looked exquisite. Neither did she ignore him as he so richly deserved, nor did anything by word or deed to make him feel guilty or ill at ease, and yet he was, desperately so. He wondered if it was his pride that was hurt—if perhaps he had expected, and even hoped, that she would appear sad and listless—but he had to believe he was better than that. As it was, he drank too much and tried not to watch Lottie, who by contrast was every bit as quiet and withdrawn as he might have expected of her sister. His chest ached with the desire to speak to her, to hold her, for tonight all the life and vivacity that usually shone in her eyes was gone. She looked lost and vulnerable, and so lovely that looking upon her hurt his heart.

"But where is your brother?" Eliza asked the comte, her tone nonchalant. "I expected to see him scowling at me over dinner. I am quite disappointed to discover him absent, for I had been determined to fence with him again if he gave me the opportunity."

Louis César frowned and shook his head. "I am afraid I must apologise for my brother once more, my lady. He has gone."

Shock flashed in Eliza's eyes, there and gone before her usual self-possession returned, but Cassius saw and wondered at it.

"Gone?" she said, with the cool lift of one eyebrow. "So suddenly? My, he *must* find me reprehensible to have allowed me to drive him away."

"*Non!*" Louis César replied, shaking his head. "I promise you, nothing could be further from the truth, though I admit Nic has not been himself of late. No, indeed, he had business which needed attending to in London. I still hope he may return, but... we shall see. He sends his sincere apologies to everyone for his abrupt departure."

"Of course," Eliza said. "But you must call me Elizabeth, for we are friends now, are we not?"

Louis César smiled at her, the kind of smile that had enticed women into scandal and fighting duels over him, and Cassius could not blame Eliza for the blush that rose to her cheeks as the full force of it was turned upon her. Damn, but the man was a bloody menace.

"*Eleezabet*," Louis said, pronouncing it in the French style and making her name sound intimate and seductive. "I would be honoured."

Chapter 10

Dear Diary,

I think I ought not wish for such amusements as I had hoped to see this summer. Falling in love and finding a husband is far harder than I thought.

Eliza is not herself and poor Lottie is pining for Cassius, who no one has seen at the house for almost a week. He's hiding down at the summerhouse. I tried to speak to him, but he was in quite a surly mood and, though he was not the least unkind, I was not welcomed in his studio. He has thrown himself into a frenzy of painting and drawing and refuses to return to the party, despite his mother speaking to him quite sternly. I swear I did not eavesdrop only I was passing the summerhouse and the door was open and it was impossible not to hear the tone of her voice, even though I did not stay to hear what was said. I was proud of myself for it was very tempting to listen in, but I carried on walking and did not look back.

I just want everyone to be happy again. Papa says I must not interfere and that everyone will find their own way without my help. I am

*trying to be good and believe him, but everyone
is making <u>such</u> a mess of things.*

**—Excerpt of an entry to the diary of Lady
Catherine 'Cat' Barrington, youngest
daughter of the Marquess and Marchioness
of Montagu.**

6th July 1838, Holbrook House, Sussex.

Lottie stared up at the moon and sighed. Everyone had gone to
Mitcham Priory to visit with Baron and Lady Rothborn and their
son and daughter, Larkin and Grace. They would have dinner
together and stay overnight, returning mid-morning the following
day. Matilda and Montagu's sons would be there too and, in usual
circumstances, Lottie would have loved to attend, but her heart was
not in it. She had pleaded a headache and told her mama and Eliza
that she would go to bed early, a lie she was ill at ease with, but
what could she do? They kept plaguing her to explain what the
matter was, and she could not tell them. Her mama had given her a
very direct look and told her that whatever the trouble was, she
could be trusted to keep it to herself if Lottie wanted to speak to
her about it. Lottie knew that was true, but she felt such shame for
the situation that had arisen, she could not bear to. She did not
think she was to blame for what had happened, but… but she could
not be certain, and that uncertainty made her feel sick and
wretched.

She had to go to bed, in truth, for her maid was far too canny
not to know she was telling fibs if she did not. Yet, after an hour of
tossing and turning, she was so thoroughly tired of her own
thoughts she got up, decided on a visit to the library to find a book.
It was too early to sleep after all, so she put on her wrap and
slippers and went downstairs. Someone had left a copy of *The
Legend of Sleepy Hollow* out on one of the side tables, and Lottie
picked it up. Perhaps if she frightened herself to death she'd stop
feeling so sorry for herself. It took her precisely ten minutes to

discover she'd read the first page three times and still didn't know what it said. With a sigh, she set the book down and spied a tantalus on the sideboard with three crystal decanters. Remembering how her mama would often take a glass of brandy to help her sleep the night before the publication of a new book, she got up and went to investigate. Fortune was smiling upon her as she discovered the tantalus was unlocked.

The first measure was barely more than a couple of sips as she accustomed herself to the taste, which was not at all nice. The second went down rather easier and a pleasant glow began low in the pit of her belly. The third was a proper measure, and as she found the library suddenly stuffy and too hot, Lottie drifted out into the garden to enjoy the fresh night air and walked with no direction in mind.

Though it had not been her intention to do so, she found herself in front of the summerhouse before she realised what she had done, and she could not force her unwilling feet to make her turn around again. She was not so foolish as to spy on her beloved, though, nor to go inside as she longed to do. Instead, she sat down on the grass beside the lake and listened to the night creatures chirp and scurry. Lottie stared unseeing across the dark water spread out before her, knowing Cassius was close by... and that was as much as she was to be allowed.

❀ ❀ ❀

Cassius flung down the charcoal with a curse and walked away from yet another botched attempt. He could settle to nothing, producing in the past week what he considered to be a mediocre still life, and a tolerable painting of the sun rising on the lake outside the summerhouse. He'd spent the day trying to decide upon a new project, but nothing inspired him. Nothing but her, that was. In his heart, all he wanted was to paint Lottie. He yearned to capture the way the sun had caught her hair and lit it like a halo as she stood in the doorway to the studio, or how she had looked at the picnic with her pink skirts arranged in soft swathes around her.

With a curse, he strode to the large sheet of paper he'd pinned up and tore it down, putting a clean sheet in its place. He snatched up the charcoal again. This time the image came with laughable ease, the elegant line of her neck, the soft swell of her breasts and the lush curves of her waist and hips. Despite working purely from memory and imagination he knew he'd captured her, the essence of her, vibrant and full of life. The image of her was one he had never seen in reality, though he'd dreamt it every night since he'd returned and seen her for the first time. The look in her eyes was everything he longed for, her posture provocative. He stood back, breathing hard, longing rising inside him, hot and fierce and suffocating. With a groan, he flung the charcoal aside once more, disgusted with himself, and flung open the door, stalking down to the lake and casting his shirt aside as he went. He doubted a swim would do much to cool his ardour, but he had no better ideas.

Cassius was moving so fast and with such single-minded determination, that he almost tumbled headfirst over the sleeping figure, and was forced to sidestep to avoid it.

"What the devil?" he exclaimed.

The figure at his feet squeaked with alarm and sat up, staring at him. Cassius's heart jammed in his throat.

"Lottie?"

"Cassius!"

The two of them stared at each other, neither moving nor speaking. For his part, Cassius did not dare. To see her out here, asleep on the grass, all in virginal white like some fairy queen, was more than his willpower had been prepared for. Keeping away from her and far from temptation was one thing, but resisting what was right in front of him quite another.

"I must have fallen asleep," she said as Cassius tried to keep his gaze from the heavy blonde plait that had fallen to lie between her breasts, or to notice that her nightgown and wrap were of the finest lawn cotton and not as opaque as she might think under the moonlight.

He swallowed, forcing his brain to grind into motion and think of something to say that would not result in him behaving badly. It was not easy.

"By the lake?" he managed, hoping he'd achieved the amused tone he was striving for and the desire-roughened, gravelly sound of his own voice was all in his head.

"I went for a walk and found myself here. I... I don't remember choosing to come here only... once I was here, I could not make myself leave."

"Lottie," he said, meaning to tell her to go straight back to the house, but the words died in his throat as she stood up and took a step closer to him.

"I've missed you," she said. "I wish you would not hide down here. I'm certain Eliza feels wretched about it, too. She does not want you to be unhappy."

He snorted at that. "That is because she does not know the truth. If she knew, she would understand just how badly I have behaved."

"You did not," Lottie said at once. "*We* did not. Nothing happened, and we did not choose to feel this way on purpose. Why must we feel so wretched?"

"Because hurting Eliza is unthinkable," he said with a shrug.

Lottie sighed. "Yes."

"You should go."

"I know."

But she only gazed at him, temptation incarnate, dressed in gauzy white, and with such longing in her eyes that his body hurt and he ached with the need to touch her. Every particle of his being seemed to incline towards her as if drawn by some unseen force, even though he held himself still.

She turned away suddenly, walking purposefully towards the summerhouse.

"Lottie!" he exclaimed, not daring to follow her, for his self-control was fraying fast, and then he realised with a jolt just what she would see if she went in. "Oh, Christ!"

He took to his heels, but she was already at the door, moving inside. He crashed in behind her, hoping to tear the sketch down before she laid eyes on it but too late.

"I'm sorry," he began, feeling like an utter blackguard for having drawn her in such a way.

She was staring at the image, eyes wide with shock, her mouth open in a little 'o' of surprise.

"That's me," she said, her voice trembling. "T-That's how you see me."

"Lottie, I…." He did not know what to say, for it *was* how he had imagined her, tumbled among the sheets of his bed, her expression inviting him to come back and make love to her again.

She moved towards the drawing, and he wondered if she would tear it down and fling it at him in fury. Had he not only lost his best friend, but also the woman he was falling in love with, both gone in the space of a week? Yet she made no move to destroy it. She only gazed at it, her chest rising and falling too fast.

"It's a very good likeness," she said after a long moment, during which Cassius realised he'd been holding his breath. "But…."

He braced himself, awaiting the furious set down, or the caustic reprimand that must surely follow.

"But if you are preparing sketches for a painting, I think you ought to work from life."

"W-What?" The breath he'd been holding escaped him in a rush, as he saw the wrap fall from her shoulders and her nightgown follow it down to form a soft heap of white cotton at her feet. He gaped, his mouth dropping open as he took in the elegant curve of her spine, her dainty waist and then… and then the most delicious, most perfectly plump bottom in the world. His gaze snagged there, and it was a long moment before he could even consider the long, shapely legs. Then her golden hair tumbled free down her back and he realised she had released it from its plait.

Cassius could not move, could not think, could do nothing but stare in stunned awe at the image before him, an image that would be burned upon his brain until the day he died. She glanced over her shoulder at him, her cheeks pink but her blue eyes calm.

God, she was brave. She threw herself at life, at the things she wanted and was always so completely honest, no matter the risk to herself. She would make herself vulnerable rather than hide behind rules and propriety as most people did. He admired her for that, more than he could say. It was only now that he realised that he always had admired that about her, that fearless spirit, the joy she took in life, making even an ordinary day brighter. Being with her would always be an adventure, no matter where they were.

His breathing picked up, his heart thudding erratically behind his ribs as she moved to the daybed he'd had brought down from the house. He'd draped it with rich fabric, velvet and satin, and cushions in vibrant colours, and it was all he could do not to moan with longing as she laid herself down upon it. She raised one arm above her head and Cassius made a strangled, whimpering sound he wasn't terribly proud of, but that any man with a pulse would have well understood. Her breasts were full and creamy and tipped with delicate pink nipples and oh, God… Oh, dear God in heaven, he was going to hell. He ought not look. He… He looked. He looked and looked and could not stop. He ought to throw his coat over her and turn his back and… and run like hell, but he wasn't going to.

"Like this?" she asked, her voice faint and nervous as she arranged herself for him.

Cassius swallowed, finding his mouth dry.

"Lottie," he rasped, his chest rising and falling like a damned bellows.

"Don't you want to draw me?" she asked with challenge in her eyes.

"*Want* to?" he said with an incredulous laugh. "Of course I bloody well want to."

He ought not to have spoken so, but he was so far beyond proper behaviour it hardly seemed to matter. What he wanted was to join her on the day bed and feel all that warm silken skin along the length of his body, to kiss every satiny inch and map her curves from head to toe with his tongue.

"Well, then," she said, putting up her chin. "Th-Think of me as a bowl of fruit. You are a professional, are you not?"

"Lottie, if anyone were to see—"

"Then make very sure that they don't," she said, her tone fierce. "It is for your eyes only, Cassius."

"Of course it bloody is!" he exclaimed. "You think I would let anyone else see—"

"No," she said, before he worked himself into a passion over the idea. "No. I do not. So… this is for you, Cassius. Paint me as I am, with no flattery, no disguises, or clever tricks. Paint the truth and know that you alone have seen what I really am."

"Do you think I know?" he asked, curious about that. "Do you think I see everything that you are?"

A slow smile curved over her mouth. "Do you remember the summer before you left? We were all out on the terrace. It had been a long, hot day and everyone was sleepy, dozing in the sun. You told me of all the places you were going to visit in France. I was so envious, and I told you that I wanted to travel too, especially to see Egypt and visit the pyramids. We talked about it for hours."

Cassius nodded. He did remember, with startling clarity. Had it begun then perhaps, without him realising, for he remembered the passion in her eyes as she'd spoken about the great Italian explorer, Belzoni and all his discoveries. He'd been as caught up in the conversation as she had, but then it had been time to dress for dinner and... had he forgotten? Or had he known he was playing with fire? Either way, he'd been about to go away for two years so perhaps he had just not allowed himself to think... to consider...

"I don't know everything about you," he said, finding himself breathless, as much with excitement at his sudden understanding as with the glorious creature laid out before him. "No more than you know everything about me, but I think we both like adventure and surprises, and walking into the unknown. I think you could live a different life and find joy in it. I think we could do that... together."

She let out a breath, her eyes sparkling with happiness and he knew he was right, knew this astonishing woman was brave enough to face the life he wanted to live. No, not only to face it, but to relish it, just as he would. Eliza wanted to change the world in which she lived but that world was in England. Cassius wanted to see everything, to record the world in its entirety, and Lottie wanted that too, and that was the difference between them.

"You want to leave again, don't you?" she asked.

Cassius nodded, knowing he could admit it to her. He was so happy to be home, to see his family and the people he loved, but there was an itch inside of him too, something that tugged at his soul and beckoned him to pack up and go.

"So do I. England is stifling sometimes. There are so many rules, and I'm so often in trouble for breaking them. I should like to see places where life is different."

"We shall," he promised her, though he had no right to, not yet. "Somehow. We'll figure it out, Lottie."

"I hope so, Cass. I'm counting on it. Now, you'd best get on and draw me, warts and all remember," Lottie said with a laugh. She gave a happy sigh and stretched on the day bed, and Cassius swallowed a groan. Perhaps he was weak. He was most certainly reprehensible not to force her to dress and send her back to the house, but Cassius could have no more turned away from the sight before him than he could have flown to the moon. Even his desire for her was set to one side as he worked, though it simmered in the background, revealing itself in every sumptuous sweep of his hand as he reproduced the beauty before him with loving attention to detail. As the hours passed, he produced sketch after sketch, each one finer than the last, his heart singing with joy, with love for this beautiful creature, this goddess, who made him come alive and inspired him to reach higher than he'd ever dared dream.

The last sketch was his favourite, the image he would carry in his heart always, engraved there for all time. For his beloved had fallen asleep, her lovely mouth parted on a sigh, her hair tumbling over her breasts, the nipples peeking shyly through. She was relaxed, safe in his presence, and the honour of her trust in him was enough to make his throat tight. He gathered up her night gown and wrap, and told himself sternly that she would get dressed and he would escort her back to the house. That was all. Good Christ, as if he hadn't been villain enough for one night.

With that thought in the forefront of his mind, he moved to the day bed and covered her with the wrap before leaning down to wake her.

"Lottie," he said, his voice low, not daring to touch her, to shake her awake, for if his skin touched hers he would surely be lost. "Lottie, darling, wake up."

"Hmmm," she mumbled, hazy with sleep as her eyelids fluttered.

Cassius saw a dazzling flash of lapis lazuli blue that made him long to reach for his paints, even if he'd not slept and it was almost dawn. He smiled at her, the desire to pull her against him greater still, though he denied himself that too.

"Wake up, love."

She blinked, focusing on him at last as her mouth curved and she reached for him, coiling her arms about his neck.

"Lottie," he said, sounding more a croak of desperation than her name as she tugged at his neck, pulling his head down, and pressed her lips against his.

Chapter 11

Wulfric,

You are insane to consider returning and stirring up another hornet's nest. For even were it not your intention, your presence will inevitably cause trouble as it always does. Keep your anonymity, my friend. It has served you well this many years.

I must tell you at his point that Nic has deserted me. Though I find it hard to fathom after he has been my shadow for so long, something has driven him from my side, and I do not know what. I have a suspicion that a woman is at the bottom of it, but you must agree it seems so ludicrous I can hardly believe it. We have been here days only, and… but I must do something to fix the situation. If only I knew what.

— Excerpt of a letter to an anonymous friend, from Louis César de Montluc, Comte de Villen.

Dawn. Morning of the 7th July 1838, The Summerhouse, Holbrook, Sussex.

Cassius was lost the moment her lips touched his, reduced to a quivering schoolboy in the arms of his first sweetheart. He had never been short of female attention. His father had attained a wicked reputation as a young man, though he protested it was far from true, but he was still acknowledged one of the handsomest men of the *ton*. Cassius had been made in his image, as anyone would tell you. Though his father had given him many a stern lecture on the perils of dallying with the female household staff—which he had heeded—it had not been easy. Women liked him and were drawn to him with little effort on his part, and he liked them too. There was nothing that pleased him more than tumbling into bed with a willing partner, especially one who knew what they liked and was prepared to ask for it.

Lottie, though....

Lottie made him giddy. When he saw her, he could think only of poetry, of the need to capture her image in every aspect, of the desire to take her to his bed and never let her go. She called to something inside of him that wanted to pack up his paints and head off on an adventure with no set destination in mind.

Eliza would not care for such a life, he knew, and so he had decided on the two years he had taken to cure his wanderlust before he settled down. Not that it had worked. His time away had only cemented the knowledge that a settled life would drive him mad. He'd tried to pretend otherwise, tried to tell himself it was just cold feet and would wear off, but the closer to home and Eliza he'd got, the more despondent he'd become.

Lottie would not want that of him. She would not ask him to stay in one place, but she would follow him in a heartbeat. He knew that now. Now she'd reminded him the memories returned, tumbling over each other. He remembered the days before he'd left with Lottie pouring over maps and asking him if he would visit this place and that one. He remembered now, the longing in her eyes, the yearning to go with him. How the hell had he forgotten? She had been so excited for him, so obviously envious and he... he could give her that. Lottie would not care about uncomfortable carriages or sleeping in rooms that were not quite respectable or going to places that had seen nothing resembling a tourist. Lottie would live it with him, would *demand* she go with him and not be left behind, just as she had when they were children, determined to be included.

"Darling," he murmured against her lips, trying to pull back, knowing it was dangerous to them both in so many ways… but he made the mistake of looking down at her instead.

Cassius found himself drowning in a sea of blue, in the swathes of Mary's cloak, the brilliant flash of a kingfisher skimming the lake on a clear summer's day.

"Oh, God."

He moaned and pressed his lips to her temple, her nose, her cheek. He sought the warm, delicate patch of skin beneath her ear that made her breath hitch when he kissed it, and he forced his hands to remain braced against the day bed and not on her. His palms itched to feel her warm skin, to fill his hands with her and lose himself in the pleasure of her. Yet, he had made such a mess of everything already. He would be a bloody, damned gentleman if it bloody, damned killed him. It really might too.

"We can't do this."

Lottie made a sound akin to a sob of frustration and he wanted to weep too, for he would surely run mad if he could not have her. Now. At once.

"We can't… Eliza…." he said helplessly.

It was the one thing he could say that would bring them back to their senses, as brutal as a bucket of ice water flung over their heads.

"Yes," Lottie said, resignation in her tone. "I know."

Cassius let out an uneven breath and forced himself to move away. He turned his back as Lottie stood and dressed, the rustling of fabric providing his imagination with quite enough information to torment him.

"I'll see you in the morning, then," she said, her voice dull.

Cassius turned, wanting to take away the sorrow he could see in her eyes. "I'll walk you back."

She shook her head at once. "No. Someone might see. It's only the garden, and I got here easily enough. It's quite all right. Goodnight, Cassius."

A thousand words crowded on his tongue: protests, demands that she stay, love words and promises he had no right to speak. In the end, though, he said none of them. He'd botched everything and he'd not botch this. If he had to wait to declare his intentions, then so be it. He must wait. So he simply nodded and watched her go, watched her until she was out of sight, the soft white fabric of her wrap fading into the darkness like some lovely, ghostly dream.

At least no one doubted she was ill, Lottie thought with a wry smile. She'd found her bed in the hour before dawn and fallen into an exhausted sleep, not waking until gone midday. When she finally opened her eyes, it was to discover her temper fraying and a dull headache that pulsed at her temples. It was all well and good for her and Cassius to speak of and dream about a beautiful future, but this morning reality seemed far too big an ordeal to overcome. Despondency settled over her, dampening her spirits like a sodden wool blanket. She felt lethargic under the weight of it and cross with the world at large, and it was too easy to pretend she had come down with some mysterious malady. After breaking her fast in her room and discovering that heartache did not affect her appetite, she made her way down the stairs.

The afternoon was a little cooler than previous days, with soft cotton wool clouds scudding about the sky and, at intervals, hiding the sun from view. As she did not much like her own company at present, she judged it best she not inflict it on anyone else, and headed for the library. Though it was a lovely room, it would usually be empty on a summer's afternoon, when the countess had arranged entertainments for her guests. There was archery set up today and there had been murmurs of taking boats out on the lake, but Lottie had not bothered herself to discover what they had decided upon. Instead, she drifted into the library, intending to sit herself down and gaze out of the window. She was thinking about last night and the fact she had completed her dare already, not that she could tell anyone. Oh, good heavens no, but… but she *had* been wicked. There was no doubt of that.

To her chagrin, and with the unpleasant jolt of a guilty conscience, Lottie discovered Eliza had beaten her to it. Her sister was curled up in a comfy chair with a book in her lap and her gaze fixed on the sky outside. Lottie hesitated and had almost decided to bolt before Eliza looked up and saw her.

"Do stop dithering in the doorway and sit down. I won't bite."

Shame rose inside Lottie as she realised Eliza probably wished for her company, for a confidante to discuss Cassius and his rejection of her. Lottie had not offered that, as she would have done in any other circumstance.

"Are you well, Eliza?" she asked tentatively.

Her sister turned her expressive green eyes upon Lottie, one dark eyebrow lifting. "No, I am considering throwing myself in the lake and having done with it."

At Lottie's gasp of shock, Eliza snorted and rolled her eyes, something so out of character that Lottie could only gape.

"Oh, sit down, Lottie. You're making the place look untidy," Eliza said, shaking her head.

She made an impatient gesture towards the chair beside her and so Lottie took it, regarding her cautiously. It was unlike Eliza to make sarcastic comments and cynical remarks, and this new version of her sibling was unsettling.

"Did you have a nice time last night?" she ventured, too cowardly to tackle this unknown creature head on.

Eliza shrugged. "I suppose so. Louis César was most amusing, very attentive. Everyone thinks he will propose to me."

"So soon? Will you accept?" Lottie asked.

Eliza plucked irritably at a loose thread on the overstuffed chair she was curled into.

"I don't know. Do you think I should?" She turned her gaze upon Lottie, a frown tugging her dark brows together.

"You don't love him," Lottie said, startled to discover Eliza would even consider such a thing.

"No."

"Well, then."

"Well, then," Eliza said absently, turning away and watching the clouds as they drifted past, her finger tracing the embossed pattern on the leather cover of the book she wasn't reading. She was quiet for a long moment. "Do you think he'll join us again, or have I frightened him away?"

Lottie blinked at the sudden change of subject but then grasped at the opportunity to mend fences. "You haven't frightened him. He just feels horribly guilty for having upset you so. He never meant to you know. He would rather die than hurt you, that's why he couldn't bear to tell you. I know he misses you. You're his best friend, Eliza and now he can't face you because he feels so wretched. We both know it isn't in Cassius to be cruel or unkind."

She let out a breath, relieved to have been able to say something to defend him.

Eliza turned a puzzled expression in her direction.

"Cassius?" she murmured and then her expression cleared. "Oh. Yes, Cassius."

A slight blush of colour tinged her cheeks and she set her book aside, getting to her feet.

"Where are you going?" Lottie asked, baffled by her sister's odd behaviour.

"Going? Oh, umm… for a walk, I suppose," Eliza said with a vague wave of her hand as she left Lottie alone.

Lottie stared after her, utterly perplexed. She was not alone for long. Why on earth was the library so popular this afternoon?

"Ah, here is sleeping beauty," Ash said, walking into the room and throwing himself casually down in the chair beside her.

Somehow, he still looked exquisitely elegant, sprawled with his long legs stretched out before him and his arms flopped out on either side, even with the addition of his outrageous waistcoat. It was lilac silk today, with ivy leaves twining across his chest embroidered in gold thread. His sister followed behind and tsked at his abandoned pose, before turning her gaze upon Lottie with a mischievous twinkle in her eyes.

"Look at him. He thinks he's as glamorous as a Maharajah, as impressive as a magnificent Indian prince. I'm afraid no one is going to recline on silken pillows and peel you a grape, Ashton dear, no matter how you long for it."

"I long for no such thing," he said, indignation in his blue eyes. "I only wish to be adored unconditionally. Is that too much to ask for?"

"Yes," Lottie and Vivien said in unison.

"But I *am* adorable," Ash replied, looking mystified by their response.

"Yes, my dear," Vivien replied, her tone soothing and more than a touch condescending, as if she were placating a difficult child. "On occasion that *might* be true, but the only kind of girl who would adore you unconditionally would also bore you silly.

You need someone aggravating, someone to shake you up a bit and make you exert yourself."

"That doesn't sound the least bit comfortable," Ash replied, folding his arms.

"No," Vivien said with a smug smile. "It doesn't, does it?"

"Why do you want me to be miserable?" he demanded of her, sitting up straighter now.

Vivien laughed at the look on his face. "Oh, you silly creature. I don't. I want you to be happy, and you never will be if it's too easy. You are too like me, too like Mama, truth be told. We bore easily."

Ash snorted, and then as if by mutual accord—though nothing was said—they turned their attention to Lottie.

"Well, then?" they asked.

She had noticed before now that they often seemed to know what one another was thinking without saying a word. "You do know it is creepy when you do that," she groused, glaring at them.

They laughed and Lottie huffed. "Very amusing, I'm sure."

"Answer the question," Ash said impatiently.

"Was that a question?" Lottie demanded, wondering if she'd missed something.

"Oh, come, come," Vivien said, giving a dramatic sigh. "Cassius did not come with us last night and at the last moment you cried off with a megrim, which I've never known you to have in your life before. You're always disgustingly healthy and full of the joys."

Ash nodded his agreement. "Which means you had an ulterior motive."

Lottie flushed. Really, it was quite unfair that she felt so wretchedly guilty, for she had not stayed behind to snatch at an opportunity to see Cassius. She felt ashamed enough without plotting to see him behind her sister's back. Nevertheless, she *had* seen him, had kissed him, had stripped bare and allowed him to gaze upon her as no man had ever done before. Worse than that, she had desperately wanted him to do a great deal more than gaze. She still did. Lottie was restless and fretful and agitated, and she felt very much as if she might burst into flames. He'd barely touched her, but the look in his eyes had been eloquent enough, and now the aching need for him was so distracting she didn't know whether she wanted to scream or cry. No... she knew. She wanted to run down to the summerhouse and demand that he put her out of her misery. Now. At *once*!

"Oh, my. It's worse than I thought," Ashton murmured, a knowing look in his eyes that made her feel hot all over.

"It isn't." She put up her chin, glaring back at him. "I did *not* stay behind to see him!"

"Keep your voice down," Vivien hissed, gesturing to the open door.

Lottie groaned and put her head in her hands. "Oh, I'm horrible. I'm a horrible person and I don't deserve to be happy."

"Well, I know you're horrible, obviously," replied a matter-of-fact voice that could only belong to a sibling.

Lottie sat up straighter as her brother strolled in. She'd not seen much of Jules, who had been very vague about his whereabouts since they arrived and could never be found. She suspected the barmaid at The King's Head. Whispering among the staff led her to believe she was a pretty girl and 'vastly accommodating.' This was usually said with a wink and a tone of amusement that led Lottie to draw her own conclusions.

"Oh, go away, Jules," she said crossly.

"Why should I?" he demanded. "You've just admitted you are a horrible person, which I've been telling you for years, but I'm fascinated to know why you've suddenly realised I'm correct."

Lottie glowered at him. At nineteen he had all the swagger and self-confidence a handsome, wealthy, and titled young man might feel permitted to own. He was tall and had looks as dark and arresting as his father, but had not yet grown into his shoulders. He was all long limbs and athletic grace, and it made her furious how her friends twittered about him like a lot of silly birds, when he was an utter blockhead. They had always been at odds, though, perhaps too similar and too close in age to be friends.

"Perhaps now isn't the best time," Ash began, as he was a sensible human being and was aware of the rising tension in the room.

"Now is the perfect time if my sister is going to unburden herself of her sins," Jules said with a grin.

Ridiculously and much to her dismay, Lottie felt her eyes burn. Why? *Why*, when Jules was just being Jules, the vexing, impossible younger brother she regularly wanted to hit with a heavy blunt object? Yet he struck too close to the truth. She did wish to unburden herself of her sins, for she truly loved her sister, and Eliza was hurt and she… and she had….

Lottie burst into tears and ran from the room.

Chapter 12

Dear Diary,

The summer ball cannot come soon enough. We need more guests. Perhaps if the house is filled with our friends and their families this odd atmosphere will disappear. I want so much to do something, but Papa scolded me and said if I interfered he would be very disappointed in me, and everyone knows having Papa disappointed in you is the worst feeling in the world. It's far worse than him being cross, which he almost never is.

—Excerpt of an entry to the diary of Lady Catherine 'Cat' Barrington, youngest daughter of the Marquess and Marchioness of Montagu.

8th July 1838, Holbrook House, Sussex.

It took Jules less than twenty minutes to track her down. Lottie muttered a curse. She ought to have known. He had always been far better at hide and seek than any of them as a child. He had that kind of mind.

Jules stared up at the hayloft and her legs dangling over the edge and put his hands on his hips.

"Shall I come up, or will you be a sensible creature and come down?"

"I'm not coming down," she said, folding her arms.

Jules sighed and gave the mirror shine on his boots a regretful glance before climbing up and crawling through the hay to sit beside her. He unfolded his long body until he too was sitting with his legs swinging over the edge. They sat in silence for a long time, with Lottie staring at nothing and Jules casting her anxious glances. In other circumstances it might have been amusing, for he obviously regretted upsetting her. For all he was her obnoxious brother, he really wasn't a bad person, just an annoying one.

He leaned over and bumped her shoulder.

Lottie glowered at him and said nothing before turning away.

He did it again.

And again.

"Oh, for heaven's sake!" she exclaimed. "Is this your idea of an apology?"

"Of course it is," he retorted. "You don't expect me to *actually* say the words, do you?"

She stared at him in disbelief and he groaned.

"Oh, very well," he said, folding his arms. "I'm sorry I upset you, Lottie, but honestly, I don't understand how I did. I always talk to you like that, and you've never started blubbering before. You usually hit me."

She snorted at that. It was true.

"It's all right," she said, not looking at him. "It wasn't your fault."

"Wasn't it?" Jules brightened at once. "Marvellous! Well, then…."

He caught her expression and clamped his mouth shut.

"Oh, just go," she said, her shoulders slumping.

Jules fidgeted for a moment before leaning in and putting an awkward arm about her shoulder. "Is there something wrong, sis?"

To her horror, Lottie felt her lip tremble. She nodded.

Jules looked vaguely horrified but drew in a deep breath and squared his shoulders. "Oh, Lord. Well, I suppose I must do something about it then. I am your brother, after all."

"Younger brother," she sniffed. "Doesn't count."

"Of course it does!" he retorted. "Brothers look out for their sisters, no matter if they are older or younger. It's one of those unwritten rule thingies. They... well, they just do. So, tell me who I need to hit. I assume there's a fellow somewhere at the heart of it?"

"Somewhere," she agreed.

"Oh!" he said, obviously not having expected that answer. "Oh. Well. Right, then. Tell me who the blackguard is, and I'll pound him."

"Can't."

Rather to her surprise, she gave the matter some thought, though. Well, not the pounding bit—Cassius had done nothing wrong—but perhaps telling her brother about her unhappiness and this dreadful situation. That she would ever consider confiding in Jules rather than Eliza was just laughable, until she considered why she couldn't confide in Eliza.

There went the urge to laugh.

"Is this why you didn't come last night?" Jules asked, once more reminding her he wasn't quite so dim as she liked to make out.

She nodded. There was a short silence.

"You spoke to him, didn't you? Last night."

Lottie turned her head in surprise and, as Jules's green eyes met hers, she discovered she couldn't hide her blush.

"Bloody hell, Lottie!" he exclaimed in obvious shock. "You did? How the devil—"

Lottie held her breath, realising too late that her brother wasn't the least bit dim and it would only take him a short while to figure things out.

"The bastard!" he exclaimed, scrambling up and heading for the ladder.

"Jules! Jules, no… *no*! You don't understand…."

"I understand plenty," he muttered, leaping from halfway down the ladder to the floor.

Lottie was still struggling to wrestle with her heavy skirts and a ridiculous number of petticoats. Getting up the blasted ladder had been nigh on impossible and very unladylike, getting down was looking even more awkward.

"Cassius has broken Eliza's heart and now he's dallying with you, and I'm going to damn well kill him."

Lottie watched in horror as Jules stalked from the barn. She yelled after him, telling him he'd got it wrong, that he was a pigheaded idiot, and a dozen other insults… all of which had no effect whatsoever.

Oh, good heavens. What on earth had she done?

Cassius fixed his eyes on the blank canvas before him and tried not to allow his gaze to travel to the corner of the room. Stacked behind canvases and tied in a leather carrying portfolio were the drawings of Lottie. He wished there were somewhere safer for him to put them, but he could not take them to the house where curious maids might peek at his work. None of the staff were allowed in here to clean, and none of his friends or family would poke about without permission. His fingers itched with the desire to get them out, to use them to create a painting of the woman he was now certain would be his muse until the day he died.

She did things to him. Odd, marvellous things that he could not account for. Her laughter made his heart trip about and her smile lit him up with happiness. Now that he reflected on the life he'd lived before he'd gone away, he remembered dozens of occasions when she had made him laugh so hard he could hardly breathe, when she had persuaded him and Eliza to let her join them and then talked them into some silly escapade that had ended with one or all of them getting scolded and having not a single regret about it. Being with her was like being swept up in a wave and tumbled about. It left one giddy and disorientated, and damned glad about it.

Why, then, had he been so certain Eliza was the one he ought to marry? Because he'd been happy, happier than he'd realised in their company. Eliza was wonderful, her company soothing, and she was his friend. Everyone knew Eliza would be the perfect wife. She had received dozens of offers already, none of which she'd even considered for a moment… because of him. She was flawless, the kind of girl titled men would give their right arm to marry, and she'd been his for the taking. He'd just assumed their friendship would grow into love. They'd both been too young to understand the kind of magnetic attraction possible between two people, the kind they did not have.

Yet it had not been Eliza, though she was his dearest friend and confidant, the one he told of his hopes and dreams, with whom he had fallen in love. Whatever the reason, there was no denying the truth of it. He had made an error of judgement, a bad one, and now he was hurting two of the people he cared about most in the world and it was making him wretched.

"So, this is where you're skulking, is it?"

Cassius turned to see their brother Jules in the doorway. He turned with a smile despite his despondency as he liked Jules very much. The devil-may-care attitude hid a good heart, and a fellow who took things a deal more seriously than people might have thought. Cassius stood to greet him and then paused as he saw the furious glint in his eyes.

"Jules," he said, feeling his heart pick up as the tension in the room became palpable.

"I didn't break your nose when you broke things off with Eliza because I understood that two years apart had changed your feelings. I knew you'd never made a formal offer, and I felt certain you'd never hurt my sister on purpose," Jules said, walking into the room and inspecting some items arranged on a table by the door. It was a mess of paint-stained rags and brushes and empty pots, and things that had taken Cassius's eye: a badger's skull, a large yellow vase he'd liberated from the house, a broken mirror. Jules trailed his hand over a few things, picking up the skull and inspecting it. He tossed it back to the table and looked back at Cassius. "You'd not do that, would you, Cass? Mess about with my sisters? You'd not make them fall in love with you and then break their hearts?"

"No," Cassius said, with a sick sensation roiling in his stomach as he knew that was exactly what he had done, what he was doing. No, he had not meant to do it. He would have cut out his heart before hurting either of them, but....

"So tell me, why is it Eliza is acting so strangely? Sweet, patient Eliza is now brittle as a Lucifer match, and about as likely to burst into flames, and then there's Lottie...."

Jules held his gaze and Cassius felt heat crawl up the back of his neck. He could see Jules's desire to punish him for his crimes. It burned in the young man's eyes and Cassius could not blame him. A part of him welcomed it, felt he deserved it, but still he moved around the studio, edging towards the door. If they were going to fight—and that appeared inevitable—he'd just as soon not destroy his studio.

"I left her in the hayloft, crying," Jules remarked lightly, though there was no doubting just how angry he was that his sister had been hurt.

"Crying?" Cassius repeated in alarm. "B-But why? What—"

"Why don't you tell me?"

His tone darkened, the demand curt and angry. Cassius swallowed. Did Lottie regret what she'd done? Well, of course she did. It had been mad of her, mad and reckless, and would ruin her if anyone discovered it. He ought to have stopped her. He'd known that, damn it. God, Jules was right, he was an utter bastard. Had... Had she *told* her brother? No. No, if he knew he'd not be standing there discussing it. There would have been no prelude to violence, no chance for Cassius to explain himself.

"Jules," he began, startled to discover he sounded a little breathless.

Not that he was afraid of a fight. He'd got himself into a few scrapes over the past years, and before that it had been a part of life, for boys at school always scrapped with each other. He could hold his own. In truth, though they were about the same height, he was heavier than Jules, who still carried the lanky frame of early adulthood. No, it wasn't fear, it was because Jules was right. Jules was defending those he cared about, the furious desire to protect his sisters radiating from him, and how could he fight that?

"What, Cass? Are you going to tell me you didn't meet her last night? Didn't take any liberties?"

"No, I... I...."

Well, he might not have made love to her, but he *had* taken liberties. She'd been naked, for heaven's sake.

Jules made an incoherent sound of fury and lunged at him. Cassius dodged and ran for the door.

"Come back here, you bloody coward!" Jules yelled after him.

Well, hold on now.

"I'm here," Cassius said, standing on the lawn before the summerhouse. "And I'm not going anywhere. You can have your fight if you want it, Jules. God knows I deserve it, but I need to tell you—"

He didn't get to say anything else as he was tackled to the floor. Jules's shoulder hit him square in the solar plexus and he went down with such a thud the air was knocked from his lungs. Cassius hauled in a breath and had just enough wit remaining to block the fist speeding towards his nose. He twisted, dislodging Jules, but only temporarily. A fist caught him on the jaw, snapping his head sideways.

"Jules," he shouted, trying to make himself heard, but he was short on air still and Jules was in no mood to let him catch his breath. "Jules, wait...."

In a move Cassius was not prepared for, Jules wrestled him back to the ground. Cassius broke free and struggled away, but Jules got a hold of his arm. He wrenched it up behind his back, which dashed well hurt. Aggrieved, Cassius flung his head back, not hard enough to break the fool's nose, but enough to give them both a headache.

Jules yelled in pain and Cassius took advantage of his distraction, thrusting his free elbow into the fellow's stomach. There was a curse, and the grip on his arm faltered. Cassius pulled free and scrambled to his feet, putting distance between them.

"Jules, wait," he rasped, bracing his hands on his knees. "I know you're angry, and that's understandable...."

"How good of you to be so bloody accommodating," Jules growled, moving in for another go.

His nose was bleeding and his clothes were awry. Cassius had fared little better; he was dirty and covered in grass stains, and the arm of his shirt had ripped at the shoulder.

"I love her!" Cassius exclaimed.

"Which one?" Jules demanded with a snort. It was a fair question.

"Both of them," Cassius replied, before quickly realising this had been the wrong answer. He spoke quickly, trying to get the words out before Jules got serious and bloody murdered him. "But I'm *in* love with Lottie. I want to marry her."

That pulled him up short, and Cassius let out a ragged breath.

"I love her," he said again, just in case Jules hadn't understood the first time. "I thought it was Eliza, and I do love her too, but… only as a friend, Jules. My dearest friend in the world, but… but with Lottie…."

Jules held out a hand, his expression one of disgust. "Spare me the details, old man, but if that's true, if your intentions are honourable, why was Lottie crying?"

Cassius shrugged. He was not about to tell Jules about last night, but that would not be the only reason for Lottie's misery. "I can't say, but… but I think this whole situation is hurting all of us deeply. Neither of us can bear to cause Eliza any further harm, but that means we can tell no one how we feel and… and that means we are lying to everyone. Lottie is wretched about keeping secrets from you all. We both are."

Jules stared at Cassius for a long moment, obviously weighing up how badly he still wished to break his nose. He let out a breath and raked his hands through his dark hair, which was all in disorder after their tussle.

"Hell and damnation, Cass," he muttered in disgust. "And now I've been dragged into it, too."

"Been dragged into what? What on earth is going on here?"

Both men jolted as the feminine voice called them to account. They exchanged a panicked glance before doing their best to straighten themselves, for what good it did them. They turned and met Eliza's suspicious gaze.

"Have… Have you been *fighting*?" she asked, staring at them in outrage.

"Only a little," Jules said, sullen as a boy as he regarded his older sister, who was looking at him as if she intended to send him to bed with no supper.

"What on earth about?" she demanded, her astonished gaze darting from one to the other and back again.

Ah, now there was a tricky question to answer.

"*Well*?" Eliza folded her arms, glaring at them both.

"Art," Cassius said, as it was the only thing he could think of and about the only subject he ever got riled up about enough to lose his temper. "Jules said a lot of idiotic guff to wind me up and I reacted rather foolishly. Silly of us. All over now. No harm done."

He did not dare look at Jules.

"It *was* foolish of you," Jules retorted, a sarcastic edge to the comment that promised retribution in one form or another in the near future. "I was only ragging you. There was no need for you to act like a blasted caveman, now, was there?"

Cassius gritted his teeth.

"I apologise, Jules," he said, knowing he owed the devil that much, no matter how annoying he was. "I behaved badly, but I *will* put things to rights. You have my word."

Though, how the hell he was supposed to do that, he really had no idea.

Jules made a disgruntled sound but seemed to accept his apology.

"See that you do," he muttered, and stalked away.

Cassius swallowed as Eliza turned her attention back to him. She gave him a penetrating stare, direct enough that he felt she could see right through him.

"I didn't know you at all, did I?" she said, her voice full of sorrow.

"Yes, you did, Eliza. Better than anyone. We were just too young to realise we wouldn't suit. We want different things."

Eliza nodded, staring out over the dark water of the lake. "You want to travel, to see the world. I always knew that but… I suppose I thought it was a boyish whim, that you would grow out of it. That's not it though, is it?"

Cassius shook his head. "No."

"You never said."

"You always seemed to know what was right, Eliza, and I was excited by all the plans you made for us. I know you are capable of great things and I looked forward to playing my part. You were always so certain of everything when I was unsure, I believed in your vision of the future, of the better world you want to make, but I'm a man now, not a boy. I know what I want and this…" He swept a hand at the bucolic landscape about them. "This isn't it. At least, it isn't yet. Perhaps one day it will be. I hope it will, but not, I think, for some time."

"I could not live like that, always on the move."

"I know."

They were silent for a long moment and Cassius felt the chasm between them like a physical weight, an ache in his soul.

"I miss you, Eliza. There is so much I wish I could say to you. I want to explain everything and talk it though and listen to your sensible advice but…"

"But…" she said sadly.

"Will you ever forgive me?"

She smiled at that, a crooked, sorrowful quirk of her lips. "Yes, but my pride has taken a blow, Cass. You must wait for the bruises to fade."

Cassius watched her walk away and wondered how on earth they could endure inflicting any more hurt.

Chapter 13

Nic,

*Where the devil are you? I'm addressing this to
our rooms in town in the hope that you are
there, and not off God knows where and doing
God knows what. I pray you are not getting
yourself into trouble. You might remember you
are supposed to be with me, helping me, not off
sulking about whatever it is you've got yourself
all worked up about. I still do not understand
why you did not confide in me. We always tell
each other everything, do we not? It is how we
have survived this long. Brothers in arms, yes?
I am no child and I know I have been impatient
with your fussing over me like some old woman,
but I confess I am hurt by the manner in which
you have abandoned me. I agreed to do this even
though I do not want it. I agreed that this
should be my fate but I thought you would help
me see it through.*

*I must tell you I have discovered Eliza and
Cassius were to be married. Though nothing
was formally announced, it was acknowledged
in the family to be their intention. Cassius has
since told Eliza that he does not wish to marry
her after all. For my part it is a relief, for had I*

known he was my rival I should not have felt easy in my mind. I like him and should have regretted making an enemy of him. However, Eliza appears to have taken it hard. She is not at all the serene, happy young woman she was when we arrived. I am doing my best to revive her spirits but even I cannot mend a broken heart. Fear not, though, brother. I will do my duty and make her forget him.

—Excerpt of a letter from Louis César de Montluc, Comte de Villen to his half-brother, Monsieur Nicolas Alexandre Demarteau– translated from the French.

14th July 1838, Holbrook House, Sussex.

"Everyone is arriving, Papa!"

Lottie looked up from the copy of The Lady's Magazine she had been forcing herself to attend to, easily distracted by Cat's excited announcement. Her father, the Marquess of Montagu, withdrew his gaze from the letter he'd been writing and caught his wife's eye. She smiled at him, such an intimate smile Lottie felt she ought not to have seen it, nor especially the answering light of wickedness that danced in the marquess's eyes. Still, he put his letter aside and got up to stand by his daughter at the window.

"So they are. Will you burst with excitement before tonight, do you think?"

"It is possible," Cat replied gravely. "I cannot wait."

"Are you going to attend?" Lottie asked in astonishment, to which Cat replied with a gurgle of laughter.

"Of course not, silly. I'm far too young to attend a ball, which is so unfair, but Mama said I might watch from the balcony."

"For a little while, *if* you were very good," her father amended, with a stern tone that did not match the look in his strange, silver eyes, which shone with amusement.

"Oh, but I have been, and I will be," Cat said, her little face solemn as she gazed up at the father she clearly idolized.

Montagu nodded his approval. "Shall we go down and greet them, then? I believe that is Helena and Gabriel's carriage, so your friends are here."

"Yours too," Cat said excitedly, taking her father's hand and dragging him from the room. "For Gabriel is your best friend, I think, even though he vexes you dreadfully. It's just like with Emmeline, you see. I do like her, but she makes me so cross sometimes...."

Montagu chuckled as his daughter towed him away and Lottie watched his wife, Matilda, as she stared after them, her adoration obvious. How must it feel, to be married to a man you loved so deeply, to have weathered storms, to have raised children and experienced years together, and to still feel just the same as you had years earlier? Would she always feel this mad jittering in her heart whenever she saw Cassius? Would her breath always catch and her pulse race with giddy excitement? She believed it would, and so this feeling would not simply go away, and if Cassius felt the same....

They could not keep their secret indefinitely. They had kept quiet to save Eliza pain, but what if she found out anyway? How furious she would be to have been kept in the dark again.

Oh, what to do?

Cassius and Jules had nearly ruined everything with their stupid fight last week, for which she was still beyond vexed with them, the idiots. Why did men always think that going around hitting each other was a valid method of solving problems? They were imbeciles both, and so she'd told them, though in truth she'd been touched to discover Jules would ride to her rescue without a second thought. Yet Eliza had come upon them and only some quick thinking from Cassius had defused the situation. Lottie could not help but wonder if they had done right, if they ought not to have confessed all from the start. Oh, lud, what a coil.

"You must be excited for this evening."

Lottie looked up again, torn from her tangled thoughts by Matilda's soft voice.

"I remember the excitement of a ball, of getting ready and looking forward to seeing all my friends, *and* wondering if I would see a certain gentleman, of course," she said with a smile. "Will you dance with Cassius?"

Lottie drew in a sharp breath. Oh, Lord. She knew.

Matilda shook her head. "Don't look so appalled. I've not said anything, and nor will I, though I don't think you will keep your secret for long. You wear your heart on your sleeve and you look at him like he hung the moon for you."

Lottie swallowed.

"Eliza is too preoccupied to notice, or she would have done by now. I cannot help but feel it would be better if you just told her the truth. She is your sister."

"I c-can't bear to hurt her," Lottie said. "I wish I didn't love him. I wish I could make it stop, that it could be anyone else, but...."

Matilda returned a smile of such understanding Lottie's throat grew tight. "But love comes where it will and we may not understand the why of it, only that it *is*."

"Yes."

"I know," Matilda said with a sigh. "I remember as if it were yesterday. I hated Lucien for such a long time, but there were so many secrets, so many lies and things I did not understand. The truth made it so much easier to love him, even though it was far from easy."

She rose to her feet and smoothed down her gown. "And now I had better think about getting ready for the ball this evening. It is sad to own, but it takes me far longer than it used to."

"I cannot believe that," Lottie said, meaning it. "You're beautiful, and so very elegant."

Matilda flashed a dazzling smile. "Why, thank you, child. You've made the evening quite perfect before it has even begun."

"It's true, and thank you," Lottie said sincerely. "For your advice. I shall think on it."

Matilda nodded, moved towards the door, and then paused.

"Did you take a dare?" she asked.

Lottie flushed as she remembered, but nodded.

"How perfect," Matilda said happily. "And so we begin."

And, with that enigmatic comment, she left Lottie alone.

"How do, Cass."

Cassius turned at the hand on his shoulder to see his Uncle Jerry grinning at him.

"It's good to see you," he said, shaking his uncle's hand. "Is Aunt Bonnie here?"

"Oh, yes. Causing havoc among your guests, no doubt, or trying to encourage our girls into it. I see your mama is as organised as ever."

Cassius looked over to where his mother was ticking the final items off a list as long as her arm with calm precision while the staff leapt to obey her. His father was lounging in a chair, idly turning a glass of wine in his hands and watching her with a rapt expression. Cassius smiled.

"Wellington could not better her."

"There," his mother said, putting down her list with a satisfied smile and pushing her spectacles back up her nose. "I do believe everything is in order, and I deserve a glass of champagne."

"Harriet, you are quite terrifyingly efficient," Jerry said, but dutifully poured her out a glass.

"I am, aren't I?" she said, accepting the glass with a smile and taking a sip. "Oh, that's better. Now, Jasper, Cassius, we had better go down. The guests will be arriving soon."

Though many of their closest friends had arrived earlier in the day and would stay over, many more would come from the surrounding area to attend an event considered one of the high points of the summer. The Countess of St Clair was considered something of an oddity, and no one seemed to have the slightest clue how she'd captured the heart of the most eligible man in the *ton* all those years ago, but her summer balls had become legendary. Some even said she did a better job of it than her predecessor, the late Dowager Countess St Clair, which was the highest praise any of them could give.

Cassius usually enjoyed the ball very much. It was a chance to catch up with his friends and family, to laugh, and to flirt and dance with a lot of pretty girls. Tonight it would be a test of endurance, for he did not dare spend too much time with Lottie, for fear of what he might reveal. Staying away from her had been damned near torture this past week, and Cassius had decided enough was enough. They must tell Eliza as soon as possible. Keeping secrets would only make matters worse in the long run and he must learn by his mistakes. Tomorrow afternoon would likely be the earliest opportunity and they must take it. He intended to snatch time enough with Lottie tonight to gain her acceptance of the idea. She would not like it, he knew, but she hated deceiving her sister more, and he felt it would be a relief to her to get it all out in the open. Surely Eliza could not stay angry with Lottie for long? He knew her well enough to be certain of that. Or, at least, he *had*. She was acting so strangely of late.

"I didn't know you at all, did I?"

That had hurt more than she could know. For she did know him, better than anyone except Lottie. Though perhaps he ought to tell her the same, for he did not recognise the girl she had become in the days since he had admitted he didn't wish to marry her. She was preoccupied and short-tempered, just as Jules had said. Was that all his fault?

He had no time to consider as it was time to greet their guests.

Cassius was so distracted most of them passed in a blur of polite nothings, but some stood out.

Cat's oldest sister, Phoebe, and her husband, Maximillian Carmichael, The Earl of Ellisborough, were among those he was only too pleased to welcome.

"Your father is in the ballroom," he told Phoebe. "He's been worse than little Cat for demanding what time it is, he's so impatient to see you."

Phoebe laughed with delight and tugged at her husband's arm. "Oh, do come along, Max. I can't wait to see them all."

Cassius watched in amusement as she bore her husband off in search of Montagu and her mama. Minerva and Inigo de Beauvoir arrived next, with their adopted son, Hartley, who was some years older than Cassius.

"Cass," Hart said with a grim smile, looking very much as if he was being escorted up the scaffold to have his neck stretched. Balls were really not his idea of fun. His father wasn't enamoured of them either.

"Mother has laid a selection of titles that may interest you in the library," Cassius whispered to Hart's father, Inigo. The man brightened perceptibly at this prospect until his wife scolded him.

"Don't you dare disappear yet. You promised me two dances at the absolute minimum," she said, tapping his arm playfully with her fan.

"Oh, how you torment me, wife. How shall I endure the tedium?"

From the glittering look in his eyes, Cassius felt certain the man would manage with no problem at all.

Cassius laughed and was about to greet Baron and Lady Rothborn and their son, Larkin, when something made him turn. His breath snagged in his throat as he saw Lottie come down the stairs, and all the rest of their guests faded into a dull, murmuring blur of sound and movement behind him.

Oh, God.

Oh God, how could he endure another second of hiding his feelings? Yet he wasn't hiding them, not in this moment. He *could* not. His breath was short and his mouth was dry, his heart thudding erratically in his chest. Intelligent thought of any variety held up a white flag and surrendered to feelings. There were too many of them—love and lust and pride and guilt—playing havoc with his equilibrium, sending jolts of desire lancing through him with the burn of a thousand lightning strikes, melting what little remained of his brain to a thick syrup, like sugar poured into hot water.

She was dressed in pink. Her gown and bodice, which exposed her shoulders and a teasing glimpse of décolletage, was a lush pink satin. The waist was tight, revealing her curves, and the open robe revealed a madly flounced lace petticoat that fluttered enticingly as she moved. She looked edible: the prettiest confection that ever was, just waiting for him to unwrap her.

Cassius swallowed.

She must have correctly identified the look in his eyes for colour rose in her cheeks.

"Good evening, Cassius," she said, and then lowered her voice. "Don't look at me so."

"Can't help it," he rasped. "You look…. You're…. That dress…."

She glanced down at herself and smoothed a pink silk glove over the ruffles with a sigh of pleasure that didn't help him a whit. "It *is* lovely, isn't it?"

"It's wicked," he said helplessly. "You've done it to torment me."

She looked up at him, a quizzical expression in her eyes.

"I would never…." she protested and then laughed as she realised he was teasing.

"How shall I bear it, watching you dance with all those other fellows whilst I must stay away?"

Her bright expression dimmed, and he cursed himself for diminishing her enjoyment of the evening.

"It's all right," he said quickly. "I shall bear it. I want you to have fun."

"We can't keep on like this. I can't. I must tell her," she said, her lovely face determined though there was fear in her eyes.

Cassius experienced a flood of relief as he realised he'd not have to persuade her into it. "I know. Me either. Tomorrow. We'll do it together, though, love. Not you alone."

She let out a breath and nodded.

"Run along, then," he told her, though it ate at him to send her away. "Go and have fun."

"Will you dance with me?" she asked, pleading in her eyes. "It will look odd if you don't dance with me once, at least."

Cassius nodded. "Yes. Save me the last waltz."

She flashed him a brilliant smile that made him feel dazed and light-headed and was gone with a flurry of beckoning pink lace and ribbons.

Lottie waved up at the balcony where her younger siblings and Cat were gathered, leaning over and watching the fine ladies in their lovely gowns and the men in dramatic black-and-white eveningwear as they danced. She turned to smile at Cat's oldest sister, Phoebe, as she joined her, waving at the viewers above. Phoebe had children of her own now, not much younger than Cat, who had come as something of a surprise to her parents.

"Heaven help us when she comes of age," Phoebe said with amusement dancing in her blue eyes. "I believe Papa is more alarmed by the prospect than he was about my come out and that's no small thing. She's got some dreadfully dangerous ideas about love and romance and redeeming wicked men. It quite terrifies me to consider it."

Lottie laughed, though she suspected Phoebe's concerns were valid enough. Everyone knew Cat had a thirst for romantic novels and would hunt them down, no matter how her parents scolded her. Their own story was legend, though, immortalised by Lottie's mother in her romantic novel, The Eagle and The Lamb. The book had caused a sensation and was never out of print. Was it any wonder the girl had ideas?

"How's Eliza?" Phoebe asked, the concern in her eyes making guilt settle in Lottie's stomach like a cold lump of lead.

"Oh, she's fine. Looking astonishingly lovely, of course," Lottie said lightly and hating herself for it.

Phoebe gave her a searching look that made her feel rather ill.

"She's recovered from what happened with Cass, then?"

Lottie swallowed.

"I don't know," she said miserably. "To be honest, we've not spoken of it much, but… but she's not herself at the moment."

"No. I didn't think so. I greeted her earlier and she's quite lost her sparkle," Phoebe said thoughtfully and then her expression changed to one of undisguised delight as she spied Louis César with Eliza on his arm, moving towards them.

"Louis César!" she exclaimed as the man laughed with equal pleasure.

"Comtesse Ellisborough. My word, but it seems like yesterday. You have not changed at all."

"Oh, what a plumper," Phoebe said, laughing as she gave him an unashamedly frank look up and down. "You have certainly *matured* in ten years, but then you were a beautiful young man, so I ought not be surprised. My, my, my."

Louis César chuckled. "Have a care for my life, madam. I have no wish for your husband to call me out."

"Is she flirting again?" demanded a deep voice from behind Lottie.

She turned to see Phoebe's husband, Max, join them. He took a firm hold of his wife's hand.

"You are incorrigible, you dreadful creature. Put the poor man down and come and dance with your boring old husband."

Phoebe gave a snort of mirth but allowed herself to be dragged—though far from unwillingly—onto the dance floor.

"Perhaps we might join them?" the comte asked Eliza who inclined her head and gave him a smile which Lottie did not think showed in her eyes.

"I should be delighted," she said.

to hide what he was. Why she was so struck with a fellow who seemed to hate her, she could not fathom. Was it injured pride, perhaps? Did she expect every man she met to admire her? Perhaps discovering one who did not was like a stone in her shoe, a constant irritation. Eliza considered this idea, trying to be honest with herself. No. No, she was not so very conceited as that. It was just so unexpected. She had been polite and welcoming, and the look in his eyes when he'd first seen her….

Oh, she was a great ninny. There was no other word for it.

"Good evening, Eliza."

She jolted, discovering herself startled to be addressed directly by Cassius. It was so ridiculous a situation, especially after he had been her friend for all her life, that her throat grew tight.

"Cassius," she said, her tone a little cooler than she'd intended. She forced a smile to make up for it.

"You look lovely tonight."

She smiled for real then, though she wanted to cry. Usually he insulted her, in the way very good friends did, teasing words that made her laugh, that made the serious business of being the perfect lady a little more bearable.

"Not like an over-decorated bride cake, then?" she said sadly.

Something lit in his eyes. Was that hope?

"Well, I didn't like to say."

His voice was grave, his expression serious and, despite everything, Eliza laughed. Oh, what a relief it was to shake off a little of her turmoil and laugh with a friend—her best friend.

"And blue, Eliza? Really? There are other colours in the world."

"Ah, but I have no imagination, as you are well aware."

It had always been what he'd teased her for. Lottie was the one with the imagination. Lottie, who made up wild stories and thought of ridiculous escapades that Eliza never really understood. Who wanted to get all wet and muddy and then scolded for the pleasure, when you could just as well have a perfectly nice time and keep clean without getting into trouble at all? Except now she wished she *had* got into more trouble. Perhaps if she had, this odd, unexpected sensation of being caught in a trap of her own making would not plague her so.

Cassius stared at her and suddenly the atmosphere between them was awkward again. She wished he would go away. It was too upsetting to be with him, this man who had been her friend but was now a man she felt was keeping secrets from her.

"Eliza," he said, a pleading note to her voice. "What you said—"

"Ah, and here you are, Cassius, and the beautiful Lady Elizabeth too! My cup runneth over."

Eliza groaned inwardly as some relation of Cassius's appeared. The man was a distant cousin of his father's if Eliza remembered rightly, but her attention drifted, their conversation washing over her as she sought an opportunity to get away.

Cassius wanted to thump his father's cousin in frustration, a reaction he knew his father would sympathise with, as the fellow was a prosy old bore. As good manners not only would not allow that, but forced him to endure the man's droning with a smile on his face, he just seethed with impatience. He could see Eliza awaiting the first opportunity to make her escape. At any moment she'd be off like a whippet after a rabbit. For a moment there, it had been like old times and he wanted that back. If he'd fallen in love with anyone but Lottie, he knew he could have handled this whole affair much better. No doubt by now Eliza would have been offering him advice on how to manage this ridiculous situation, except if she'd known there would have been no situation to manage.

Argh.

It occurred to him then how odd it was to see that Eliza was clearly bored with the situation and wanted to get away. Until these past few weeks, she would have listened attentively to the awful fellow with every appearance of interest. Even if she had been desperate to get away from his father's dreadful cousin and a boastful story about how much money he'd spent on some magnificent horse and what a terrific horseman he was, no one would have been able to tell. Lottie would have fidgeted and done her best to be courteous before concocting an urgent excuse to be elsewhere. Eliza would have endured. Until now.

He saw her draw in a deep breath, preparing to interrupt the man's endless stream of babble and make her escape, when her eyes grew wide. All the colour drained from her face and then returned in a hectic rush of pink that rose over her chest and neck and sat high on her cheeks.

Cassius followed her gaze to see Louis César approaching them, with his brother Nic.

"Would you excuse us?" he said, grasping the opportunity to leave the tedious conversation. "I see a guest I have not yet greeted, and I must not forget my manners. Come along, Eliza."

He tugged at her arm, looking down at her in surprise when she did not leap at the opportunity to escape with him. She was rooted to the spot and, when he placed her hand on his arm, he felt certain she trembled.

"Eliza? Are you well?"

"Yes," she said, her voice faint, and then she drew in a deep breath and put up her chin. "Yes, of course I am."

Cassius frowned at her, but she gave him an impatient glare and they walked to meet Louis and Nic.

"Nice of you to join us, old man," Cassius said, shaking Nic's hand. "Was it something we said?"

Nic's dark eyes were hooded, revealing nothing but he shrugged. "I 'ad business to attend to."

Slowly, his gaze drifted from Cassius to Eliza. "I owe you an apology, Lady Elizabeth, for leaving so abruptly. I 'ope you will forgive me?"

"Indeed, you owe me nothing," Eliza said, her voice cool and tart. "You must apologise to Lord and Lady St Clair for your disappearing act. I am merely a guest here. Your comings and goings are of no matter to me, I assure you. If you would excuse me, gentlemen, *Mr Demarteau.*"

Cassius gaped in undisguised astonishment at the slight, staring at Eliza's haughty profile as she stalked away. He turned back to see Nic watching her go, something glinting in his eyes Cassius was not certain he liked. Louis César gave a bark of laughter.

"*Mon Dieu*, Nic, you have certainly made an impression there, and not for the first time."

Nic grunted and stared down at the glass of champagne in his hand in disgust. "It's too damn 'ot in here, and I need a proper drink."

"*H*ot, Nic. Do not drop your 'h's. We must speak English properly," Louis said with a mocking tone.

His brother glared at him and Cassius grinned.

"Come down to the summerhouse," he suggested. "I've got a bottle of cognac stashed there I think might meet with your approval."

It was obvious Nic was in an uncertain mood this evening and, in Cassius's experience of the man, that invariably led to trouble. In the circumstances, it was best to take Nic as far away from the guests as he could get.

153

Cassius filled his glass again. No doubt he would regret this in the morning, and he had no doubt whatsoever he would receive the devil of a dressing down from his mama for having disappeared so early in the evening. Yet it was good to be with his friends again. It reminded him of many nights in France with the brothers, drinking too much and talking nonsense half the time, arguing fiercely about art and books, and life in general. It usually ended with him talking about home as the longing for it rose in proportion to how drunk he was. He would wax lyrical about Holbrook, about his life there and his family, and most often about Eliza and Lottie and how he missed them both. How strange, then, to be back here at last, with his friends, and still missing Eliza and Lottie so badly his chest hurt. He must go back to the house soon though, for he had promised Lottie a dance. Though it was a dangerous thing to do, he would not miss it, not for the world.

"This is dreadful," Nic said, looking down at the still life he'd managed the other day in disgust.

Cassius flushed. Nic had a good eye for art and knew what he was talking about. His opinion mattered to Cassius and the comment stung, for he knew it was true.

"Yes, it is. I know," he said, frowning into his glass. "Can't seem to settle to anything."

"Guilty conscience?"

Cassius looked at Nic in surprise, a little unsettled by the fellow's tone, he sounded angry. He glanced then at Louis César, who cleared his throat.

"I told him about Eliza."

"Are you out of your damned mind? *Fils a Putain*!" Nic snapped, with such fury Cassius could only stare at him. "And why the devil did you never tell us you were engaged to her?"

Lottie swallowed.

"I don't know," she said miserably. "To be honest, we've not spoken of it much, but... but she's not herself at the moment."

"No. I didn't think so. I greeted her earlier and she's quite lost her sparkle," Phoebe said thoughtfully and then her expression changed to one of undisguised delight as she spied Louis César with Eliza on his arm, moving towards them.

"Louis César!" she exclaimed as the man laughed with equal pleasure.

"Comtesse Ellisborough. My word, but it seems like yesterday. You have not changed at all."

"Oh, what a plumper," Phoebe said, laughing as she gave him an unashamedly frank look up and down. "You have certainly *matured* in ten years, but then you were a beautiful young man, so I ought not be surprised. My, my, my."

Louis César chuckled. "Have a care for my life, madam. I have no wish for your husband to call me out."

"Is she flirting again?" demanded a deep voice from behind Lottie.

She turned to see Phoebe's husband, Max, join them. He took a firm hold of his wife's hand.

"You are incorrigible, you dreadful creature. Put the poor man down and come and dance with your boring old husband."

Phoebe gave a snort of mirth but allowed herself to be dragged—though far from unwillingly—onto the dance floor.

"Perhaps we might join them?" the comte asked Eliza who inclined her head and gave him a smile which Lottie did not think showed in her eyes.

"I should be delighted," she said.

Lottie watched with a troubled heart as they joined the others on the dance floor.

Chapter 14

Dear diary,

Balls are marvellous. I cannot wait to grow up and wear beautiful gowns and have fun with my friends – oh and fall in love, of course! There are so many people here, all our friends and family and lots I don't know too. My brothers, Philip and Thomas have come and are certainly the handsomest men here tonight, except for Papa of course, and I suppose, Louis César. I may be a little prejudiced in Pip and Tom's favour though for they are the best brothers in the world.

— Excerpt of an entry to the diary of Lady Catherine 'Cat' Barrington, youngest daughter of the Marquess and Marchioness of Montagu.

14th July 1838, Holbrook House, Sussex.

Eliza glanced behind her, relieved to discover she had evaded Louis César. She must be out of her mind. He was gorgeous, witty, charming, and there was a dangerous edge to him that he mostly hid, but she had caught the odd glimpse of it. Far from being off-putting, it only added to his appeal. Yet she could not keep her thoughts from a man far more dangerous, one who did not bother to hide what he was. Why she was so struck with a fellow who seemed to hate her, she could not fathom. Was it injured pride, perhaps? Did she expect every man she met to admire her? Perhaps discovering one who did not was like a stone in her shoe, a constant irritation. Eliza considered this idea, trying to be honest with herself. No. No, she was not so very conceited as that. It was just so unexpected. She had been polite and welcoming, and the look in his eyes when he'd first seen her....

Oh, she was a great ninny. There was no other word for it.

"Good evening, Eliza."

She jolted, discovering herself startled to be addressed directly by Cassius. It was so ridiculous a situation, especially after he had been her friend for all her life, that her throat grew tight.

"Cassius," she said, her tone a little cooler than she'd intended. She forced a smile to make up for it.

"You look lovely tonight."

She smiled for real then, though she wanted to cry. Usually he insulted her, in the way very good friends did, teasing words that made her laugh, that made the serious business of being the perfect lady a little more bearable.

"Not like an over-decorated bride cake, then?" she said sadly.

Something lit in his eyes. Was that hope?

"Well, I didn't like to say."

His voice was grave, his expression serious and, despite everything, Eliza laughed. Oh, what a relief it was to shake off a little of her turmoil and laugh with a friend—her best friend.

"And blue, Eliza? Really? There are other colours in the world."

"Ah, but I have no imagination, as you are well aware."

"Because I wasn't!" Cassius retorted. "It was just a foolish arrangement we made as children, and lucky for you, for Louis César seems to have stepped into the breach fast enough."

He knew at once it was the wrong thing to stay as Nic stiffened, but before things could go badly wrong, Louis César intervened as he usually did when Nic was about to erupt.

"Cassius, I think we should get some air. We shall leave Nic to enjoy criticising your work in peace. Thinking up some cutting remarks will make him feel better. When we return, he can tell you how awful it is, and you can tell him he's an idiot, and all will be well, yes?"

Not waiting for an answer, Louis took Cassius by the arm and towed him forcibly outside. He did not stop until they stood beside the lake, staring out over the glinting black water.

"What the bloody hell is wrong with him?" Cassius demanded.

"I'm damned if I know," Louis said. "He won't tell me. You know him well enough now to understand Nic has a dark spirit. His is not a quiet soul. He is not by nature easy-going, and his temper is uneven at best, but... but this I am not certain I understand. Unless...."

Louis César shook his head in frustration and stared at the lake, deep in thought.

They stood in silence for a long while.

"Do you mean to marry Eliza?"

He felt Louis César turn to look at him.

"If she will have me," he said quietly. There was a soft huff of laughter. "Which, I am chagrined to discover, is by no means certain. I do not think your Eliza is terribly impressed by my charm. It is a dreadful blow to my ego, I assure you."

"She is not *my* Eliza," Cassius said.

"No. Much to my relief. I should not have wished to have you as an opponent for her affections."

"Will you make her a good husband?" Cassius turned to look his friend in the eyes. He'd never seen eyes of quite such intense blue as Louis César's and had painted the comte more than once, trying to capture the mercurial spirit he saw there.

"I do not know," Louis replied with his usual candour. "I can only promise you that I will try."

"I hope you will try very hard, Louis," Cassius said, knowing Louis heard the threat behind his words. "She is my friend, and I won't see her hurt or embarrassed."

Louis quirked one eyebrow and Cassius felt sick.

"You do not need to tell me I've done just that. I've made a confounded mess of everything. Believe me, I know I'm an utter bastard. I hate myself."

Louis shrugged. "You cannot help it if you do not love her, or… is there more to it than that? Another woman perhaps?"

It wasn't the first time Cassius had cause to curse Louis's perceptiveness. He could only hope he hadn't guessed who the woman was. Hoping to turn his attention to other matters, he gestured back to the summerhouse. "We'd best go back. He's seen everything I did in France and there's not much else. If we don't hurry, he'll decide it's all worthless and set fire to the lot."

Whether Louis was truly diverted from the subject he did not know, but he went with Cassius back to the summerhouse. As they approached, Cassius saw Nic in the open doorway, candlelight at his back, and a leather portfolio open in his hands.

Chapter 15

My dear Kitty,

I shall miss you at this year's ball. Do you remember that summer here at Holbrook years back, when we dressed Jasper's stuffed bear in evening clothes? My word, what a long time ago that seems, and yet it's like yesterday too. The summer always seems to have an element of romance, of the air being full of possibilities, as if it only needs a spark to ignite it. Goodness, listen to me writing of romance! Jasper is rubbing off on me after all these years. Still, I cannot help but wonder what excitement this year's ball will bring us. There is certainly something in the air.

—Excerpt of a letter from Harriet Cadogan, Countess St Clair (mother of Cassius) to her old friend and Peculiar Lady, Kitty Baxter, Countess of Trevick.

14th July 1838, Holbrook House, Sussex.

Lottie glanced up at her father. It had become dreadfully stuffy inside and he had brought her and Eliza out for a walk in the garden to get some air. Cassius's father, the earl, had come too, and both men were deep in conversation.

Lottie and Eliza trailed behind them, relishing the cooler air. Lottie had danced all evening, doing her best to appear as she usually did, as though she was having fun, but her heart was with Cassius. She could not keep her thoughts from him, try as she might. Oh, but he'd looked splendid this evening. The stark black-and-white evening wear suited his golden beauty and had been perfectly tailored to his impressive physique. She allowed her mind to drift back to the day she'd caught him skinny dipping in the lake and remembered his broad shoulders, those powerful arms and muscular chest, and the way the water had slid down his body, trailing towards….

"There's a light on in the summerhouse," Eliza said, amusement in her tone. "Cassius has escaped."

Lottie felt heat crawl up her neck as Eliza spoke of Cassius just as she'd been thinking of him naked and wet and splendid and… oh, Lord. Something low in her belly contracted with longing as she thought of the summerhouse, of his gaze upon her, hot and liquid with desire as he sketched her, sprawled against the silks and velvets of the daybed.

"Are you friends again?" Lottie asked, making a valiant effort to keep her thoughts from straying to such wicked subjects and failing miserably. All she could see was Cassius, all she wanted was to feel his skin upon hers, the weight of his body pressing her down. Oh, heavens she would combust if this kept up.

"Not quite," Eliza said with a sigh. "But we shall be. I'm just…. Oh, Lottie, I just wish he'd been honest with me. I realise he was right, we were not in love, not in that way and he was right to say so, only now I wonder about so many things. How could I have been so blind to the truth, and as I was, how well I really know myself. All the things I had relied upon are gone and I'm… I'm adrift."

"Eliza," Lottie said, her heart beating very fast. She knew Cass had wanted them to tell Eliza together, but she could not bear it a moment longer. "Eliza can I tell you something, please?"

"Of course," Eliza said, concern in her gaze, and there was the sister Lottie knew and loved, the one who would do anything for those she cared about. "You know you can trust me, Lottie. So, please, will you tell me why you've been so out of spirits these past days? I hope you've not been fretting on my account?"

"In part," Lottie admitted, gathering her courage. They were drawing close to the summerhouse and she could see two figures walking up from the lake. "But let's not discuss it here. Can we go back inside? Come to my room and—"

She broke off as there was a bellow of fury. The sound was raw and primitive and they both looked to the summerhouse to see....

Good heavens, was... was that Mr Demarteau and....

Lottie watched in horror as Demarteau flew at Cassius and punched him in the gut. Cassius doubled over, staggering back, and then straightened and threw himself at Mr Demarteau.

Eliza screamed and ran forward, but their father and the earl were faster, wading in and pulling the two men apart with difficulty as they thrashed and struggled, and Louis César got between them to help.

Lottie ran to Cassius, whose lip was bleeding. He was breathing very hard, his colour high. Somewhat to her astonishment, she saw Eliza run towards Mr Demarteau and then stop dead some distance from him.

"What were you thinking?" she demanded of him.

Demarteau said nothing, his gaze fixed on Cassius.

"What in the name of God is going on here?" their father demanded, and Lottie shivered.

Most of the time this fierce man was simply *Papa*, whom they adored. He was loving and indulgent and dreadfully overprotective, but now and then they were reminded of exactly who and what he was.

Neither man spoke, only glared resentfully at each other.

"*Well?*" their father bellowed. "Answer me, damn you!"

As they remained stubbornly silent, he turned his attention to Louis César.

"I have no idea," the comte said, looking as stunned as everyone else.

"Cassius," the earl said. "What is this about?"

Lottie saw his jaw tighten, but he said nothing, so the earl turned to Mr Demarteau.

"I think you should leave."

"No," Cassius said, breaking his silence. "No. It… It was not his fault."

"Not his fault?" their father retorted. "We saw him storm out of the summerhouse and attack you!"

Cassius gritted his teeth but spoke again. "He was provoked."

The duke waved this away. "Nonetheless, we cannot have such behaviour. A gentleman does not go about knocking seven bells out of his host at a ball. You could at least wait for the proper time and place, and go about it like gentlemen."

"Pistols at dawn," Demarteau sneered, not helping himself a great deal.

"*Ta gueule!*" Louis César muttered under his breath, glaring at his brother.

Demarteau clamped his mouth shut, a muscle in his jaw ticking.

"Will someone explain what is going on!"

Everyone stared at Eliza in surprise, astonished by her outburst.

"Well, something is," she said, throwing up her hands. "We all know it, we just don't know what it is."

"There is nothing going on," Mr Demarteau said, though he seemed to vibrate with the effort of speaking and not lunging at Cassius again. "It is only that I am not a gentleman, as you see, and I have the oddest notions about honourable behaviour. My apologies once again, my lady. I shall leave you to your entertainments."

He gave her a stiff bow and stalked away. Louis César hurried after him and Eliza watched them go for a long moment. Then she turned back to Cassius.

"You're all mad!" she exclaimed in fury and ran off with a frantic rustle of skirts.

By the time Lottie had seen Eliza to her room and allowed her to vent her feelings about idiotic men and their ridiculous, barbaric behaviour, it was late. Most of those guests who had come by carriage had made their goodbyes, and those staying had drifted up to their rooms. Thankfully, only her father and the earl had witnessed the scene between Demarteau and Cassius, and so no one was any the wiser. It appeared Mr Demarteau had left at once, returning to London, she imagined, or wherever he'd been all this time. For the life of her, Lottie could not understand why he had attacked Cassius. They were friends. It made no sense.

Though she was tired, Lottie did not wish to go to bed. She wished the ball was not yet over, for she had missed her dance with Cassius as his father had towed him off to his study. She had no doubt the earl would want a full and frank explanation of what had gone on, and could only pity Cassius having to endure it. With a sigh of frustration, she wandered the vast house until she arrived at the schoolroom. It was empty now, the children having gone to bed ages ago, but it was full of memories. This was the backdrop to many of her childhood reminiscences, when the weather was too bad to play outside, or if Lottie could not persuade Eliza into whatever mischief she'd suggested.

There was a battered old sofa in the corner, with a table on either side of it. The table was stacked with books, just as it had always been. They had snuggled up together here to listen to Eliza read to them, as she was the best at it. She would act the parts, changing her voice to suit the characters and having them in whoops sometimes at the comical way she said things. Eliza might not have much of an imagination, but she was a keen observer of people and their mannerisms. Lottie plopped down on the sofa with a flurry of skirts and petticoats and sighed, leaning her head back and closing her eyes.

"Funny, I knew I'd find you here."

"Cassius!" she exclaimed, wide-eyed. "What on earth happened?"

He shook his head and came to sit down beside her. "I'll tell you in a moment. Just… give me five minutes. My head is still ringing after my father's little *talk*."

"Was he terribly angry?"

"Not terribly. I don't think father *gets* terribly angry—well unless someone upsets Mother. No, he was just frustrated because I refused to tell him what it was about."

Lottie desperately wanted to ask the same thing but he'd said he needed a moment, so she held her tongue. She stared at him, at the moonlight as it caught the strong lines of his profile, the long straight nose and the hard line of his jaw, those sculpted lips that were so very soft and….

"Damnation, Lottie, don't look at me like that. We're in enough trouble," he said ruefully.

"Sorry," she whispered. "I can't help it. I can't stop thinking about you, about the other night."

"Me either."

He reached out and threaded their fingers together.

"Tell me something amusing," he said with a sigh, leaning his head back and staring up at the ceiling. Lottie did the same but turned her head to watch him.

"I was just remembering this room and being here as children. Do you remember Eliza reading to us and making all the voices?"

Cassius chuckled. "I do. How funny she was. Does she still do it?"

"Not often," Lottie admitted. "Though she will for the little ones if no one else is around to listen. She's too afraid of making a fool of herself."

He turned his head to meet her gaze and, though the room was dim, she did not need light to remember the exact shade of his eyes, that distinct turquoise that made her think of hot, sunny places and exotic seas.

"You've never cared about that, have you?"

Lottie shook her head. "I don't think about it. I just react, which is not always a good thing. I'm too impulsive."

"Like taking off your clothes in a summerhouse in front of some wicked fellow."

"In front of the man I love," she amended, and she heard his breath catch.

"Do you, Lottie?"

She nodded, emotion tugging at the words. "I always have, and it's been so dreadful, Cass, pretending that I didn't mind it was Eliza you wanted. I w-was so horribly jealous, and I felt so wretched for being such a hateful creature, to envy my own... my own *s-sister*."

Her voice grew thick and trembled, and Cassius slid his arm about her and pulled her close.

"You could never be hateful. You've done nothing wrong. It's all my fault for being such an imbecile and not seeing what was right in front of me."

Lottie shook her head, unable to agree with that. "Oh, no. I never faulted you. Of course you wanted Eliza. She's so much nicer than me. She's kind and patient and never loses her temper, and she's... s-so bloody perfect it makes my teeth hurt!"

Cassius laughed and Lottie made a sound of exasperation.

"You see? I told you I'm not nice."

"I think you're nice," he said softly. "And I think you're perfect too, just a different kind of perfect."

"Yes, the imperfect kind," she retorted with a little sniff.

"Perfect for me." He reached out and traced the shape of her lips with a fingertip. "When I was away, I had the most marvellous time. For the first six months I was immersed in my work and in everything I was discovering. I made new friends and travelled, saw the most beautiful scenery, but little by little I noticed this longing for... for something. I thought I was just homesick at first, for my family and friends, then I decided it was you and Eliza, and it was. Only... It was you Lottie, and it wasn't until you burst onto the terrace that day that I realised it."

Lottie felt her face heat.

"I meant to be well-behaved and act like a lady. I did, truly. Only I had bottled up my feelings for so long and when I saw you it... it all sort of exploded out of me." She shook her head. "Papa says I'm about as subtle as a brick, and he's right, you know."

"I know," he said, smiling as she flashed him an indignant glance. "I like it!"

"Oh, you can't," she protested. "I'm horribly gauche."

"I like it," he said again, his voice firm. "It's honest. You are honest about what you feel, and you say what you think. I admire that."

She was silent for a moment, considering. "Do you remember the Peculiar Ladies and their hat?"

"You mean our mothers' friends and their hat of dares?"

Lottie nodded. "Cat found it, and Eliza and I took one. Mine... Mine was to be wicked. That's why I undressed for you. Well, partly why. It *was* wicked, wasn't it?"

Cassius grew very still, and she saw his Adam's apple bob.

"Yes," he said, his voice low and gravelly.

Lottie became aware of a shiver running over her, excitement stirring in her belly.

"I'm not sure it was wicked enough, though. You know... to complete my dare."

She held her breath, watching him watch her.

"Was it not?"

Lottie knew she ought not, it was... well, it *was* wicked, but that had been the dare, had it not? And what was the point of accepting a dare if one was going to be hen-hearted about it?

Eliza paced her room. There was something going on, something she was not being told and it was making her wild. Everyone had known about Cassius not wanting to marry her and she was dashed well not going to be taken unawares again. This time, she would be the first to figure it out.

When she had seen Mr Demarteau and Cassius together earlier in the evening, they had been perfectly amicable. They had escaped the ballroom together with Louis César, no doubt after she'd been so shockingly rude to Mr Demarteau. She still could not quite believe she'd done it. Worse than that, she'd enjoyed it. She had wanted to provoke him badly and it had been… liberating. After years and years of being polite and nice and holding her tongue, she'd been deliberately rude and… and it had been marvellous. She wanted to do it again. As soon as possible, and preferably to Monsieur Demarteau. Her breath caught as she remembered the look in his eyes.

Stop that.

Not now.

Now she wanted to know why he'd attacked Cassius, when they'd been so friendly just moments earlier. Mr Demarteau had been in the summerhouse alone, so it could not have been something Cassius had said, unless perhaps it had been written down or….

Eliza stopped her pacing as she considered this. Could it have been a drawing or a painting that had lit his temper? But what could possibly…?

Well, there was only one way to find out.

※ ※ ※

Cassius was about to suffer a heart attack. This beautiful, dreadful girl would kill him, and even if she didn't, if anyone found out about them, the duke undoubtedly would. The duke would rip off his head and stick it on a pike outside the front door of Beverwyck as a warning to any other presumptuous fool who thought to dally with one of his daughters. Bedwin was notorious for being protective of his girls. Only the rules had never applied to Cassius because he was family. They'd all grown up together, squabbled and rough and tumbled and climbed trees, and… and how was that girl with scabby knees and a gap between her teeth the same as the siren calling to him now, tempting him to dash himself to pieces on the rocks when he fell? He *would* fall, it was inevitable. Hell, he'd already fallen, he'd tumbled head over ears into whatever this was the moment he'd laid eyes on her again.

Again.

How could it be 'again' when it was like seeing her for the first time? Yet it truly was Lottie, yet not Lottie. She was still in there, that mischievous girl playing hide and seek, and peeking out of the eyes of this new creature she'd become, this unholy temptation. He could see the devilish glint in her eyes, see the naughty tilt to her lips, tugging at the corners. Cassius wanted to kiss her there, at the corners of her mouth, along the elegant line of her neck, the swell of her breasts....

"Not wicked enough?" His voice was deep and rough with desire, his breathing picking up.

She shook her head, making the golden curls bounce. As if of its own accord, his hand lifted to take a hold of one, tugging it lightly and watching in fascination as it sprang back again.

"You took all your clothes off," he said, remembering the scene with far too much clarity for his peace of mind. "Every stitch."

"It wasn't difficult," she said. "I was only wearing my night gown and wrap."

He nodded. "Barely. They were see through."

"Were they?" she asked, her eyes wide.

He nodded again. Speech was becoming complicated and needed far too much brain power when his blood was being redirected to deal with more pressing demands.

Lottie sat up, getting to her knees on the sofa beside him. He ought to leave. Oh, Lord he'd been here before, with *what he ought to do* and what the devil on his shoulder knew he was damn well going to do. Her dress rustled as she moved, the copious layers of petticoats and tulle and silk and those provocative flounces beckoning him, tempting him closer, tempting him to touch.

"Teach me something wicked," she whispered in the darkness. "Teach me something those foreign girls liked, for I am horribly jealous of them."

Cassius was aware of his heart picking up speed, anticipation working on him as his body grew tight and visions of everything he could teach her danced in his mind.

"You've no need to be jealous," he said, meaning it. "They were lovely and fun, and we enjoyed ourselves together but… but it wasn't… it wasn't *you*, Lottie, it didn't mean…."

He hesitated and then blurted the words out.

"I love you. I think I must have done for a long time, but I didn't know it. How did I not know it?"

He knew he sounded bewildered, and he was. How could this feeling, that had swallowed him whole the same way the whale had swallowed Jonah, possibly have escaped his notice? How could something so overwhelming not have been blindingly obvious? He had no illusions about his intellect. With a mother like his, he was too aware his mind was nothing out of the ordinary. He had inherited his father's artistic skill, but he'd not been blessed with his mother's brains. Nonetheless, he was intelligent enough, he certainly wasn't a bloody idiot, nor a halfwit, or at least he'd never thought so before now. Yet the most important thing that had ever happened to him seemed to have done so without him knowing it. This vast emotion had settled inside him and lay there like some sleeping beast, only to leap out and shake his heart in its slavering jaws when he was least expecting it.

"You don't need to, Lottie," he said, though the little voice in his head was threatening to beat him with the nearest heavy object if he didn't shut up. "You don't need to do this, to do anything, I…."

But before he could say anything more, she had leaned in and kissed him and his brain turned to mush, whilst it had quite the opposite effect on other parts. She pulled back and he was falling into her eyes, which glinted like a moonlit sea in the darkness, and into the scent of her: some teasing mixture of jasmine and that beguiling thing he could not identify, something green and herbal that made his mouth water.

"Show me something wicked."

"Come here," he rasped, his voice cracking, tugging her towards him, urging her to straddle his thighs. She did and layers of fabric billowed up as she sat, making him feel as if he'd embraced a cloud, a sensation not helped as her scent grew stronger and mingled with the warm, fragrant perfume of a woman, of *her*. It invaded his senses, potent as opium smoke, diminishing what little ability remained for rational thought.

"Cassius," she said, looking down at him, a little daunted but determined too, and it was so like her to push herself into something reckless for the sheer hell of it, because she was more alive than anyone he'd ever known.

"Tell me to stop and I will," he promised, praying she'd not tell him to, as he reached beneath the acres of fabric.

But beneath the dress were too many layers, layers and layers with lacy edges fluttering as he tried to find his way in and was foiled, each time discovering a new level of torment as her skin was kept from him. The provoking fabric rustled as he tossed each petticoat aside, his hands frantic to find a path beneath them.

"God above, Lottie, what manner of devil's device is this?" he demanded, laughing in frustration as he tried in vain to bury beneath them. "Are you trying to drive me out of my mind?"

"It's the fashion," she said with an impatient sigh. "It's such a nuisance too, they're so heavy and difficult to walk in, let alone dance and… *Oh!*"

Finally he made it, and felt a surge of victory as great as if he'd climbed a blasted mountain range. He was certainly just as breathless. How could he not be, though, as his hands encountered warm, slender limbs as satiny as the finest silk? His hands lingered on the delicate skin behind her knees, trailing his fingers back and forth. Lottie shivered.

"I've longed to touch you," he said, struggling to speak, for his breath was coming so fast. "The image of you laid out on the daybed is etched on my mind. I see it constantly, it's a torment to me, to have you so close and—"

He didn't get another word out. Lottie had clearly decided he'd said enough. She bent her head and pressed her mouth against his and Cassius sighed. He gave himself over to her, allowing her to take the lead, as she was wont to do. She kissed him, tentatively at first and then with growing confidence. Their tongues tangled, sliding and playing together, and all the while Cassius allowed his fingers to roam up and down the backs of her thighs, each time venturing a little higher. Her breath caught as his palms slid over her impeccable bottom and she drew back, staring at him.

"This is certainly perfect," he said with a grin, squeezing an agreeably plump handful as she giggled and then rearranged her face, looking down with a haughty expression.

"I'm so glad you approve," she muttered tartly, though laughter danced in her eyes.

"I don't *approve*," he said with a tut, making her narrow her eyes at him as he trailed one finger down the crease of her bottom.

She shivered.

"Surely a goddess seeks more than mere approval? You require worshiping at the very least. When we are married, I shall lavish such attention on this exquisite piece of art that you shall have no doubts of my devotion."

"Married?" she repeated, a little breathless.

"Of course, married," he replied gazing up at her. "You cannot have believed I would dally with you for sport? I love you, and so we must be married. Well, that is… if you'll have me?"

She stared down at him, her eyes very bright. "*Yes*! Yes, please. Of course, I will, but…."

"*But*?" he repeated indignantly. "There's never a but!"

"Well, there is this time." She tsked and pressed a finger to his lips to silence him. "But… you must help me accomplish my dare first."

He relaxed, delighted by her. "Ah, yes. Something wicked."

"Yes," she breathed rather than spoke the word and Cassius moved, finding her hips beneath the layers and layers and tumbling her sideways onto her back. She squealed and he hushed her as he lay down alongside her. She sniggered, covering her mouth with her hand.

"You are quite dreadful," he said, shaking his head as his hand slid up, up, over her knee, over her satiny skin.

"Yes."

"Don't ever stop being dreadful," he murmured, as his palm found the tender skin of her inner thigh, impossibly soft.

"I won't."

"Promise?"

"Promise," she said, and then gasped as his fingers trailed through the little triangle of curls that he knew to be a glorious shade of gold.

"Oh," she said as his delicate touch explored, moving lower, seeking the place he had longed for. "Oh, Cassius, that… that is *wicked*."

He chuckled, burying his face against her neck and laughing for the pure joy of it, of her, intoxicated by her scent, by the feel of her, by the sheer brilliance of being in her presence.

His fingers caressed, seeking the place that was the centre of her pleasure, and teased her gently, slowly, circling and sliding deeper, dipping into the heated core of her as he muffled a groan of wanting. He imagined the night when he could do more than this, take more than this, as he pleasured her, revelling in the soft sounds she made until he had to make himself stop painting such wanton pictures in his mind before he came undone. Her breathing hitched and she grasped at him, her hips canting towards his touch, seeking more as she chased the sensation. Cassius watched her, overwhelmed with love, with desire, humbled by her trust in him, knowing he was a wretched devil for taking this before they were even engaged, and all the world knew of his intentions. Yet she had asked, and he could deny her nothing, least of all something he wanted so desperately too.

She cried out, her body arching and trembling and he hushed her, soothed her, easing her through and helping her find every last tremor of pleasure until at last she was still. She gazed up at him, her expression soft and hazy and she gave a sigh, her warm breath fluttering over him.

"That was… splendid," she said, a satisfied smile curving over her delicious mouth.

To his amusement, she looked smug, the little devil.

"I'm glad you approve."

"Oh, certainly. A goddess always approves such shows of devotion. Didn't you know?"

Cassius snorted, pulling her against him as he leaned down and kissed her.

"Wretch," he said affectionately.

"Well," came a cool voice from the doorway as they leapt apart to see Eliza staring stonily at them. "At least I'm not the last person to know this time."

With that, she flung the leather portfolio to the floor of the school room and turned and walked away.

Chapter 16

Dearest Eliza,

I am so profoundly sorry. Please, won't you come out and talk to me?

—Excerpt of a note from Lady Charlotte Adolphus to her sister, Lady Elizabeth Adolphus, slid beneath her bedroom door.

The afternoon of 15th July 1838, Holbrook House, Sussex.

"Come in and sit down, please."

"But, Mama, I…." Lottie began, frantically searching for a reason to escape as her instincts prickled, telling her that her mother wanted to speak about something very specific.

"Now, please," the duchess said, her tone brisk and no-nonsense as she opened the door wider and gestured for Lottie to go in.

Lottie's instincts proved to be spot on as she took a reluctant step inside the room and stopped. Cassius was standing by the fireplace, looking about as awkward as a man could, and Eliza sat in the chair by the fire.

"Now, then." Mama closed the door and ushered Lottie to the chair opposite her sister. "I think we need to have a little chat, don't you?"

"Really, Mama," Eliza said, her most polite expression fixed on her face. "I do not see—"

"Elizabeth Minerva Adolphus, unless you are prepared to speak honestly and openly to me, you may sit there in silence and listen."

Eliza gaped at her mother, colour burning high on her cheeks.

"Now," the duchess said, folding her arms. "You may think me a witless old woman, but I assure you I am not. I was young once—and not *so* very long ago as you may suppose—and I am well aware of all the recklessness and idiocy involved in affairs of the heart."

"Really, Mama," Eliza protested, shifting in her seat. "I do not think that I need—"

Her mother sent her an incinerating glance and Eliza snapped her mouth shut.

"This morning, Cassius called on your father," she continued, addressing Lottie. "And asked for your hand in marriage."

Lottie gasped, her hand moving to cover her poor heart which was beating erratically now. Her gaze flew to Cassius, who sent her a small smile and then they both glanced at Eliza, who was very carefully not looking at either of them.

"W-What did Papa say?" Lottie ventured.

For a moment her mother's face softened. "He said yes, of course, you little fool. We have long hoped that Cassius would be a part of our family, only…."

Eliza gave a mirthless snort and they all turned to look at her. She put up her chin, folding her arms and glaring back.

"Quite," their mother said. "It has come as something of a surprise to all of us, I think, that it is not Eliza he is marrying."

"I don't wish to marry him either," Eliza retorted.

The duchess gave a wry smile. "I'm sure that is a relief to everyone. The problem is, I've suspected that for some time and it does not seem to account for the fit of dismals Eliza has been experiencing. I have been trying to discover this past week or more what is making her so out of sorts and this morning I discover her in the midst of a temper fit, the likes of which I have never seen before."

"Mama, I apologised for that already...." Eliza began, her mortification obvious.

"Stuff!" her mother said crossly. "It was about time. I've long despaired of you, my girl. I have never liked nor understood the passive face you show the world. It may well be the fashion for young ladies to act like a cross between a martyred saint and pretty watercolour painting, but I do not subscribe to it. Such behaviour will attract entirely the wrong sort of man, for one thing, one who expects docility and a woman who never challenges him. Where in heaven's name was my temper, my defiant spirit? You've spent your entire life trying to please the world, Elizabeth, and it is about time that stopped. I was never more relieved to see anyone indulge in a fit of pique than I was this morning."

Despite everything, Lottie giggled at the look of astonishment on Eliza's face.

"Oh, shut up," Eliza snapped at her.

Lottie shut up.

"Don't push your luck," her mother said, her tone dry. "The point remains that the temper tantrum and Cassius's sudden proposal of marriage obviously have a connection, and I am not leaving this room until I know what it is. I assume that until recently you, Eliza, like the rest of us, were unaware of any romance between your sister and Cassius?"

"Until last night, yes."

"And what happened last night that made you aware of the situation?"

The duchess looked around the room: at Cassius, who was studiously studying the empty grate as though it held the answers to the universe; to Eliza, who was approximately the colour of a ripe tomato; and then to Lottie, who knew she must be an identical shade of mortification and now edging towards puce. She squirmed under her mama's enquiring gaze.

Her mother made a sound that Lottie was almost certain was a snort of laughter but that turned so swiftly to a cough she could not be sure.

"Cassius, fetch me a drink," the duchess instructed, her voice somewhat strained.

Cassius leapt to do her bidding, reaching for the sherry.

"No, not that muck. The brandy, for heaven's sake."

Cassius fumbled the decanter, almost dropping the stopper, but poured out a generous measure. He handed their mother the brandy glass and took a deep breath.

"This is all my fault," he said, his countenance pale and grave. "I've made a mess of everything. I truly believed I wanted to marry Eliza until I got closer to home. The closer I got, the more uncertain I was, and then… then when I got here and saw her, I realised how dear she was to me, and that I could not marry her because she *was* my dearest friend, and she deserved more than friendship from her husband. I am so sorry for the hurt that has been caused, and that I caused it makes my heart hurt, but she deserves to be loved, fully and unconditionally, by a man who can appreciate just how extraordinary she is."

The duchess smiled. "Well said, Cassius. Eliza?"

Eliza looked up at her mother, her eyes very bright, and then she looked at Cassius, Lottie suspected for the first time since she'd entered the room. She nodded at him, in acceptance of his words, and of his apology.

"And what of Lottie?" asked mama.

Cassius gave a soft laugh.

"I wasn't prepared," he said. "It was like being hit by a locomotive. Any sense I considered I had deserted me, and... and I love her. I did not mean to, I certainly did not expect to, but I do."

"Lottie?" Her mother gave her an expectant look.

Lottie nodded, her throat too thick to speak, though she knew she must. "Yes. I always have. I kept it secret all these years, for I knew I c-could not h-have him, but... yes."

Eliza stared at her sister in outrage. "You loved him? You've always loved him and... and you never *said*?"

"How could I?" Lottie demanded. "He was yours, and I love you too. So much. I couldn't bear to hurt you."

Lottie jolted as if she'd been slapped at the scathing sound Eliza made.

"Eliza," Cassius began, moving to intervene, but the duchess held him back, glaring at him to hold his tongue.

"When *precisely* did you decide you could bear it after all?"

Eliza's voice was clipped and meticulous, her expression cold, and Lottie burned with shame, and with terror that her sister might never forgive her.

"I didn't plan it," she said, her voice barely a whisper. "But when I realised he... he felt the same, and once he had t-told you he wouldn't marry you...."

"Was that when you took your clothes off for him?"

Lottie gasped, clutching her arms about herself, still stunned that Eliza of all people should betray her in front of their mother.

"Still think I'm trying to please the world, Mama?" Eliza demanded, though her expression was stricken, tears pouring down her face.

With that, she leapt to her feet and fled the room, slamming the door behind her.

There was a spectacular silence.

"Well," the duchess said with a sigh. "That went rather better than I expected."

Lottie stared out at the lake and wondered how many other people had come to the water's edge with despair in their hearts. She ought to be overjoyed. Cassius had asked to marry her, and her parents had agreed, and that… that was everything she had ever dreamed of. How could she enjoy it, though, if it came at the expense of her sister's happiness? She knew she was not stealing Cassius from Eliza, and she was certain Eliza did not view it that way either, but the way it had happened….

She groaned and prised up a small stone from the ground, lobbing it furiously into the water where it fell with a disconsolate plop, which was most unsatisfying. She wished she were a man and could go and hit something.

"Lady Charlotte?"

Lottie turned in shock, not having heard anyone approach and frustrated to discover someone had tracked her down as she wasn't feeling the least bit sociable.

"Oh, good afternoon, Louis César. I hope you'll forgive me, but I'm not very good company today. I should leave while you have the chance."

He gave a soft laugh and shook his head. "I believe this is why Cassius has fallen head over ears for you. There is nothing but honesty in your heart, and it makes its way to your mouth with very little to moderate it."

Lottie flushed, a little indignant, but Louis César held up a hand.

"That was a compliment, if you missed it. After all, you could have pretended to be pleased for my company and let me prattle on, which would have been mortifying. Your way is by far preferable."

"Well, it is true, so you may do as you please, but I warn you I may well pick a quarrel with you, or even cry. So there."

He arranged himself on the ground beside her and pulled out a handkerchief, placing it on his knee.

"I enjoy a good quarrel, and I always come prepared for such eventualities," he said, gesturing gravely at the handkerchief.

Lottie snorted.

"Nic found the drawings," he said, giving her an apologetic glance.

For a moment, after everything that had happened in the past twenty-four hours, Lottie did not realise what he was saying. Then understanding dawned and, for the second time that day, she felt herself grow hot and an unattractive shade of red.

"Oh!" she said, mortified. "Oh, my…."

Louis César shrugged. "I did not tell you to cause you discomfort, and you need not fret that either of us will ever breathe a word about it for we never shall, upon my honour. Only, I did not wish you think badly of my brother for what he did. He can be… *difficult*, but he never acts without reason, and he felt Cassius had not treated Lady Elizabeth with the respect she deserves. Nic did not know, of course, that Cassius was in love with you, or meant to marry you. I have now explained matters, and he knows he acted rashly—*félicitations à vous deux,* by the way."

"Thank you," Lottie replied, though she could barely meet his eyes.

When she did, she saw amusement there.

"We are French, my lady," he said, a teasing note to his words. "I promise you we are not the least bit shocked. I am only impressed that you managed it under the eyes of so many chaperones."

"They would never think I needed chaperoning with Cassius. They assumed he was like a brother to me. So did Eliza," she added sadly.

To her surprise, Louis César reached over and patted her hand. "Do not fret, *ma chère,* your sister is not the kind to hold a grudge. I know she is hurt and angry, and perhaps her pride is wounded most of all, but she will forgive you. Lady Elizabeth is too good-hearted and kind not to."

"She is, isn't she?" Lottie said, her voice quavering, and she was uncertain if she was agreeing or asking a question. "Eliza is so kind, the very best sister in the world, and I... I couldn't bear it if...."

Silently, Louis César handed her the handkerchief. Lottie buried her face in it, laughing and crying at the same time.

"I hope she marries you," she said, once she'd gathered herself again. "It was very nice of you to come and speak with me, to explain, *and* to bear my weeping. Many men would run a mile rather than endure that."

Louis César pursed his lips, considering this. He gave a little laugh, which Lottie thought held a note of bitterness.

"*Non, non.* No, I do not think I am *very nice,* but then I am not so *very* bad, and I hope she marries me too."

There was a twinkle in his eyes as he winked at her, and Lottie laughed as she was supposed to, but wasn't entirely sure what to make of him.

"Come," he said, getting to his feet and holding his hand out to her. "It is unacceptable for a beautiful young lady to be alone in her sadness. I shall escort you back to the house and endeavour to lift your spirits. Perhaps I might help bring about a reconciliation between you and Lady Elizabeth."

Lottie smiled and allowed him to help her up.

"I don't know. For all her easy nature and mild manners, she can be remarkably stubborn when the mood takes her. Only she does it so prettily no one notices. Not that I can blame her," she added quickly.

Louis César nodded. "She is a clever young woman, far more so than one might realise at first glance, but I think—for now, at least—she is not in the mood to play nicely."

"No," Lottie said wryly. "I noticed that too. I don't think I've ever seen her lose her temper before. None of us have. We were never more shocked. As a child, I was the one who had temper fits and Eliza was a model of good behaviour."

She took his arm and they walked back to the house together. As they entered through the main doors, Lottie took a breath, relieved by the cooler air inside the great house, and then paused as she saw Eliza watching them.

"Ah, there you are, Monsieur le Comte," Eliza said. "I have been looking for you this age, as we have a guest awaiting you, and here you are... *with Charlotte.* How amusing."

Lottie flushed at the irritation glinting in her sister's eyes, aware of her implication. After all, Louis César was supposed to be courting Eliza now.

"Yes, a happy circumstance," Louis César said smoothly. "I was walking down by the lake and found the poor child crying, so I thought I had best bring her directly to her sister for comfort."

"Oh," Eliza said, her cool expression faltering and her voice faint. "Oh, Lottie, I...."

She took a step closer, holding out her hands, but before she could say another word, a strident, heavily accented French voice cut through the great hall.

"*Alors*! *Enfin*, and why am I not surprised to discover I 'ave been kept waiting whilst you entertain a pretty young lady?"

Lottie turned in surprise towards the throaty voice to see a ravishing woman. She was exceptionally lovely, perhaps in her mid-thirties, with raven black hair that clustered in thick curls about her face. Her carriage gown was the height of fashion and made of a deep emerald green *pou de soie*. The sleeves bore an extravaganza of ruffles and puffs, and a lavish line of ruffles and bows flounced down the front of the gown and trembled with fury as the lady swept towards Louis César like an avenging angel.

Louis César stiffened and did not look the least bit pleased to see her.

"Madame Lafitte, I was unaware you had been invited to Holbrook House."

She tsked at him and snapped open the black silk fan she carried, waving it furiously and putting up her chin. It dawned on Lottie that this lady was not entirely respectable, and she wondered at her temerity in chasing Louis César down at a private house party. Bold was not the word. Was she his mistress?

"Of course I 'ave not been invited, but this is what I am reduced to. *Regardez-moi, chères dames*," she said, turning beseeching eyes upon Eliza and Lottie. "This is what a man can do. I am forced to follow this one and 'is wicked brother across the seas for the sake of my 'onour."

Louis César made a choked sound and she glared at him.

"*La Manche, ma chère*," he said dryly. "The Channel is not quite the Atlantic Ocean and I fear you have wasted your time. My brother is not here, and he owes you nothing."

"'E owes me *everything*," she hissed. "And do not think I will not tell all your sordid stories if 'e does not do as 'onour demands."

"Come, Eliza," Lottie said, for once remembering her manners long before her sister, who was staring at Madame intently. Truly, it was better than the opera, though, so Lottie could hardly blame her. "We had best leave Louis César to speak to Madame in private."

"But Madame abhors privacy," Louis César said coldly. "She wishes for an audience, before which she may pour her vitriol to the maximum effect."

"I do not comprehend this…." the lady said, feigning ignorance though her colour had risen enough for Lottie to deduce she'd understood plenty. Instead she turned her attention to Eliza and Lottie once more, her eyes narrowing. "My English it is not so good, but 'ere is a picture so pretty, so *innocente*, I wonder… *Non, do not tell. I guess. Voila, c'est* the lady *Elizabet, n'est-ce pas?*"

Lottie moved closer to Eliza as the woman drew towards her sister.

"Madame," Louis César said, and he was moving too, addressing her angrily. "The ladies have no part in this. Leave them be. If you wish to discuss it—"

"But this child is too sweet for a man of your nature, Louis. She is not the type to please you," she said, her voice low and seductive. "You would be a fool to marry 'er. You will find 'er dull, and you, *ma jolie fille*, 'e only wants you to make his dirty name all clean and pretty again."

Eliza gasped at the bitterness in the woman's voice, and Lottie clutched at her hand.

"What the devil is going on here?"

Lottie let out a sigh of relief as her father and Lord St Clair appeared, emerging from the earl's study, clearly drawn by the woman's forceful voice. Madame Lafitte took a step back, but did not quail in front of the duke, for which Lottie had to give her credit.

"Who are you, madam, to come in here and speak to my daughter so?" he demanded, drawing Eliza and Lottie behind him.

Madame Lafitte sank into a deep and lavish curtsey, lowering her lashes and glancing up shyly at their papa. Lottie knew he was still a handsome man and could hardly blame her for trying, but the lady was all about in her head if she thought any manner of coquetries would influence him.

"*Monsieur le duc*," she murmured, putting a trembling hand to her forehead. "Forgive me. I am fatigued and I forget my manners, but this one… 'e and 'is brother, they treat me very bad, so cruel. I come only to warn *la pauvre demoiselle,* to 'ave a care for zhey are wicked and false."

The earl looked at Louis César with a frown of consternation. Lottie was not surprised. The comte's brother had already caused a scene with his son, and now this. She wished Cassius was here, for she felt sure he could smooth things over.

"Monsieur le Comte?" the earl said, his tone polite but clearly displeased. "Do you know this woman? Does she speak the truth?"

Louis turned a scathing look upon Madame Lafitte. "Yes, I know her, Lord St Clair, and I remain convinced that Madame would not know the truth if it sat in her lap, let alone understand the concept of honour. However, I fear I have caused a disagreeable scene and I have no desire to outstay my welcome. I will order my carriage. If you will be so good as to have my valet follow on with my belongings."

"Of course," the earl said, obviously relieved. "Madame Lafitte?"

Madame Lafitte shot Louis César a look of such volcanic fury Lottie half-expected it to singe his immaculate cravat, but he only met it with one of glacial coldness.

"You will regret this, Louis, and you may tell your brother your downfall will be on 'is conscience."

With this, she swept out of the hallway in an angry swish of heavy skirts: a dramatic exit fit for any wronged heroine in an overblown theatrical.

"My word," Lottie breathed, once the woman had disappeared and Louis César was hurrying up the stairs to ready himself to leave. Eliza watched him go, a little frown puckering the smooth skin between her eyebrows.

"Oh, Eliza, I am so sorry."

Eliza waved this away. "It is of no matter. I refuse to listen to anything the dreadful creature has to say. Imagine, chasing a man to a private party and embarrassing him so dreadfully. No matter how angry one is, a lady never behaves in such a vulgar fashion."

"That was no lady, my dear," their father said, his anger apparent.

"No," Eliza replied, her tone thoughtful. "That was done to cause the maximum damage to the comte and his brother. I shall set no store by it."

"Still," said the duke, his countenance hiding none of his displeasure at the unpleasant scene. "I shall make it my business to discover more about these brothers, and until then you are to stay well away from them. Is that clear?"

To her astonishment, rather than meekly agreeing with her father's command, Eliza bristled.

"No, Papa. It is doubtful I shall see either of them again until the season, but I will not avoid them. The comte has been kind and charming, and most considerate, and I shall not repay that by listening to gossip and cutting his or his brother's acquaintance, and if you thought about it above a moment, you would realise Mama should be very cross with you for suggesting it."

She flounced away in a manner Madame Lafitte could not have bettered and left her astonished papa and Lottie gazing after her.

"Mercy," her father muttered. "This more spirited version of your sister might please your mama, but I predict she's going to be dashed uncomfortable to live with."

Emma V Leech

"There, there, Papa," Lottie soothed, taking his arm. "If you can handle Mama, I'm sure Eliza is nothing to trouble yourself about."

"Hmph," her father grumbled as she led him away to find her mother.

Chapter 17

Dear Phoebe,

I do not know if you have yet heard of all the drama of the past few days but I am about to enlighten you.

In case the gossip has not yet reached your ears, I shall inform you that I am not to marry Cassius. Lottie, however, is. I admit it was something of a shock to my system, but I think perhaps it is as it ought to be. They are clearly very much in love, which Cassius and I never were. I cannot pretend otherwise.

I admit I am still all at sea, but I shall rally soon enough, no doubt.

However, far more interestingly your mysterious Comte Louis César and his brother are at the heart of the latest scandal at Holbrook, not that anyone outside of the family knows. So, in return for my giving you every minute detail of what happened, I must insist that you reply to this letter at once and tell me everything you know!

—Excerpt of a note from Lady Elizabeth Adolphus to The Right Hon'ble Phoebe Carmichael, The Countess of Ellisborough.

17th July 1838, Holbrook House, Sussex.

Lottie gathered her nerve as she stood outside the door to her sister's room. Though Eliza had certainly thawed towards her, they had not had the opportunity speak privately, or perhaps the opportunity had been there, but neither of them had been quite ready to take it. Now Lottie knew they must address the lingering tension between them, for fear that it would fester and damage a relationship which she prized above anything. She raised her hand and knocked, waiting until Eliza called for her to enter.

Lottie found her at the window seat, staring out at a day that had dawned misty and damp and threatened to bring rain.

"I brought that book back," Lottie said, holding out a novel that Eliza had lent her some weeks ago.

"Oh, thank you. Did you like it?"

Lottie hesitated and put the book down on the bedside table, perching on the edge of the mattress. "Actually I… I haven't read it yet only I wanted an excuse to come and see you."

Eliza stared at her. "You needed an excuse?" she repeated.

Lottie looked away from her sister's wide-eyed gaze and smoothed out her skirts nervously, discovering her palms were damp. "Yes."

"Why?"

"B-Because I wasn't sure you'd want to see me," Lottie said, appalled to discover her voice quavering. Her bottom lip trembled.

"Oh, love!" Eliza surged to her feet with a rustle of skirts and rushed to her sister.

It was quite awkward to sit closely without crushing both of their voluminous skirts but neither of them cared. Eliza embraced Lottie, who burst into tears, throwing her arms about her sister with such relief she felt a weight had been lifted from her.

"I'm s-so sorry, Eliza," she wept, as Eliza thrust a handkerchief into her hand, for of course Eliza had a handkerchief ready for such an occasion. Lottie always lost hers. "I hate myself for making you unhappy."

"Oh, no. Oh, Lottie, don't. I've… I've been pettish and spiteful, and I'm quite ashamed of myself."

Lottie gave her nose a forceful blow and sat up, regarding her sister. "Don't say that! Mama is so proud of you for speaking your mind."

Eliza snorted. "Speaking my mind is one thing, and I must admit… oh, Lottie, it is so liberating to do so. I never realised… but never mind that. One does not need to be unkind to be truthful, only I was so very angry."

"With me," Lottie said, nodding.

"*No*! Well," Eliza said with a rueful sigh. "If I am being honest, then yes. Yes, I was angry, but only that it seemed you were keeping secrets from me. When I thought about it, I realised I had no right, when… when I have been doing the same."

Lottie sniffed and sat up a little straighter, regarding her with interest. "You have?"

A flush of colour tinged Eliza's cheeks and she and got up, moving to the chest of drawers and taking out another clean handkerchief.

"Here," she said. "You've mangled that last one."

"Thank you," Lottie said, wiping her eyes and giving her nose another blow. "But what secret, Eliza?"

Eliza hesitated. "Tell me what happened with Cassius. Tell me everything, and… and I shall tell you my secret in return."

This time Lottie blushed, heat crawling up her neck and scalding her cheeks. Eliza smirked at her.

"And well you might blush, you dreadful creature. I was never more shocked to find those drawings of you in... in... well, in the altogether! How did you dare? I cannot imagine ever having the courage to do such a thing."

Lottie giggled. "It *was* my dare."

Eliza gaped at her. "Charlotte! You never took your clothes off for a *dare*!"

Lottie crowed with laughter at the outrage in her sister's eyes. "No! Well, at least, not just for the dare, but it gave me a reason, the courage to do it. But I wanted to, Eliza, I... oh, my dear. I have such a lot to tell you."

Eliza climbed back onto the bed, and the two of them sat very close as Lottie explained everything that had happened since they had arrived at Holbrook. As she spoke, all the restraint and resentment that had grown between them fell away, and it was as if the past days had never happened. By the time Lottie had whispered the most delicate of details of what she'd experienced in the past few days, Eliza was round eyed with wonder.

"Good heavens," she said, staring at Lottie. "Truly?"

"Truly," Lottie said, grinning at her.

"Good heavens."

Both of them were pink-cheeked and, when Eliza caught her sister's eye, they burst out laughing. They laughed and laughed until they were clutching at their corsets and begging for mercy because everything hurt.

"Oh, my," Lottie said, wiping her eyes. "Stop it. I shall do myself an injury if you set me off again."

"Serves you right for lacing your corset too tightly," Eliza observed, to which comment Lottie stuck out her tongue. Eliza replied in kind.

"Oh, Eliza, I have missed you."

"And I you, Lottie," Eliza said, reaching out and taking her hand. "Let's never be so angry with each other again."

They sat in happy silence for a moment until Lottie remembered their agreement.

"Now then," she said, fixing Eliza with her most piercing gaze. "Tell me everything."

"Oh," Eliza said, suddenly looking awkward as she traced a finger over the pattern on the bedspread. "Well, there's really not a great deal to tell, only… only…."

"Yes?" Lottie said, bouncing with impatience.

Eliza sighed and flung herself back onto the mattress. "Oh, Lottie, I'm such an idiot, but… but I think I'm infatuated with a man who despises me."

Lottie gaped at her.

"Not really," she said. "You can't mean…?"

Eliza nodded sadly. "Yes, I can. I'm the worst ninny, but I cannot get him out of my mind, and then Papa went and forbade me to speak to either of them and—"

"Mr Demarteau," Lottie said, wondering how on earth Eliza could fall in love with a man she not only barely knew, but who had been nothing but awful to her.

Eliza nodded. "And don't ask me to explain, for I swear I cannot. I am not a foolish, fanciful creature. I have never dreamed of knights in shining armour, or a Prince Charming… which is just as well, for he's none of those things."

"No, he's not. Indeed, I think he's dreadfully intimidating."

"I know!" Eliza wailed. "He's wicked and dreadful, and every time I think of him I get the oddest sensation, low in my belly, and I go all hot and it's hard to breathe."

"Oh, dear," Lottie said faintly, wondering how her sensible sister had got herself into such a pickle.

"Quite," Eliza said.

They sat in silence as Lottie digested this.

"I'm not sure you ought to do anything about an infatuation of this kind," she said, feeling dreadfully anxious on her sister's behalf.

"Well, and what could I do anyway?" Eliza demanded with a huff. "It's awkward and hopeless, especially now Papa is so furious with them both, and Louis César is supposed to be the respectable one! After that scene with Madame Lafitte, I shall be lucky to get within a mile of him, let alone his brother. Though perhaps that is for the best."

"I think it really is, Eliza. You want to accomplish something with your life, remember? Think of all the plans you'd made, all those charitable organisations you wish to set up, not to mention the Chartist Movement. You had plans to marry a duke or a marquess so you had influence enough to get things done, and Mr Demarteau is barely tolerated in society. He's illegitimate, and barely respectable. If he and his brother weren't so handsome and intriguing, and Louis César wasn't so charming, they'd never be received."

"I know!" Eliza exclaimed, so irritated that Lottie knew she had considered this herself.

"Well," she said soothingly. "You are unlikely to see him again for some time. Perhaps it was just an eccentric episode. Like the summer Fred wouldn't eat anything red. The feeling might have worn off by the next time you see him."

Eliza cast her a doubtful glance. "Perhaps."

They both looked up at the sound of a knock on the door. Their mother strode in.

"Ah, perfect," she said, beaming at finding them together. "I'm so pleased you've made up. You have made up, haven't you? I'm not missing broken china or pointy objects hidden under the pillows?"

Lottie rolled her eyes. "Yes, Mama."

"Excellent, and don't you roll your eyes at me, young lady. We need to arrange this wedding, and the sooner the better, it would seem, if what Eliza says is true... and when *exactly* did you take your clothes off, you wicked girl? And if there was anything more than posing for a drawing going on, you'd best tell me at once."

"No, Mama!" Lottie went hot and cold in quick succession and was not entirely soothed by the obvious amusement in her mama's eyes.

"Oh, do stop looking so missish," the duchess said with a tsk. "You love each other, so something was bound to happen. But, Eliza, do not think for one moment I condone such behaviour, for I do not."

"*Mama!*" Eliza said, outraged by the way her mother was wagging an admonishing finger at her.

"Well," the duchess said thoughtfully. "It seems you are both more like your dreadful mother than anyone supposed, so I think we had best be prepared. Lottie, you were foolish, but Cassius is at least a gentleman, and someone to be relied upon. Far too many men are not, as unhappy women discover to their cost too often."

"I'm not stupid, Mother," Eliza replied, sounding impatient and unsettled by the conversation.

"Indeed, you are not, but the cleverest women can get themselves into tricky situations when desire raises its head. Just ask your soon to be mother-in-law," she said, winking at Lottie.

Eliza glowered, looking surprisingly mutinous. "There is no danger of that, as my only suitor has been sent away in disgrace."

"Your only suitor," her mother replied with a snort. "Just you remember, my girl: a man who marries you, owns you. Not only your money, but everything. Your clothes and belongings become his, your body is no longer your own. If he wishes to beat you or lock you in your room, he is at liberty to do so and no one can stop him. You need to be very certain before you give yourself into his keeping. I'll admit Louis César would be an unholy temptation to any woman, but you need to know a man's soul as well as his heart before allowing yourself to trust him."

"Yes, Mama," Eliza said, serious now.

They knew Mama had good reason for fearing for them, for she had seen first-hand the dangers of a bad marriage. Her father had abused her mother and made her life a misery. No. No man could be taken at face value. Lottie felt a tremor of unease as she looked at her sister and considered the ill-mannered Mr Demarteau. They had already seen that he was capable of violence. Was this the kind of man her lovely, kind-hearted sister should take an interest in? No, certainly not, and Lottie must do all in her power to ensure Eliza did not fall prey to any foolish notions about him.

Their mama had not been joking when she had said a speedy wedding was in order. By midday they had a date, two weeks hence, and had agreed the wedding could take place at Holbrook House. Many of their friends lived close by, and as the family was already in residence, it seemed pointless to go elsewhere. They had begun the invitations list and arranged a visit to a new modiste that Matilda had discovered, and was quite enamoured of, to discuss the trousseau and the wedding gown.

Lottie had fretted at first, wondering if Eliza would resent all the fuss and excitement when it ought to have been for her, but she seemed genuinely happy and eager to join in. It seemed, at last, that everything would work out for the best.

"Thank goodness the rain has stopped," Eliza said, looking out of the window after they had fortified themselves with tea, and some tempting platters of good, strong cheese served with tart green apples and plums. "I do believe the sun will show itself too. I shall go for a ride and get some fresh air, I think, for all this plotting and planning has given me a headache. Will you come?"

Lottie yawned and stretched, knowing some exercise and fresh air would be a good idea, but pondering that she'd not seen Cassius all day *and* that she had promised to visit him down at the summerhouse.

Eliza laughed before Lottie could answer. "Never mind. Go and see him before you faint with longing. You know, I realise now what a lucky escape we both had. I have never craved to be with Cassius in the way I can see you do. There is nothing the least bit romantic between us, and it is only now I appreciate the difference. Papa was right. Marrying your friend is not perhaps a bad thing, but there needs to be more than that… *I* need more than that."

"Yes," Lottie replied, quite grave in her reply. "Yes, you do."

Eliza nodded, gave Lottie a wry smile, and hurried away to get changed.

Chapter 18

Dear Diary,

I am so relieved that everyone is happy again. Cassius and Lottie are to be married! It is so exciting, especially now Lottie and Eliza have made up, and Eliza holds no ill will towards either her or Cassius. All is right in the world and they will be married here at Holbrook which means we can stay longer. The perfect summer. The twins, Ashton and Vivien are staying too, which is wonderful, for Ash is such fun. I do adore him. I only wish Louis César would come back, perhaps even Mr Demarteau for they added a little excitement, perhaps because they are new and unpredictable. Life is always more thrilling when one has no idea what will happen next.

—Excerpt of an entry to the diary of Lady Catherine 'Cat' Barrington, youngest daughter of the Marquess and Marchioness of Montagu.

17th July 1838, Holbrook House, Sussex.

"Like this?"

Cassius felt his breath catch as Lottie tilted her head as instructed. The sunshine which had begun so tentatively once the clouds had cleared was now hot and fierce and caught the thick tresses of her hair, burnishing them like old gold and illuminating her profile. She looked like an angel. It sounded trite, so much so he could hardly bear to say it out loud, but it was true. Looking at her hurt his heart, made something inside him ache with tenderness, with the desire to love and protect her always. Unable to resist the temptation, he went to her, bent his head and kissed her, just a soft press of lips that was still a mistake as it left him restless and short of breath.

"Perfect," he said, moving away with difficulty. "In fact, could you be just a little less perfect? My desire to paint you is being overridden by other, less wholesome yearnings."

"*Really?*" she said, her eyes lighting with interest. "That sounds fascinating."

"It is, but you must stop being fascinated, for your mama only allowed you to sit for me alone on condition I had work to show her when she comes to see us later. If I have a blank canvas for my allotted two hours, we shall both be in the basket."

"Oh, I don't know. She was remarkably sanguine about me having taken my clothes off for you."

Cassius blanched. "Well said. Knowing she is aware you did that, and so your father likely knows too, has focused my mind wonderfully. Now sit still."

Lottie gave a regretful sigh, and Cassius scowled at her. How he would get through the next two weeks he could not fathom, but then... then they would be married. His father had given them a beautiful old house in Aylesbury. It was a fine Tudor mansion which the earl had extensively remodelled and was luxurious and comfortable, and the gardens were magnificent. The idea of being able to live there whenever they returned from their travels was enough to make Cassius feel he truly was the luckiest fellow in the world. So, he would be good, and ensure that Lottie was just as she ought to be when she walked down the aisle of their private chapel.

For the next half an hour, Lottie did as he asked, and did not fidget or complain, and he progressed nicely with the drawing.

"It's awfully hot in here," she said with a heavy sigh, trailing a finger slowly down the side of her neck.

Cassius paused, his pencil suspended in mid-air as he watched that languid hand trail down the elegant column of her throat, along her collarbone, to the neckline of her gown. It paused at the hint of décolletage, drawing his eye there as his breath hitched. The wicked digit then trailed back and forth over the tops of her breasts as she drew in a deep breath and sighed again, wistful now.

"Lottie," he said, a warning note to his voice.

She turned melting eyes upon him, all innocence. The devil.

"What is it?"

"You know very well. Stop it."

Lottie pouted, but resumed her pose. Cassius concentrated on capturing the lush curve of her breast, the way the soft muslin of her white gown hugged her form. The dress sat low on her shoulders, revealing a great deal of creamy skin. Cassius swallowed, took a breath, and carried on. He followed the swanlike neck, to ensure that stubborn chin was quite as determined on his canvas as it was in reality, and moved onto study her mouth. His focus faltered as a little pink tongue darted out and wet her lips. The pencil hovered, close to the canvas but not touching it. Cassius cleared his throat but made the mistake of looking into her eyes. Those great big blue eyes captured his, expressive with such blatant invitation his skin prickled all over, and then he looked back at her mouth to see the corner twitch, just a little, and he was lost.

"Lottie," he said, though he could not muster the warning note this time, too dazed with longing to protest.

"Yes?"

"You are the very devil."

"But I didn't do anything."

"Yes, you did, you provoking creature."

"Did I really?"

"Yes, dash it. How is a fellow to concentrate when… when…."

He waved a hand at her.

"What did I do, Cassius?" she asked, her voice low. "Tell me."

"Why? So you can use your wiles on me again in future?"

She laughed at that, a sound that made little explosions go off inside him, tiny bursts of happiness. "Yes, of course."

He groaned and set down the pencil. "You licked your lips for one thing."

"Is that provocative?" she asked, and he wondered at the look in her eyes.

Did she really not understand the power she held over him? Probably just as well… at least, until they were married.

"It is when you do it, when I want to feel that little pink tongue on me, against my skin."

"Oh," she said, sitting up straighter.

"*Oh*," he echoed, lips quirking, and then realised he also had the power to have a little revenge. "Do you not find my tongue provocative if you think about it trailing over your skin, down your neck… to your breast? Just as an example."

She sat very still, her eyes growing wider as her colour rose. As if tracing the same path, her hand went to her neck as it had earlier, imitating the path he'd just described taking with his mouth and tongue. He swallowed.

"I want to do that, very badly. I want to kiss your breasts and take each little rosy peak into my mouth and suck."

Her jaw dropped, which might have been more amusing if he wasn't now rigid with desire himself.

"Cassius," she whispered. "Cass, p-please."

He was moving before she'd even got to the *please*, falling to his knees in front of the day bed where she sat for him and pulling her into his arms.

"Oh, love. Beautiful girl," he murmured, his mouth and tongue doing just as he'd promised and painting her beautiful skin all the way to the barrier of her gown. He growled in frustration and she gave a little laugh and then lifted her hands, undoing the buttons at the front of her bodice and giving the fabric a little tug.

"Oh," she said in frustration as the corset beneath refused to budge.

Despite his own desire to remove the blasted thing with haste, he laughed, delighted by her impatience.

"Wicked girl. You are forever taking your clothes off."

"Well, it was a deal easier in a nightgown and wrap," she retorted.

Cassius smirked and lowered his head. Slowly and deliberately he ran his tongue over the swell of each breast, the only parts available to him.

Lottie shivered and gave a little sigh, and he groaned.

"Two weeks. Two weeks. Two weeks, only two weeks," he said, muttering the words under this breath.

"That's fourteen whole days!" Lottie wailed.

"Not helping, love."

Feeling a little desperate, he got up and sat on the bed.

"Come here," he urged her, getting her to straddle his thighs like she had the other night. "We don't have long."

"I know. Mama will be here in an hour."

"Don't remind me," he cursed, pulling her down and battling through the copious layers of skirts and petticoats. "Confound these blasted things!"

Lottie giggled and he huffed, determined to reach skin. Finally... *Finally*, he put his hands on her warm thighs and tugged, pulling her down so she sat pressed against him and her skirts billowed out on all sides.

Cassius grinned at her. "You look like you're emerging from a cloud."

"It's a very hard cloud I'm sitting on," she said, quirking one eyebrow.

His breath snagged in his throat as she pressed closer and his head fell back.

"Oh, God."

Lottie gasped, her colour rising as she discovered the pleasure in friction too.

"Oh!"

She caught on quickly, thank the Lord, too quickly perhaps, as it was an embarrassingly short time before Cassius had to call a halt.

"Stop, stop."

"But I... I don't want...."

He grasped her hips, stilling her movement.

"Stop," he said firmly.

She whimpered and pouted a little but didn't argue. Cassius drew in a deep breath and then let it out again, slowly.

"Cass?"

Lottie squealed as someone knocked on the summerhouse door, calling his name. Cassius grabbed hold of her again as she moved so quickly she nearly went over backwards.

"H-Hold on," Cassius called, hastily setting Lottie to rights again and returning to his position at the easel with as much speed as possible. Though he had not yet begun painting, he grabbed hold of his palette and held it discreetly to cover his modesty as his body had not yet caught up with the fact it was to suffer a grave disappointment. "Who is it?"

"Ashton."

"Bloody hell, Ash, come in."

Ash stuck his head around the door, looking sheepish. "Sorry."

"You will be," Cassius grumbled. "What the devil do you want?"

"Well, I'm probably worrying over nothing, but Eliza was supposed to meet with us by the lake. We were going to take a boat out, but she's not come back from her ride."

Lottie sat up straighter, frowning. "But she left ages before me. She said she'd only be an hour."

Ashton nodded. "She ought to have been with us almost an hour ago, and I know she might have lost track of time, but Eliza—"

"Is never late," Lottie replied, getting to her feet. "Cassius."

Cassius went to her, knowing all too well that Eliza was a stickler for punctuality. It was dreadfully bad manners to be late, after all, and Eliza was never rude. Whilst she might have tested that truth a little in the past weeks, he could not believe she would keep her friends waiting.

"I'll look for her," he said. "I'm sure it's nothing. Perhaps her horse threw a shoe and she's walking it back."

"Yes," Lottie said, nodding, though her face betrayed her worry. "Yes, I'm sure that's it."

An hour later, Cassius was not feeling so confident. He returned to the house to see if anyone else had seen her, if perhaps she'd returned in the meantime, only to discover Lottie preparing to ride out too. Ash had also returned and gone out again with his sister. Eliza's father, as well as his own, and the marquess of Montagu, had all ridden off in different directions with many of the groomsmen accompanying them.

"Oh, Lottie," her mama said, standing with her other children gathered close about her. "Where can she be?"

"Try not to worry, Mama," Lottie said, though she too was pale and anxious. "Eliza is a terrific horsewoman. I'm sure she's fine."

Her mother nodded as she held her two youngest daughters close to her.

"Find her," she implored them, and Cassius nodded.

"We won't come back without her," he promised, feeling anxiety coil about his heart.

They set off and found that they were instinctively heading in the same direction, away from where the grooms had said she'd ridden out.

"Bayham Abbey?" he called to Lottie, who nodded.

"You know she's always loved it there, and she's been visiting often of late. It's romantic and peaceful there. She says it helps her to think."

It was less than twenty-five minutes ride to the abbey, but the hour was growing late, and they would not have much more daylight to search in. There was no question now that something had befallen Eliza, and everyone was sick with dread. He could only admire Lottie's quiet determination to find her sister, despite the terror she must be feeling.

They rode up to the abbey's ruins, which were indeed romantic, especially now with the sun sinking lower in the sky as dark clouds tumbled over one another, promising more rain. The abbey's lonely Gothic arches were overgrown with tumbling ivy and dog roses. Birds chattered among the thickly green clad walls and bees hummed about their work, but other than that there was no sign of life.

"Eliza!" Lottie called, a desperate note to her cry that pierced Cassius to the heart.

"Eliza!" he shouted, steadying his horse when it shied in agitation, disturbed by their raised voices. He prayed Eliza would hear them and reply. "Let's ride the perimeter."

Though the ruins were not vast, they were so thickly overgrown with ivy and trees that it was impossible to see through to every nook and cranny. Cassius hoped to discover some sign she had been here before they took the time to search the ruins. A shriek from Lottie gave him the answer.

"Cassius!" she cried, pointing to Eliza's horse, peacefully cropping grass close by the ruins.

Cassius leapt down and secured his mount before running to Lottie and helping her dismount. She was trembling, and tears glittered in her eyes but the moment her feet touched the ground she picked up her skirts and ran into the ruins.

"Eliza!" she screamed, running pell mell through the broken walls and arches.

"Eliza!

"*Eliza!*"

Long shadows cast them into obscurity as the sun sank lower still and the birds fell silent. Their voices echoed about the shadows, like some ghastly Gothic horror, until Cassius stopped in his tracks, a chill running down his spine on seeing the slight form crumpled on the ground.

"Eliza," he said, his voice thick.

Lottie was right behind him and saw a second after he had. She screamed and ran to her sister, falling to the ground beside her.

"Eliza! Eliza!"

Cassius joined her, desperately relieved to see the rise and fall of Eliza's chest.

"She's breathing," he said, his voice sounding too loud in the growing gloom as Lottie stroked her sister's hair.

"Cassius!" she said, showing him her trembling hand and her glove, which was dark with blood.

Cassius felt as if his heart was squeezed within his chest.

"She… She must have fallen," he said, looking up at the low, crumbling walls beside her and not comprehending how on earth she could have hit her head with such force otherwise.

But surely, she could not have been so reckless, so very foolish as to have climbed up them alone?

Whatever the cause, they did not have time to discover it and it was with huge relief that he heard his father's voice, calling out to him.

"Father! Father, we have her. *Come quick*!"

Chapter 19

Nic,

You are now deep in my debt, for this favour was by no means easy to arrange. Even for me.

Do not forget it.

— Excerpt of letter to Monsieur Nicolas Alexandre Demarteau, signed... Wolf.

20th August 1838, Holbrook House, Sussex.

Lottie stared down at her sister in despair. She looked to be sleeping, her chest rising and falling steadily, but she was like the princess in a fairy story who had pricked her finger and slept for a hundred years. It was more than a month now since that dreadful day, and Eliza had not stirred. Her frantic parents had brought every doctor from every corner of the country and, though some of them had waffled on with confidence about this or that condition, and had tried various remedies, still Eliza slept.

The one man they truly wanted and needed was a French neurologist, but the devil was caught up in some ground-breaking experiment and had such calls on his time that no amount of money or bribery could induce him to voyage across the Channel. Their father had even gone to see the man himself, to plead his case, and Dr Archambeau had been unmoved. He had patients of his own, the man said, each of whom were beloved and important in their own right, and an English duke's daughter had no more call on his time than anyone else. Their father had returned, shattered and at his wits' end.

Lottie let out a breath and grasped her sister's hand, her voice low as she spoke.

"We still don't know who your admirer is. But every day a new bouquet comes. Your room cannot hold them all, and they fill the house. We've had everything. Roses mostly, but also chrysanthemums, gardenias and...." Her voice quavered and she paused to take a breath, to steady herself, for she must not cry. "So, you simply must wake up, or I shall die of curiosity."

Lottie winced, wishing she had not said that.

"Please, Eliza. I cannot get married without my sister. Indeed, I feel I can never be happy again without you. I know Cassius feels the same. We are both utterly heartbroken, and poor M-Mama and P-Papa...."

Though she had promised herself she would not cry in front of Eliza, she lay her head in her hands and sobbed. A moment later, noise and raised voices in the corridor caught her attention and she wiped her eyes and nose and got up, moving to the door, about to reprimand whoever it was who was making such a racket when her father strode in, his face alight with hope.

"Dr Archambeau," he said, hugging Lottie fiercely. "He's here."

"H-Here?" she asked, stunned. "But he told you he wouldn't come. Not in any circumstances."

"*Oui*, and I meant it," replied a terse voice before her father could speak, and the fellow strode in. "However, there are some forces even I cannot resist. You have some unpleasant friends, *monsieur le duc*."

Her father frowned at the doctor in consternation.

"But...." he began, only to hush as his wife grasped his arm and shook her head.

Lottie agreed with her mother. Let the man think they had unpleasant friends bringing undue influence to bear, if it got this apparent miracle maker to Eliza's side. For the first time in weeks, Lottie felt her heart lift.

He was a man in his forties, prematurely bald but with monstrous white eyebrows that gave him a dreadfully fierce appearance. His eyes were sharp and intelligent, though, and compassionate, if she was any judge.

Please, oh, please. Let this man be the one.

"*Sortez*!" said the doctor, waving an irritable hand at them all. "Everyone out. You may station a footman beside the door to attend to my requirements. Other than that. Go *away*!"

The doctor remained with Eliza for most of the next three days, refusing to give them any information as to his diagnosis, though much to Lottie's relief, he did not recommend further bloodletting. Eliza was so pale, so terribly fragile, that the very idea of taking more blood from her made Lottie want to weep.

By the time he eventually deigned to speak to them, her parents were in a state of high agitation, not that you would have known it when they faced the man. Mama sat straight-backed and still with Father standing beside her, one hand on her shoulder, which she grasped with all her might. Lottie sat at her side, willing herself not to fidget, weep, or fall into hysterics, though she felt like doing all three.

"Your daughter is in a coma state due to a severe blow to the head," the doctor said, his English precise and clipped. "However, it is my professional opinion that she will make a full, if slow, recovery."

Mama made a desperate sound, clapped a hand to her mouth and got to her feet, flinging herself into Papa's arms.

"Robert, Robert," she wept, laughing and crying all at once.

"Yes, yes, my love." Her father's voice was very thick as he held his wife close.

Lottie watched them, able to draw a proper breath for the first time in what felt like months, tears streaming down her face.

"How?" she asked, hardly daring to believe him. "How can you tell?"

"She is responding to light and sound and pain."

"Pain?" her mother cried in horror.

"Just a pinprick to the fingers and toes, your grace, do not fret. The reactions are slight, no more than a flickering of her eyelids or a tiny jerk of response. Easily missed, but they are there. Indeed, they have become more apparent in the past twenty-four hours. This is an excellent sign and should become more pronounced over the following days. There is still the concern as to whether any permanent damage has been done, but I believe we have cause to be optimistic. I hope to tell you more by the end of the week."

Lottie hardly heard the rest of the conversation as the doctor gave her parents detailed instructions on Eliza's care and ongoing treatment. She was too overwhelmed with relief. A tiny voice in her head told her not to get excited, that other doctors had been wrong, had promised and failed to deliver, but her heart told her this one would bring Eliza back to her.

As soon as she was able, she ran to find Cassius.

He was down in the summerhouse, staring bleakly at an unfinished canvas, when she burst through the door. She had not questioned him when he had put the portrait of her aside, the one he had begun the day Eliza had fallen. Lottie felt the same way: their happiness must wait.

"Cassius," she said, as he stood in alarm, staring at her.

"What? What is it? Is Eliza...?"

Lottie flung herself at him, trying to get the words out. "Archambeau s-says she will g-get better. He says she will recover."

Cassius made a strangled sound and clung to her, holding her tight. "Oh, thank God, thank God."

They stayed like that for a long time, holding each other and wiping away tears.

"Do we still not know who sent him?" Cassius asked.

"No, and he won't say anything more than that he was forced. Blackmailed, Papa says."

Cassius frowned, shaking his head. "I wonder who would go to such lengths for her, and why?"

"I do not care who or why, though I should dearly love to thank whoever it was, with all my heart."

She sighed as Cassius kissed the top of her head. "As would I. Come along, though. I bet you've not eaten a thing all day. I'll take you back to the house."

Ten days later and the doctor appeared pleased with Eliza's progress. To their relief and delight, she had woken for brief intervals, only a few seconds at a time, but she had smiled at Lottie and squeezed her hand. It was enough to make Lottie sob with happiness.

Later that same day, on making her way down the stairs, Lottie was irritated to discover a close neighbour to Holbrook House, Miss Dudley, had come to call. The earl and his wife were not at home, but the butler informed her that her mama wished Lottie to join them at once. Lottie could well understand it.

Miss Dudley was a lady of middling years and very kind. For this reason alone, Lottie knew she ought not be impatient with her, but she was an odd duck with romantic sensibilities and was prone to swooning fits over dead birds or a cat carrying a struggling mouse. An epic poem could see her bedridden for days. Lottie found the weeping and overblown sentimentality vexing and incomprehensible in a woman who'd lived her entire life in the countryside. How she would carry on over Eliza she could only imagine.

"Oh, and here is Lottie," her mama said as Lottie entered the parlour.

She held her hand out to Lottie who went to her and took it, sitting down beside her. The duchess sent her a look full of apology, but it was clear she needed support, so Lottie pasted a smile to her face.

Half an hour later and Lottie was contemplating crowning the lady with the elegant Limoges teapot. At least she had stopped crying now. No matter how often Lottie and her mother reminded the exasperating creature they had just received the news they had been praying for, and her sister was waking up, she kept maundering on as though Eliza was on the brink of death. Lottie wanted to scream, and she knew her mother was holding onto her temper by a thread.

"And for her to be in such a romantic place when she fell, I did wonder, only…. No. You know I am no tattlemonger, so I should not say."

Lottie forced her attention back to the conversation. This much was at least true. Unlike some ladies—and gentlemen—of her ilk, Miss Dudley's heart was in the right place. She might act as though every trifling affair was worthy of a Greek chorus, but she never had a bad word to say of anyone, nor would she spread gossip. It was for this reason the St Clairs always made time for the lady and welcomed her into their home, even when she tried everyone's patience.

"What did you wonder, Miss Dudley?" Mama asked, frowning, for none of them had understood how Eliza had come to fall.

Lottie had been reckless enough to climb the walls in the past, but even she had never done it wearing a heavy riding habit, and certainly never alone.

"Well, I saw her at Bayham Abbey, you see, perhaps two weeks before her accident. It was just before I went away to stay with my sister in the Lake District. Such a beautiful place. Have you ever been?"

"Yes, it's very lovely," Lottie agreed, striving not to sound impatient. "But you said you saw Eliza at Bayham Abbey? I know she often rides out that way when we are at Holbrook, for she thinks it romantic and peaceful."

"Yes," the lady said, lowering her eyes. "But…."

"But?" Mama pressed.

Miss Dudley bit her lip, her expression troubled. "Well, I should not like to cause dear Eliza any hurt or… or damage her reputation."

"Her reputation?" Lottie said, aghast. Her heart thudded behind her ribs. "My word, Miss Dudley, you cannot believe *I* would do or say anything—"

"*No,* of course you wouldn't. I never meant to suggest…" Miss Dudley sighed and shook her head. She shifted closer to Lottie and her mama and lowered her voice. "It is only that I saw her there… with a *man.*"

Lottie's jaw dropped. She looked to her mother to see she too was astonished.

"Alone?" she squeaked, finding it incomprehensible that Eliza should do such a thing.

"You must be mistaken," Mama said briskly. "Eliza would never...."

But Miss Dudley nodded, her tone firm now. "Yes, your grace. I know I am believed to be a silly, frivolous creature, but I am not so shatter-brained as all that. She was there, alone, with a man. Such a wickedly handsome fellow he was, too, just the kind to seduce an innocent girl. *Oh*, n-not that I am suggesting for one moment that he succeeded."

Miss Dudley turned a dull shade of red as her mother stared at the woman in outrage.

"No. Of course not," Lottie said, moving the conversation on quickly as she remembered the day Eliza had left their picnic and ridden off in a state of high agitation, and that she had not returned home until ages after Lottie. She had been in a strange mood, too, and... and she had not been the only one who'd left the picnic early.

"What did the gentleman look like, Miss Dudley?" her mama asked, though Lottie wished she had not, as she had a fair idea.

"Oh," Miss Dudley said, her expression growing wistful. "A big, strong fellow with fierce features. Such shoulders he had, and so tall. Dark, too. Hair as black as a crow's wing."

Lottie swallowed as Mama stiffened beside her.

"Thank you, Miss Dudley," she said, giving the woman a gracious nod and proceeded to lie through her teeth without batting an eyelid. Lottie was rather impressed. "I believe the gentleman is a friend of the family, so there was no impropriety. Indeed, I believe they just got ahead of the rest of the party. If you had stayed, the others would have arrived not long after. But we have taken enough of your time. Thank you for your visit. You've been very kind, and I know I can rely on your discretion...."

Miss Dudley's kind eyes crinkled as she smiled. "Ah, well. I remember what it was to be young, and I would never do or say anything to hurt such a lovely girl. It was only when I heard of her accident and thought how strange it was that she *fell*, and…."

She trailed off and something cold and anxious wrapped about Lottie's heart. Mama did not allow Miss Dudley to remain long after that, though, and herded her out with as much haste as she could politely manage.

Once the lady was gone, Mama turned to Lottie.

"Did you know?" she demanded.

Lottie shook her head. "She wasn't meeting him, Mama, I'm sure of it. It was just that one time, when Miss Dudley saw her, and I'm certain that was… well, accidental. Certainly it wasn't planned. It couldn't have been. She left the picnic early. It was after Cassius had told her they were not to be married and she rode off alone. She was terribly upset when she left."

"You think Mr Demarteau followed her?"

Lottie swallowed. She was not about to break her sister's confidence and tell Mama that Eliza was infatuated with the man, yet she did not want Mr Demarteau to be implicated in… in what? *Could* he have been there when Eliza fell? Could he have been *responsible*, or have left her injured? No. No, she would not believe that.

"I don't know," she said. "But Eliza returned safely and did not mention having seen him."

"And she tells you everything, does she not?"

"Yes. Usually," Lottie said, knowing that Eliza had certainly not told her everything, and she could hardly remonstrate as she had kept secrets from her Eliza, too.

Yet Mama was exhausted with worry, and she could not bring her more anxiety by telling her that she feared there was more to it.

"Well, Eliza will explain it to us when she is well, but I do not think she will see Mr Demarteau again. Your father has taken against his brother as it is and, in comparison, Louis César is *almost* respectable."

There was a look in her mother's eyes Lottie well recognised, and she sighed. Papa was overprotective and Mama was stubborn, but then… so was Eliza.

Chapter 20

Dear Cassius,

We are so delighted to hear Eliza is well again. What a splendid wedding gift for you and Lottie. Of course we will come to Holbrook for the ceremony. Nothing would keep us away.

—Excerpt of letter to Cassius Cadogan, Viscount Oakley from Mr Ashton Anson — son of Lord Silas Cavendish and Lady Aashini Cavendish.

20th September 1838, Holbrook House, Sussex.

"Oh, Lottie, you look like a fairy princess," Eliza said, beaming at her.

Lottie grinned and did a twirl as the proprietress of Maison Blanchet looked on with satisfaction. Madame Blanchet was a beautiful, elegant woman in her late thirties who was a fine advertisement for her own wares. The Marchioness of Montagu had discovered Maison Blanchet last season and secured the new Parisian fashion house's future, as she was still a leading figure in the stylish world of the *ton*. If Matilda said something was fashionable, it was.

Madame Blanchet gestured to the gown. "You see, my creation is a delicate blue grey satin that brings out the colour of Lady Charlotte's eyes. There is a pattern of floral sprays and vines.

The short sleeves are adorned with furbelows and lace trim, the wide boat neck with a blonde lace bertha, and we have created a deep waist point with three rows of piping. The skirt is full with two deep gauze flounces set in furbelows, lined in stiffened gauze, and the results…."

Madame sighed happily as she looked at her creation with obvious pride.

"It is perfection," their mama said, wiping her eyes.

"Mama, you are not crying?" Lottie said in astonishment, for their mother was a practical, no-nonsense woman who was not given to tears.

"Oh, it's the baby," she said, patting her rounded belly and sniffling. "You know I turn into a wretched watering pot whenever I'm breeding."

"Mama," Eliza murmured, shaking her head in despair at her mother. "One does not speak of *breeding* any longer."

Lottie sniggered.

"Oh, lud," the duchess said in disgust. "I cannot be doing with all this sensitivity. Why can we not just call the thing what it is without causing young women to fall into a swoon? I declare it was bad enough in my day, but this excess of propriety will become intolerable if we do not have a care."

"Yes, Mama," Eliza said, her lips twitching as she caught Lottie's eye.

Lottie felt her heart lift to see her sister smile. She was still frail and horribly weak, with little energy. This trip to Maison Blanchet would likely send her to bed for the rest of the day, but she had been determined to come along for Lottie's last fitting.

"Well, Madame Blanchet, let us go over the list for the trousseau and ensure we have forgotten nothing," Mama said, taking Madame Blanchet out of the fitting room with her.

"I'm so happy for you, Lottie. It will be the perfect day," Eliza said, her pleasure obvious and genuine.

"It will," Lottie agreed, turning back to the mirror for a moment to admire her gown. She smiled at her reflection and caught Eliza's eye in the looking glass. "Now that you are well enough to be there it will, anyway."

Eliza beamed at her, and then her smile faltered.

"I remembered," she said. "What happened that day."

Lottie needed no explanation to deduce what day she was speaking of. By tacit agreement neither she nor Mama had pressed Eliza, or questioned her over Mr Demarteau. She was too easily upset and agitated, and her memory remained hazy in places. They did not wish to do or say anything to cause her anxiety.

Lottie turned and hurried to her.

"I climbed the walls," she said, staring at Lottie in consternation. "Why would I do that? I was all alone, and my skirts were heavy. Why would I be so foolish?"

Lottie shook her head. "I don't know, love but… are you *certain* you were alone?"

Eliza gave her a sharp glance. "Why would you think otherwise? Who would I be with?"

"Mr Demarteau."

Eliza gasped, one hand going to her throat. "You think… you think I went there to meet him?"

Lottie shrugged. "You told me you were infatuated with him and… well, it's the kind of thing I would do, Eliza, if I were in love with a man."

"You would, wouldn't you?" Eliza said, staring at Lottie with an expression she could not read. Then she gave a little huff of laughter. "Well, you may set your mind at ease. I never have been, nor ever will be as brave as you. I was alone. I was alone and

clearly out of my senses. I have no explanation for it, except…
except I remember feeling restless and wild, like I wanted to
escape. It was as though the abbey walls represented the bars of a
cage and…. Oh, what nonsense."

"Not nonsense," Lottie said, understanding the sensation all
too well. "And you will be strong enough soon to do just as you
wish. You may be as bold and reckless as you please, only don't
go climbing any walls without me."

Eliza laughed. "Oh, I won't. I promise."

Cassius stood back, staring at the painting. Pride and love and
a swell of emotion that felt far too large to hold inside of him
pushed at the confines of his chest. He swallowed hard and told
himself to stop being such a silly blighter, but he knew Lottie
would love it and he could not wait to show it to her. He had not
returned to it until they were certain that Eliza would recover. The
weeks had been hard on them both. He had felt guilt for his
happiness in being with Lottie and he knew she felt it too. How
could they be happy when Eliza was trapped in some sleeping
world, neither alive nor dead but somehow suspended between the
two? The relief when she had awoken that first time had been so
overpowering that he'd wept. He had missed his friend badly, and
he could not bear for Lottie to endure the loss of her sister any
more than he could bear losing someone he had loved and relied
upon since he was a small boy.

But that was over. Eliza was still as weak as a kitten, but she
was a determined young woman who hated being an invalid. She
would recover and return to being the kind, generous friend and
sister they knew and loved.

Regretfully, he reached for the cloth to cover the painting of
Lottie back up again and turned as the door to the summerhouse
burst open.

"Cassius!"

Lottie's voice filled the room, joyous and excited as she ran to him and flung her arms about his neck. Cassius staggered back a step and put his arms about her.

"What is it?" he asked, uncertain whether or not to be alarmed, yet she was smiling and happy.

"I love you!" she said, beaming at him. "And my dress is glorious, and we are getting *married* in *two days*!"

He laughed, delighted by her, and then cursed as her eyes widened and she saw the painting.

"Drat you, Lottie! That's your wedding present. You weren't supposed to see it yet."

"Oh," she said, her mouth falling open and her big blue eyes becoming very bright. "Oh, Cass."

Cassius sighed and moved behind her, sliding his arms about her waist and pulling her back against him as she stared at her portrait. He couldn't be cross with her for long, it was impossible, and he had been impatient for her to see it in any case.

It was just as he'd envisaged it. She was beautiful, almost ethereal with the sunlight creating a nimbus of golden light about her blonde hair. The white gown only enhanced the feeling of purity and innocence, yet there was a twinkle in her eyes that was entirely Lottie and promised the viewer that this young woman was no idealised image of perfection. She was a real girl, with a mischievous soul, the sort of girl one could spend a lifetime loving and being surprised by. He had every intention of doing just that.

She leaned back into him and sighed. "I thought you were supposed to paint the truth, warts and all? I'm quite sure I'm nothing like as beautiful as that."

"You're wrong," he said. "You're the most beautiful thing I've ever seen. I shall never tire of painting you. I shall paint you in Italy and Egypt and India, and here at home too, and I shall never grow bored. Not even when you are a very fat old lady, and your hair is white. I will paint you with our children, and our grandchildren and every time I shall think, *Cassius, you lucky devil*."

She turned and grinned at him. "I want a big family, like mine."

"Eight children?" Cassius said, quailing a little at the idea. "Ah, well. Whatever you like, love. You always get your own way in the end, after all."

"Do I?" she asked, all innocence as she tilted her head back to look at him.

"You do," he replied, seeing the elegant curve of her neck as it met her shoulder, the delicate, not quite there scent of jasmine rising from her skin. Unable to resist, he ducked his head, pressed his mouth to that delicious curve, and groaned. "Oh, you smell so divine, Lottie. What is it? I know it's jasmine, but there's something else… something green…."

A touch of colour tinged her cheeks which intrigued him. "I use jasmine as my scent, but my maid puts herbs in the drawers with my… my stockings and undergarments."

His mouth curved in a hopeless grin. "Is that so?"

She giggled and pushed away from him, running to the other side of the studio.

"Yes," she said, putting her chin up. "But I can't believe you can smell that. It's very faint."

"Darling, it has been tormenting me for weeks."

"Has it?" she asked, tilting her head to regard him, that wicked glint in her eyes that he loved so well making his heart pick up speed.

"What herbs does she use?" Cassius asked, praying she'd invite him to find out.

Lottie turned away from him, sauntering towards the day bed. She paused to regard the explosion of paint that still stained the stone floor and sent him a delighted smile. "I can't believe you left this here."

"It's finally dry," he said. "And I like it. It reminds me of you, of the way you burst into my life and filled it with colour and excitement."

"And made an almighty mess," she added with a snort.

She tiptoed around the paint, even though he'd told her it was dry, lifting her skirts rather higher than necessary to give him a lovely view of her pretty ankles. She sat on the day bed, looking demure and sweet for a moment, but that couldn't last, thank heavens. Cassius swallowed as she extended one leg out in front of her, and slowly… so slowly, pulled her skirts up to her knee.

"Come and see if you can figure it out," she said.

He did not need a second invitation.

Lottie cast one of the cushions to the floor and he quirked an eyebrow at her but knelt at her feet, a lowly supplicant before the goddess. She settled back among the remaining cushions as his hands slid about her ankles, delicate stockings sliding beneath his hands. A whisper of scent rose from the fine silk as Cassius lifted one dainty foot. He brushed his lips over her ankle, breathing in the perfume, so slight, yet utterly intoxicating.

"Thyme," he said, aware that his voice was scratchy and rough.

Lottie shook her head and raised her skirts higher.

"No," she said. "Try again."

His mouth was dry as he set her foot down and pressed his mouth to the inside of her knee. He pushed her legs wider apart, aware of her breathing coming faster as he trailed a line of kisses up her thigh. A billow of petticoats tumbled about her hips, hiding the prize from his hungry gaze. The perfume was stronger here and he thought he might know it, but he said instead, "Lavender."

"Wrong again," she murmured.

Cassius tsked and shook his head. "I think I need to make deeper enquiries."

Lottie bit her lip. Her cheeks were pink, and she looked torn between laughter, the desire to tease him further, and her very real curiosity as to what he would do next. He waited, uncertain as to which aspect of her character would win out.

"Very well," she said, her voice not quite steady. "But it is your last chance."

"Then I had best be very sure before I give my answer," he said gravely, and then flung her petticoats over his head and disappeared in a billow of white lace.

"Cassius!" she squeaked but he ignored her, content that she was only surprised and not voicing any objection.

It was warm and dim and sweetly scented beneath the layers of her gown and petticoats. Jasmine mingled with the herby green perfume and a scent that was uniquely feminine and fogged his mind with lust. His mouth found the tender skin of her inner thigh and he kissed her, moving higher until he got to the juncture of leg and hip and the impossibly silken skin that bracketed the soft triangle of curls. His tongue drew a fine line along that satiny flesh and she made a startled sound, jolting beneath him.

"Shall I stop?" he asked, aware he'd surprised her.

"Don't you dare!"

He chuckled, and his warm breath must have gusted over her for she gasped. Pleased, he decided his wife-to-be must be punished for ruining his lovely surprise. He flipped back the petticoats and exposed her to his view.

"It's hot under there," he said, flashing her a wicked smile. "And I want to see what I'm doing."

"But the door isn't locked," she said, breathing very hard.

"I'll go," he said, moving to lock it, but she grabbed hold of his hair. "No, don't go. It's exciting."

"Wicked, wicked girl," he murmured, his blood thrumming through his veins, though he knew as well as she did that it was unlikely anyone would come by his studio today, not with so many other things to occupy them with the wedding to arrange. "God, I love you, Lottie."

She laughed, a pleased, happy sound that made his heart feel light but that stopped abruptly as he bent his head again and pressed a kiss to the soft curls. Her hands were still fisted in his hair and they tightened reflexively. Cassius smiled and touched a finger to the springy golden thatch between her legs, tickling her gently as his finger ghosted up and down the crease of her sex.

"Cass," she pleaded, shifting beneath his touch.

There was impatience in her voice, not that he was surprised. She ever did want to run headlong towards every adventure, straight into anything new and exciting, never looking before she leapt.

"Relax, love. There's nothing you need to do, just enjoy my touch." He gave her a devilish glance and deliberately provoked then by saying, "You are supposed to obey your husband, after all."

She returned a look of outrage but, before she could ring a peal over him, lowered his mouth to that secret place and licked.

Whatever indignant words were brewing on her tongue melted into an incoherent mewling sound that only grew louder and wilder as he teased his tongue along the delicate folds, and she trembled and gasped beneath him. His ruthless mouth continued to wring the desperate sounds from her as his tongue sought the little peak of flesh that made her buck and exclaim with pleasure and shock.

"Do keep still, sweetheart," he chastised her gently. "You're a dreadful fidget."

"Oh!" she huffed. "You're the dreadful one. How can I possibly keep still with you teasing me so? Just you wait, Cassius. Once I know how I shall…I shall…."

He did not get to hear whatever it was she had in mind, though he was certainly more than keen to find out. Today was his turn to pleasure his beloved, though, and tease her a little too. The increasingly loud wails of pleasure that he drew from her made him very relieved that they were spending their wedding night in a hotel before going onto their new home. The idea of being under the same roof as her father was enough to give any man pause. Holbrook might be vast, but there was no house big enough to be sanguine about deflowering the Duke of Bedwin's daughter when he was in the same building.

Thoughts of his wedding night were only too tempting to entertain, but he wasn't about to anticipate their vows any more than he already was. It was only because Lottie was an unholy temptation, and they had waited so much longer than they first expected, that his sanity was unravelling. He ached for more, but he would not have her first time be in the summerhouse. Though, if gossip was to be believed, there was something of a family tradition there, he thought with a wry smile.

She made a soft sound, tugging at his hair. Cassius chuckled and slid one finger inside her tight heat. His own body grew taut, his breathing increasingly rapid as she shuddered and moaned. He caressed her gently.

"Shall I stop?" he enquired lazily.

"If you do, I shan't be responsible for the consequences," she warned him, breathless, gasping as he returned his mouth to the tender bud of her sex and suckled whilst he continued to stroke her intimately.

She shattered beneath him, a breathless cry of pleasure that rolled through him with the force of a lightning strike, bringing him so close to the edge that it was all he could do not to embarrass himself.

"Oh," she said, her voice hazy and indistinct once the tremors had ceased. "Oh, that… that was…. Goodness, how long until we get married? I want to do that again."

Cassius let out a helpless laugh and buried his face in her petticoats.

"Rosemary," he said, forcing the word out as the dizzying scent of her, jasmine and that tantalising green perfume made him feel drunk and happy and a little dazed that she was truly going to be his.

"Oh, you wretch. Did you know it all along?" she demanded, and then put her head back with a laugh. "I'm glad you didn't tell me."

They both stilled as the muted sound of voices reached them. Someone was coming.

"Christ," Cassius said, leaping to his feet as Lottie did her best to settle her copious petticoats and her badly rumpled skirt back into order.

"Oh, your hair," she wailed, gesturing to it as Cassius tried to smooth it down again, but to no avail.

They were both flushed and a little disarranged, and he could only hope whoever it was would keep on walking.

"Yes, well, I'm sure they'll be very pleased to come along with us," said an overly loud voice that Cassius recognised.

"Mama!" Lottie squeaked in horror.

"That's torn it," he said, lunging for the back of her gown which had not fallen properly and showed a deal of petticoat. He just got it straight as the door opened and the Duke and Duchess of Bedwin walked in. Lottie's father stilled in the doorway, his cool green gaze going from his rumpled daughter to Cassius. Despite being a grown man, one who'd seen the world and survived it, Cassius was in that moment reduced to a grubby schoolboy. He felt heat creep up the back of his neck as the duke's face darkened.

"Lottie, darling," the duchess said, sweeping to her daughter before the man could speak, and surreptitiously making an adjustment to Lottie's bodice whilst she was shielded from her father's gaze. "We need you at the house, my dear. Tedious, I know, but there are some decisions only you can make and… and…."

The duchess trailed off and Cassius followed her gaze, realising she had seen the painting.

"Oh," she said, one elegant hand moving to cover her heart. "Oh, Robert."

The duke sent Cassius a look that told him he'd not be getting within fifty feet of his daughter again before the wedding if he had anything to do with it, before going to stand beside his wife.

"Isn't it lovely, Mama?" Lottie said, taking her mother's arm. "He's flattered me dreadfully, of course, but I can hardly complain about that."

There was silence for a moment while her parents studied the picture.

"No," the duke said at length. "No, he hasn't flattered you. He's seen you just as you are, as I knew he did, for I should not have let you go away from me so soon otherwise."

"Oh, Papa," Lottie said, hearing just as Cassius had, the slight tremble of emotion in the man's voice. She ran to her father and hugged him tightly.

"Oh, stop it!" the duchess wailed, wrestling a lace handkerchief from her sleeve. "You know the slightest thing sends me off at the m-moment and how can I p-possibly withstand…."

The next moment the duke was hugging both his daughter and his wife and Cassius felt a tad superfluous.

"Cassius," the duke said, giving first Lottie then his wife a kiss before disentangling himself. He moved closer, studying Cassius for a long moment, and then held out his hand. Cassius took it. "It is a devilish hard thing to give your daughter into another man's keeping, no matter how worthy he might be, but… but I am proud of the man you have become, and I trust you to make her happy."

"I swear I will do everything in my power, sir."

Bedwin nodded, the glimmer of a smile at his lips even as something dark flickered in his eyes. "See that you do."

Chapter 21

Dear Diary,

We are returning to Holbrook House for the wedding and I'm so happy. The summer was full of excitement and drama just as I'd hoped, but I realise now that drama, which is thrilling and bone chilling in books, is not at all nice to experience first-hand. We were all so afraid for poor Eliza and are so delighted she is recovering well. Though she is terribly fragile still, like a little china doll. She will need a great deal of looking after I think, though of course all her brothers and sisters dote upon her, as do we all. Indeed I think our fussing is driving her quite to distraction.

—Excerpt of an entry to the diary of Lady Catherine 'Cat' Barrington, youngest daughter of the Marquess and Marchioness of Montagu.

22nd September 1838, Holbrook House, Sussex.

Eliza looked on with amusement as her sister ran about the room, as giddy as a child at Christmas. She had driven her poor mother and her maid quite distracted with her inability to sit still for five minutes together. The two women ran around after her trying to do her hair and fasten her corset and get her into her gown, but it did Eliza's heart good to see Lottie brimming with happiness. This was how you ought to feel about marrying the man you loved. She realised that now, and she knew she would have felt nothing like this on her wedding day if Cassius had not been brave and honest enough to tell her he would not marry her.

Finally, things were as they ought to be, and though it was a touch mortifying to have one's little sister marry before you, Eliza was not about to let such a thing disconcert her. Lottie was happy and Cassius was her friend again. That was all that mattered. He had spent yesterday afternoon with her, playing cards and talking, and pretending to be engrossed in a book when she fell asleep, something she still seemed to have no control over and would do at the drop of a hat if she dared to close her eyes. Everyone's fussing about her was tedious, though, and she wished they would stop, even if she did appreciate their care. She just wanted to be as she was before, but she knew she must be patient. Eliza gave a soft huff of laughter at that. *Patient.* Lady Elizabeth Adolphus, known to be one of the most serene and patient ladies of the *ton*, was increasingly snappy, bad-tempered, and petulant as a child.

She was a fool. No, she had *been* a fool. Climbing the crumbling walls of the Abbey, wearing a riding habit of all things, had been the height of idiocy. The trouble was she still remembered the desire to be reckless and defy the rules, to make her heart beat faster and to feel alive. She not only remembered it, she felt it still, a simmering restlessness beneath her skin. There were other things, too, like the day she had galloped across the fields with Mr Demarteau at her side, his wicked dark eyes daring her, urging her on. She *had* dared, or at least she thought she had. It was still all so hazy in her mind she could not be certain she hadn't dreamt it. It seemed too unlikely to be real, for she had dared to lead him to the abbey and once there she had watched him, spellbound, as he climbed the walls, agile as a cat. Then she had stared, not daring to breathe, as he had performed for her. He

had stood on his hands, then—impossibly—balanced on one hand, and shown her feats of strength and agility she would never have dreamed possible. He finished his performance by somersaulting down from the walls while she stifled a scream of shock lest he fall. But he had not fallen, he had come back to earth, like some mythical creature, or at the very least a performer like those at Astley's Amphitheatre. How or where he had learned such things she could not fathom, and he had refused to tell her. He had barely spoken to her at all, but the memory of his dark eyes on her lingered like a brand upon her heart, stirring her blood. Remembering it now made her heart beat too fast, skittering about erratically in her chest. *If* it was a memory. Could she truly have dreamed such a thing? It seemed no more improbable than it being real.

"Eliza?"

She jolted as her mother's worried voice penetrated her distracted thoughts.

"Are you well, love? You're flushed."

Eliza tried to swat her mama's hand away as she put it to her forehead.

"Sally, do you think she has a temperature?"

Eliza groaned and submitted whilst Sally—who was a sensible creature, thank the Lord—assured Mama that she was not about to succumb to some unknown malady.

"Well, then, if you are sure you are well, my love?" her mama persisted.

"Oh, for goodness' sake. Indeed I am well. I'm just impatient and excited to see my sister married, Mama, and if you don't let her go down at once, poor Cassius will think she's run away."

"I think Papa might help me if I decided to," Lottie said with a grin. "He's awfully tense."

The duchess sighed. "Oh, your poor father. It is difficult for him to see you leave, Lottie dear."

Lottie snorted. "Piffle. Eliza's still here, so he'll be perfectly content, though I think it will be a brave man that comes to ask for your hand, my dear. Everyone knows you're his favourite."

"Don't be so shatter-brained," Eliza protested. "I am nothing of the sort."

"Yes, you are. You're his *annngel*," Lottie said, drawing the word out and smirking. "He's never called me 'angel' in his life."

"No, indeed," their mama said with a wry smile. "As you've never given him reason to, you wicked creature. Perhaps I should take this opportunity to ask what exactly you were up to in the summerhouse. Hmmmm? You're lucky I have such a carrying voice, I suspect."

To Eliza's amusement, Lottie turned a startling shade of scarlet. Oh, she must ask her sister exactly what had gone on there before she disappeared off on her honeymoon. Mama had been forthright about explaining the mechanics of sex, and the ways in which gullible girls could get themselves into tricky situations. She believed girls ought never be ignorant of the world, or of men, and certainly not of their own bodies. She would never send them off to their wedding night with no clue of what was to happen, but one simply could not ask her about the finer details—too embarrassing for words!

"Now, don't keep that poor young man waiting any longer," the duchess instructed, handing Lottie her bouquet, and shooing them all out of the bedroom. "He looked dreadfully pale and anxious when he arrived, and I doubt your father has done anything to put him at ease."

❋ ❋ ❋

Cassius paced the length of the vast marble fireplace in the grand saloon and tried to resist the urge to check the time. Again.

"You are supposed to look resigned to your fate, old man," Ash drawled, amusement glinting in his bright blue eyes. "Not like you're desperately eager to throw yourself into the fire."

Cassius turned back to his friend and snorted. "Just you wait until it's your turn. I swear if I must delay much longer to make her my wife, I think I shall run mad."

Ash sighed, arranging his long limbs elegantly as he leaned against the mantel. "This falling in love business seems far too taxing to my mind. I think I prefer to be adored by others but to keep my heart to myself. It looks dashed uncomfortable to always be at the mercy of one's emotions."

"Says the man wearing that waistcoat," Cassius said, wincing as he regarded his friend's lavishly encased chest. Today's effort was purple silk embroidered with… with…. He squinted at the motif. "Are those lobsters?"

Ash scowled with indignation, smoothing a loving hand over the purple creation that was assaulting Cassius's sensibilities. "Indeed they are not, you cretin. That's a heart with a crown, held between two hands. It's an Irish symbol of love, loyalty, and friendship. It was a birthday gift from Lady Aisling."

Cassius raised an eyebrow. Aisling was the eldest daughter of the Earl and Countess of Trevick, Luke and Kitty Baxter. She also had an older brother—the Viscount Harleston—who guarded her and her younger sister like Cerberus patrolled the gates of hell.

"Does Conor know you've been receiving gifts from his sister?"

"No, and don't you tell him," Ash said crossly. "She's a sweet creature and, yes, she has a *tendre* for me, but I don't see her from one year to the next so there's no harm in it. And she has the most amazing skill with a needle and thread. It seemed a shame for such fine work never to see the light of day, and she made me promise to wear it on a special occasion."

"Well, you'll be wearing it while Conor pitches you off the nearest cliff face if he gets wind of it," Cass said dryly and then his heart gave an uneven thud in his chest as he saw the duchess and Eliza come and take their places.

Eliza sent him a dazzling smile and the rest of the guests looked expectantly towards the door.

"Ash," he said, groping about for his friend's arm as he could not take his eyes from the vision before him. "*Ash!*"

"I know, I know, old man. It's time for you to do your bit," Ash said, and Cassius heard a decided wobble to the fellow's voice. "Ah, and she looks a picture. I take back every word. You're a lucky fellow, so don't mess it up."

Cassius could neither breathe nor move, and he hardly dared blink. To his astonishment, he felt his throat tighten and his eyes prickle, and he had to fight to keep his composure lest he be teased for the rest of time for blubbing at his own wedding. He felt slightly better as Ashton sniffled and accepted a handkerchief from his twin, who had obviously come prepared in the full knowledge that her brother was the sentimental sort. Cassius was not, and yet... and yet, Lottie was so beautiful, so radiantly happy he wanted to weep. Her happiness shone from her, turning a beautiful girl into something quite beyond description. The force of emotion her joy provoked in him made it hard to breathe. After all, he had the soul of an artist, and did not great beauty stir such men? Beauty of this magnitude had inspired sonnets and odes, operas, and paintings of the kind that made people stare and gasp and wonder at such heights of artistic achievement. She was his heart, his soul, his muse, and he would never grow tired, never grow used to someone who was as both as constant and changeable as the sea or the sky.

The solemnity with which the duke gave her hand to him did not help his composure. Her father's green eyes were very bright, though that made Cassius feel better, for if a man like the duke was

moved to tears then surely lesser mortals were allowed the same privilege?

"You look like poetry, or a painting by one of the great masters," Cassius said, his voice not quite as steady as he would have liked, but he was determined to get the words out. "A work of art."

She gave him a fondly exasperated look and leaned in close to whisper in his ear. "I do hope not, Cassius, for aren't things like that untouchable? And I was so looking forward to my wedding night."

He gave a sudden bark of laughter, for of course Lottie would say such a thing with everyone watching them. Cassius turned towards the priest to discover the fellow's beady eyes narrowed at him suspiciously. Heat crept up the back of his neck and he shot a glance at Lottie, whose shoulders were shaking with silent laughter.

"Wretch," he murmured under his breath.

Happily, the ceremony proceeded peacefully thereafter, except for the odd sniffle as they were reciting their vows. When it was done, Cassius could not have said if it had gone on for hours or was over in the blink of an eye. It seemed to have done both somehow and left him dazed and happy as the priest finally got to the bit he'd been waiting for.

"You may kiss the bride."

He grinned at the duke who rolled his eyes, and then Cassius bent and kissed his new wife.

Though he had meant it to be a no more than a press of lips— they had an audience after all—Lottie threw her arms about his neck and held on. He laughed, knowing that she would always bring joy and merriment into his life, as well as mayhem and madness and heaven alone knew what else, but he was ready, ready for all of it.

"Oh, you do look divine. What a glorious dress."

Lottie beamed at her Aunt Helena. "It is lovely, isn't it? It's from Maison Blanchet. Madame Blanchet is so clever, she's created such beautiful things for my trousseau."

Helena sighed and leaned into her husband. "It's so romantic. Do you remember when we were first married, Gabe?"

Uncle Gabriel glanced at her father and pulled a face.

"Vividly," he said, his tone dry.

Everyone laughed, as all the family knew Helena and Gabe had eloped to Gretna Green and the duke had chased them all the way there, arriving in the nick of time to stop the marriage. He'd relented in the end, once he'd realised Gabriel was truly in love with his sister, and she with him. Gabriel Knight had a terrible reputation of course, a wicked industrialist, a self-made man who'd come from nothing, who'd had no place in the *ton*...until he'd made himself a place. With Helena's help, naturally.

"I can't believe you got married before me, Lottie," Florence grumbled, her beautiful face the picture of consternation.

Helena and Gabe's eldest daughter—Lottie's cousin, Florence—was the same age as her and they'd always been dreadfully competitive.

"Well, it's not like I planned it," Lottie said cheerfully. "Don't worry, dear, your time will come."

Florence made a show of tossing her head with an imperious sniff, her thick black curls bouncing about her face. "Oh, do stop condescending to me, or I shall stamp on your toe."

Lottie snorted with laughter, knowing full well Florence was only funning, even if she *was* a bit jealous.

"Sorry, Flo, but it's not like you're short of suitors," Lottie said, taking the girl's arm.

"Nor short of time to choose one," Uncle Gabe put in. "So stop being in such a hurry."

"Oh, Papa!" Florence said, shaking her head. "And yes, of course, I have suitors. They're all deadly."

Her father frowned.

"Dull," Lottie explained hurriedly. "She means deadly dull, and didn't I see you speaking to Viscount Roxborough at the Hely-Hutchinson party? He's dreadfully handsome, and charming too."

"And poor as a church mouse," Uncle Gabe muttered, folding his arms.

"Oh, Papa! Not everyone can be as rich as Croesus," Florence remonstrated, green eyes flashing.

"No," her father replied mildly. "But they *could* be solvent."

"You see," Flo said, throwing up her hands. "You see what I must contend with?"

Sensing a row in the offing, Lottie took Florence by the hand. "Do come and see Ash and Vivien. I haven't properly teased Ash yet for sobbing, and I've been so looking forward to it."

She towed Florence away, moving through the room and squeaking with surprise as a hand slid about her waist.

"What mischief are you about, wife?" Cassius demanded, his voice low and intimate as he whispered in her ear.

Lottie shivered with anticipation, glancing up at him. "I was being a good friend and intervening before Florence got herself locked up in a nunnery for the foreseeable," she said, finding herself blushing at the intent look in her husband's eyes. Her *husband!* Good heavens.

"She's trying to cheer me up with the prospect of mocking Ash for snivelling like a little girl during the ceremony," Florence said with a sigh. "Which might work, to be fair."

"Sounds fun," Cassius said, grinning, and offered the ladies an arm each.

They paused to speak to his Aunt Bonnie and Uncle Jerry and their three girls on the way. The eldest two were twins, though unlike Viv and Ashton, no one would guessed it as they were quite different despite their blonde hair, having taken after their father.

"Don't forget to throw your bouquet," Greer said, grinning at Lottie. Her sister, Elspeth, who was far more serious, rolled her eyes.

"Don't you sneer at me," Greer said, bristling.

"I wasn't sneering, Gee," Elspeth replied patiently. "It's just so silly. As if catching a bunch of flowers can determine when you marry."

Greer folded her arms. "It's tradition, and how do you know?"

"Well, for the same reason I know there are no such things as unicorns, or fairies," Elspeth said, throwing up her hands.

"Oh, girls, do stop bickering," their mother reproached them. "Elspeth, if it makes your sister happy to catch the bouquet then don't spoil it. Must you always be so sensible?"

"I'm not being sensible, Mother, it just stands to reason...."

Cassius and Lottie slipped away with Florence in hot pursuit before things could get heated.

Ashton groaned as he saw them approach.

"Viv," he said in a plaintive whine. "Make them stop."

Vivien only snorted. "They haven't yet begun, Ashton, dear. And, really, what did you expect? You really ought to have remembered to bring a handkerchief. You knew you would weep, surely. I certainly did. I never knew anyone so tender-hearted."

Ash scowled.

"It was *moving,* seeing two of my closest friends speak those vows—*forsaking all others.*" He sighed putting his hand over his heart. "I could not help but think—you poor fools."

Lottie smacked him with her fan, and he grinned at her.

"Just funning, Lottie. You know I thought nothing of the sort. I'm so pleased for you both. You'll be idyllically happy, if I'm any judge. It's just now the rest of us know what's possible we'll never be satisfied. You've set an impossibly high standard."

"Oh," Lottie said with a huff. "I was so looking forward to tormenting you for being a watering pot and now I can't because that was such a nice thing to say."

"I know," Ash said smugly.

"Where's Eliza?" Cassius asked, scanning the room.

"She's gone outside for some air," Lottie said, leaning into him. "She'll come back for the wedding breakfast. The poor thing was finding all the noise too much."

"She's still very weak," he said, frowning.

Lottie nodded, her heart squeezing a little as she remembered how fit and healthy Eliza had been when they had first come to Holbrook. So much had changed in such a short time. Before her accident they had planned to travel for their honeymoon, but neither of them felt happy leaving until Eliza was fully recovered.

"Yes, but she is determined to be well again, so she shall be," Lottie said, reminding herself of that fact. "She may be quiet, but she's single-minded when something matters to her."

Cassius laughed. "That's true. No doubt she'll set her sights on a duke or a marquess now, like she always said she would. I'm sure she was always disappointed I was a mere viscount. A duke would be much more the thing. All the better to enforce her plans to make the world a better place."

"If anyone can do it, she can," Lottie said, smiling up at him with such adoration that he did as she had hoped he would, and leaned down to kiss her.

They broke apart at the sound of a discreet cough as a footman approached them.

"Begging your pardon, my lord," he said to Cassius. "But the Comte de Villen is here. He is waiting in the yellow saloon. Should I tell him the family is not receiving today?"

"Oh, no," Lottie said. "We'll go and see him, won't we, Cass?"

Cassius nodded his thanks to the footman and dismissed him. "He can't have known we were marrying today. It's not been announced yet. Only the family and a few of our closest friends knew."

Lottie followed him out of the room. "That's true. I wonder what he wants," she said. "Papa won't be pleased."

"Neither will mine, but they need not know. Come along, let's go and find out before we're missed. They can't have a wedding breakfast without the bride and groom, after all."

Chapter 22

Dear Aunt Minerva,

Thank you for your kind letter. I am indeed faring much better and am determined to be well again by next season. Pray do not listen to Mama and Papa, who are fussing far too much. It is true I get tired, but they exaggerate the matter, Papa especially, and they get all worked up over nothing. Mama at least has an excuse, for it is her condition that makes her fret so. I shall be glad when my newest brother or sister arrives, and their attention is diverted.

We shall be so sorry not to see you at the wedding, but we all understand how important Uncle Inigo's work is. I do hope you enjoy your time in Scotland. It is very beautiful at this time of year.

—Excerpt of a letter from Lady Elizabeth Adolphus to her mother's cousin, Mrs Minerva de Beauvoir.

22nd September 1838, Holbrook House, Sussex.

Nic stared up at the vast building that was Holbrook House. He half-expected the earl, if not the duke himself, to come storming out of the front door and throw him bodily from the premises. Not that they ought to know Nic was here. He'd kept out of sight, allowing Louis César to go in alone. It was his part to play, after all. He was supposed to be the respectable brother, the one courting Eliza, if the duke let Louis within a mile of her again after Madame Lafitte had done her best to ruin everything. Nic ought have known she was determined enough to follow him here, not that it would do her any good.

He kept to the shadows, something he was used to and adept at. It was still remarkably hot, even under the trees, though there was the scent of autumn in the air already, and a tinge of gold creeping over the countryside and burnishing the trees. It was something he was not entirely accustomed to, having spent most of his life in one filthy, stinking city or another. The countryside, especially this pleasantly manicured, green, English countryside, was a foreign land for him. He moved towards the garden, drawn by the sound of water splashing and the scent of roses. That scent would always make him think of her, of that day on the terrace when he'd seen her for the first time. Well, outside of a little pencil sketch Cassius had shown him, and his too vivid imagination, at least. She'd been all too real, surrounded by pretty china and crystal bowls of perfumed sweet peas and roses, and she'd turned his life inside out and upside down without even knowing it. Why, and for what? For some silly chit of an English girl, when society believed him not fit to kiss her hem, let alone any other part of her.

A girl destined to marry his brother.

Bloody fool.

Yet he could not bear to keep away. He had been beside himself when he'd heard of her accident. His fault. His damned fault. Why had he done it? Performing tricks he'd learned in his youth, like a trained dog, like some idiot boy, showing off to the girl he was besotted with. He'd barely been in her company yet, somehow, he'd influenced her enough to climb those bloody walls, and she… and she….

His throat tightened.

Don't think of it.

All the reports said she was well, and getting stronger. Yet he'd needed to be certain, to see, if not with his own eyes, then through Louis César's. Louis had not wanted to come. He had written to her and her family, and sent flowers every week, as a concerned and respectful beau ought to, but he had not wished to visit. Neither of them understood why the family were still here and had not returned to their own home. Nic worried that Eliza was not as well as they were making out and could not yet travel. Louis had shrugged and just reminded him the two families were close, but Nic refused to be reassured. Louis had protested, certain he would be met with cool civility at best. His brother would be furious with him now, as it had become clear that they were intruding on some family event and their visit was ill-timed. Louis had believed it better to wait until the next season, when tempers would have cooled, and he could ease his way back into the family's good graces. Nic had persevered, though, wearing down each argument but never giving himself away, never letting Louis know why they must go back, why *he* must go back. Just to be near her, just for a moment, just until he knew....

"Monsieur Demarteau?"

He stilled. That voice. That familiar cool English voice pronounced his name, clipping the syllables and making them sound so different, odd to his ear, and yet strangely charming. His heart skittered about in his chest and he told himself not to be such a stupid bastard. He was no schoolboy infatuated with his first girl, yet he might as well have been. He'd been infatuated with her before he'd even met her, beguiled by the description Cassius had given of her, and by that little sketch he had shown of the lovely Elizabeth.

Nic's ideal.

His perfect English rose.

No. Not his. Never that.

"Lady Elizabeth."

He bowed, aware that his manner was stiff and awkward but unable to do a thing about it. No matter how he had learned to ape the manners of a gentleman, he felt clumsy and brutish before her, unrefined. Unworthy.

"I did not expect to see you here," she said, and Nic hardly heard the words for he was drinking in the sight of her.

His heart clenched, worry making his chest tight as he noted how pale she was, how fragile she looked. She had lost weight, far too much, and those green eyes—which had promised him he was in far over his head—were too large in a face as delicate as that of a china doll. A protective instinct rose in him, so overwhelming he had to clench his fists to stop himself from picking her up and carrying her off. He wanted to care for her, to keep her safe, to wrap her up in tissue paper and ensure the world could never harm her again. *Mon Dieu,* that was a great joke, was it not? It was likely his fault she'd been hurt, and being anywhere near him would cause her more harm than anything else.

"Monsieur?"

He realised he'd not answered her question. He had only stood looming over her, glowering at her, though she did not back away.

"My brother was worried for you," he said gruffly. "He came to see how you fared."

Those green eyes studied his face, assessing him. He fought to hold her gaze, when he wanted to turn away in case she saw too much.

"You were not worried for me, then?" she asked, still scrutinising him, too perceptive.

His jaw tightened.

I haven't been able to breathe, have not had a moment's peace since I heard of your accident, he didn't say. *My heart hurts. I have been living in a nightmare, an agony of suspense, unable to do anything for you, unable to come to you, to take care of you. I have been so unspeakably miserable it defies description.*

"Of course," he said. "My brother would have been devastated if you had not recovered."

"Yes, your brother. Of course," she said, a tight smile at her lips. She turned her head away from him, her profile so lovely to him it was like an arrow shaft piercing his heart.

She looked unhappy. Was she unhappy? Did she want him to care?

"Are you well, Eliza, truly?"

The words escaped him before he could stop them, before he could crush them and force them back down into the darkness. That was his brother's question to ask, not his, and there had been too much emotion there, the words revealing too much. She might… she might think....

She turned sharply towards him, her beautiful eyes alight with a question he wanted to answer but could not, but the movement seemed to unbalance her, and she swayed.

He moved, sweeping her up into his arms as he had longed to do from the first and, good Lord, she weighed nothing at all. She fit against him so perfectly, her hand a fist on the lapel of his coat as she stared up at him in astonishment.

"You m-must put me down," she said, a sunrise blush of colour at her cheeks, upon skin as fine and pale as porcelain.

Nic shook his head. He could not speak, did not dare. He could not even look at her, certain he would give into the overwhelming desire to steal a kiss if he did. Instead he carried her back towards the house. What the devil was she doing out here alone? Was no one taking care of her? What were her family thinking? Did no one look after her as they ought? Instinct demanded he take her back to the carriage and drive away with her and never come back, but that was madness. He was not mad. He was not uncivilised either, not anymore.

"Put me down, sir."

He ignored her. His heart was beating too fast, panic and fear competing for dominance in his heart. What if he'd not been here, what if she'd fainted? They ought never to let her out of their sight. They ought to fetch a doctor. Dr Archambeau ought to have stayed longer. Why had the devil left when she was still so frail, so ill? She needed caring for, she needed—

"I can walk!" she protested.

Her hand was still fisted upon his lapel, against his chest and he was desperately aware of it there, close to his heart. The ridiculous organ seemed to be trying to get even closer, beating almost out from behind his ribs. Nic's jaw felt too tight and he could not open his mouth. His chest was a snarl of emotion that he did not know what to do with, had no experience of.

"Mr Demarteau."

That clipped English voice again, speaking his name in that delicious way, like a governess. He experienced a savage desire for her to scold him. Well, she'd have to do better than that if she wanted him to put her down. Someone had to take care of her.

He walked on.

"Nic."

His breath caught and he hesitated, chest heaving. He dared to look down at her to see something soft and understanding in her eyes.

"I was just dizzy for a moment. Do not worry so. I know I have lost weight, but I am not so frail as I look, I assure you."

"You would have fallen. You're too weak, there's nothing of you," he ground out. "Don't they feed you? What did the doctor say? Isn't anyone—"

The words stopped as she raised her hand to his cheek. His breath caught in his throat, at the impossibility of it, that she would touch him, voluntarily, and with such tenderness. Though she wore a fine silk glove, the contact seared him, branded him as hers. Despite himself he closed his eyes, savouring the moment as her thumb moved gently over his skin. Oh God, if she knew… if she had the slightest idea what her touch did to him, she would not give away her caresses so easily.

"I am well," she said gently. "Now put me down before someone sees."

He did not want to. Every instinct rebelled against the idea, but he could not resist the gentle command. Nic set her down as carefully as if she were made of spun glass, and she smiled at him. Inwardly he cursed her for it, for tying his heart up into a tighter knot, for binding him to her so inextricably.

"I must go back to the house before they worry for me. Lottie and Cassius got married this morning, and the breakfast will begin shortly."

She smiled at the outrage in his eyes.

"I'm happy for them. Cassius was right, we would never have suited."

Nic could say nothing. If he tried, he'd say something ridiculous and make a fool of himself and then she'd *know* and she'd pity him or be kind to him and… and he'd rather die.

"Did you send me all those lovely flowers?" she asked.

To his horror, he felt heat prickle down his spine, his face growing hot at her having guessed. Him. Of all men. *Blushing?* Good God, he was in a world of trouble, but he was damned if he'd confirm her suspicions. Instead he turned away, forcing himself to leave her. She was safe now, close enough to the house.

"Will you come and see me again?" she called after him.

Nic ground to a halt, hardly daring to believe she had asked him—*asked* him—to come to her again. Was she out of her mind? But she *had* asked him.

No.

No.

Too dangerous.

He shook his head before his senses deserted him completely, scowling at the ground and avoiding her eyes. "No."

She walked around so she was facing him again, her voice soft, cajoling. "Not even if I ask nicely?"

Though he knew better, he looked at her. He wanted to plead with her not to put temptation in his way when every fibre of his being wanted to do just as she asked, but… it was impossible.

He folded his arms.

"*Non.*"

"Oh," she said with a sigh, and… was that *disappointment* in her eyes, the foolish girl? "Then I must wait until the season begins. No doubt our paths will cross again."

"No," he said, fighting to hide the regret in his words. "They will not."

And he forced himself to turn and walk away.

"There you are, Eliza," Lottie said, relieved to see her sister had returned from her walk. "Oh, the fresh air has done you good. There's some colour in your cheeks at last, and look, I have a surprise for you!"

Eliza smiled as Louis César moved to greet her but did not look as surprised as Lottie might have expected.

"How lovely to see you," she said, as the comte raised her hand to his lips and kissed her fingers.

"The pleasure is entirely mine, Lady Elizabeth. We have been so dreadfully worried about you. I simply could not stay away a moment longer without seeing with my own eyes that you were recovering well. Yet, I seem to be intruding on a family celebration."

Cassius smiled at him, his arm going around Lottie. "Not intruding, but it is certainly a celebration."

"So I see," Louis said, his bright blue eyes studying them both for a moment before glancing at Eliza.

Eliza laughed. "I am delighted for them. Cassius is my brother at last, just as he was always meant to be. Everything is perfect."

Louis nodded, smiling. "In that case, I believe I shall take my leave of you before your fathers discover my presence and decide to throw me in the lake for disturbing this wonderful day. I am very happy for you both, and delighted to see you looking so well, my lady. I shall hope to see you again, *very* soon."

❀ ❀ ❀

Finally. *Finally,* the wedding breakfast was done, and the family gathered in front of the house to wave them off. Not a moment too soon for Cassius, who was far too eager to get his wife to their new home and, more importantly, into their new bed. Tonight, though, they had a lovely suite of rooms booked in a hotel in London, to break the journey to Aylesbury.

"Thanks for taking her off our hands, old man," Jules said, slapping Cassius on the back and smirking, their fight long since forgotten. "Life will be so much more peaceful."

Lottie stuck her tongue out at her brother, who tsked and rolled his eyes. "Such a perfect young lady you've got yourself. Good God, to think she's Viscountess Oakley now."

Cassius laughed. "All right, Jules, quit whilst you're ahead or she'll find something to hit you with."

"I won't," Lottie retorted. "I shall just kick him in the—"

"Best if we leave it at that," her father remarked dryly, giving his son and heir a look. "It is your sister's wedding day, Blackstone."

The reproving tone and the use of Jules's title was indication enough that Jules had better be nice.

Jules gave a long-suffering sigh, but held his arms out to his sister. "Good luck, Snottie. I suppose I'll miss you."

Lottie huffed but hugged him back. "I suppose I'll miss you too, Crackedstone."

"Ha-ha, that's a good one! Crackedstone, because he's cracked in the head," chortled their thirteen-year old-cousin, Felix, Florence's little brother.

Jules sent him a glacial look and the boy turned a startling shade of scarlet, subsiding at once.

"Yes, yes, that's enough familial affection," drawled the long-suffering duke. "Away with you now."

Cassius could not have agreed more. He turned to where his parents were waiting to see them off.

"Promise you'll write," his mother said thickly as she accepted the handkerchief his father handed her. "More than you did when you were in France you dreadful boy."

"Harry, they're going to Aylesbury, not India. Not yet anyway," Papa said fondly, hugging his wife and kissing the top of her head.

"I know, I know," she said. "But he's still my little boy."

Cassius shared an amused glance with his father before hugging his mama tightly. "You may come and visit us soon, Mama, so do stop it."

"But not too soon, hmmm?" his father murmured before adding a *sotto voce* whisper into his mother's ear. "We have the house to ourselves." Mama blushed furiously and Cassius cleared his throat, deciding it was certainly time to go. Gathering his new wife, he hurried Lottie into the carriage.

"The bouquet!" all the girls squealed, running forward as Cassius gave the driver the nod.

Lottie laughed to see little Cat pushing to the front. He watched as Lottie stood in the open carriage with her back to them all before tossing the bouquet over her shoulder. She sat down with a shriek as the carriage jerked into motion, tumbling into Cassius's lap, much to his amusement.

She scrambled up before he could enjoy it though, looking to see who had caught the flowers. Cassius watched a slight scuffle between Greer and Florence, and then saw the bouquet go sailing again, landing at Eliza's feet.

"Oh!" Lottie exclaimed, clapping with delight. "You're next, sis! Just you wait."

Eliza laughed as Jules picked up the bouquet and shoved it at his sister, looking faintly disgusted. Eliza took it and waved it at Lottie.

"Write to me!" she called, before mouthing the words *and tell me everything.*

Chapter 23

Dear Florence,

It was so lovely to see you at Lottie's wedding and so nice to have someone sensible to talk to. Greer is such a henwit. I swear I shall murder her if I am forced to be cooped up with her all winter. Oh, my dear friend, please be my saviour, rescue me from the prospect of sororicide (yes, I looked it up) and invite me to stay with you for at least a few weeks. I promise to help entertain Felix and little Emmeline.

Either that, or Greer's demise will be on your head. You have been warned.

—Excerpt of a letter from Miss Elspeth Cadogan (daughter of Mrs Bonnie and Mr Jerome Cadogan) to Miss Florence Knight (daughter of Lady Helena and Mr Gabriel Knight).

22nd September 1838, on the London Road.

Cassius had arranged the open carriage for their departure as it was romantic and beautiful, and it was a lovely sunny day. He knew his bride would be delighted by the picture they made as they drove down Holbrook's impressive driveway, and she could wave goodbye to their family in style. However, being a sensible chap at

252

heart, and taking on board a word of advice from his father, he also had a closed carriage waiting a few miles down the road.

"Oh," Lottie said, as the carriage halted and she spied the luxurious closed carriage that would carry them to London. "It's such a lovely sunny day. It seems a shame to be shut up in a stuffy carriage."

Cassius said nothing, only helped her down from one carriage and up into the next. The moment their new equipage was in motion however, he dragged her into his lap.

"It might be a lovely day for an open carriage," he said, his tone dry. "But one cannot do this."

He slid his hand to the back of her neck and pulled her close, pressing his mouth to hers.

Lottie sighed, at once pliant in his arms.

"Silly me," she said dreamily, blinking at him through thick golden lashes when he finally let her go "Whatever was I thinking?"

"You weren't thinking, love," he chastised her, knowing she could tell he was only teasing. "But I was. Indeed, I've thought of nothing else but getting you alone since… forever!"

She snorted at that. "You didn't know I existed until a few months ago."

"Oh, come now. You know that isn't true."

"Hmmm," she murmured. "I'm not sure I believe that, but never mind. I insist you show me what it is you've been thinking of."

Cassius was not about to make love to his new wife in a carriage, but he was not averse to giving her a taste of what was to come. By the time they got to London, she was flushed and rumpled and utterly delicious.

They were staying the night at Brown's in Mayfair, far from one of the most lavish hotels in the capital, but Lottie had been desperately curious to see it. The place had been open barely more than a year, the proprietors being a Mr and Mrs Brown, previously valet and personal maid to Lord and Lady Byron. Cassius had heard good things about the comfortable and well-run establishment, and so was more than happy to accede to Lottie's wishes.

They were shown up to what Mr Brown himself proudly informed them was their best suite of rooms. It was light and airy and beautifully furnished. Lottie's flattering comments on the style of the décor clearly pleased Mr Brown enormously and he promised to pass this onto his wife, who he said was responsible for much of it. If they hadn't been due it before, Lottie had guaranteed them exemplary service, not that anything was wanting.

Flowers adorned several surfaces in pretty glass vases, a small intimate table was laid with a selection of delectable pastries, cold meat, cheese, bread, and fresh fruit, and a bottle of champagne. More importantly, as far as Cassius was concerned as he moved through to their chamber, the bed was large and inviting.

"Are you hungry?" Lottie called out to him, plucking a grape from the fruit bowl and popping it into her mouth.

"Famished," Cassius replied.

Lottie tugged another grape free and turned to look at him. She stilled, the grape suspended halfway to her mouth. Her lips quirked upwards and one eyebrow lifted. "You… are not speaking of the food."

"I am not."

"Oh."

She put the next grape into her mouth, watching him and chewing thoughtfully. "Can you be hungry for… well, *you* know?"

"Do I?"

"Certainly, you do," she said, tart now, though her eyes sparkled. "Don't tease me."

"But it is my ambition to spend the entire night teasing you," he said, leaning against the door jamb and watching her pull another grape from the bunch.

"I would have thought you'd done enough of that on the way here," she remarked, a subtle tinge of colour at her cheeks.

"Oh, love," he said, shaking his head. "Not nearly enough. Indeed, I regret to inform you that I suspect there is no such thing as enough where you are concerned."

"Really?" she said, pursing her lips.

"Really."

"Oh, well. In that case… I am your wife after all, and duty bound to please you." She lifted her chin and spread her arms out wide. "You may ravish me."

Cassius snorted. "Not with all that lot on, I can't. I nearly died of suffocation the last time. Death by petticoats."

"What a way to go," Lottie retorted, walking to him and rustling her petticoats at him in a provocative manner.

He gave a bark of laughter and pushed off the door jamb. Cassius crossed the room and swept her up in his arms as the froth of lace and silk rustled and swished.

"Have I told you how extraordinarily beautiful you look today? That gown is quite breathtaking. Indeed, I could not breathe when I saw you for the first time. In truth, I was perilously close to weeping. Happily, Ash beat me to it and diverted attention."

Her eyes grew wide and soft with adoration and he was glad he'd told her, even if he felt a little silly doing so.

"I'm glad," she whispered. "For my heart was beating out of my chest and it was the hardest thing not to just run across the room and throw myself at you, but I promised Papa I should behave like a lady, not a hoyden, and I *almost* managed it."

"Almost?" he replied, grinning at her.

She nodded. "Until you kissed me and I couldn't let you go. Those kisses are supposed to be shy and demure."

Cassius chuckled. "Well, we were among family and friends, so I don't think they would be so dreadfully shocked, though I'm glad enough to put distance between me and your father."

"Poor Papa," Lottie said with a sigh.

Cassius shook his head, carrying her through to the bedroom. "And that is the last mention we shall have of him, I thank you."

Lottie glanced at the bed as Cassius carried her through. Despite everything they'd done together, her heart was beating very fast. Mostly, it was anticipation. After all, Mama had said it was more discomfort than pain, and only for the first time, if the man was an attentive lover and prepared the way well.

'And his father is St Clair, after all,' she'd said with a devilish smile.

"Did your papa have a dreadfully wicked reputation before he married?" Lottie asked as he set her down.

"Yes, he did. Though he denies much of it was true," Cassius replied, turning her around to peruse the fastenings on her gown. He made his way along the buttons, undoing them with startling speed. "Why?"

"Oh, nothing," she replied as her gown slithered to the floor with a soft shushing sound and a flurry of lace. Lottie undid the ties of her little linen bustle and tossed it away. "Just something Mama said."

The fingers that had been making quick work of her heavy crinoline petticoat stilled. "Lottie."

"Yes?"

"Your mama, she… she did tell you…?"

Lottie glanced over her shoulder to see an expression of horror on his face. It was so comical she burst out laughing.

"Oh, Cass," she said, clutching at her corset, which was suddenly far too tight. "Oh, take it off, take it off!"

"Well, I would if you'd keep still," he grumbled, snatching at the ties of the crinoline again. "But there's about two dozen petticoats to get through yet. I declare whoever designs women's fashions is a damned sadist."

Finally the crinoline sagged, though it was too stiff to fall, made thickly of horsehair and linen. Lottie pushed it down and stepped out of it, then waited impatiently as Cassius fought with the two remaining cotton petticoats. He muttered wrathfully under his breath and Lottie bit her lip, trying not to laugh or fidget. Finally, they were gone, and his clever fingers were tugging at the corset strings.

"Thank the Lord," he said with a sigh as the corset came loose. Lottie threw the busk aside and pushed the corset to the floor, folding her arms over her breasts as she turned to him, aware that her shift was so fine it was nigh on see-through.

"You're not shy, Lottie?" he asked in surprise. "Not with me?"

"N-Not shy exactly," she said, and then saw the wonder in his eyes as he looked at her, the tinge of colour high on his cheekbones, the way his chest rose and fell.

"My God." He breathed the words, reverent.

"No," she said, as any last inhibitions fell away, because this was Cassius, whom she'd adored her entire life. This was perfect and there wasn't the slightest thing to be shy or anxious about. "No. Not the least bit shy."

To prove it, she stripped off the chemise and let him look at her, watching him as he took her in. His throat worked, his beautiful turquoise eyes darkening with desire.

"No words," he said, his voice hoarse.

He shook his head helplessly and laughed, a slightly choked sound that made her heart soar. So she ran to him, flinging her arms about his neck as she always wanted to do when he was near. His arms tightened around her, the cold press of buttons a shock against her overheated skin as he pulled her flush against him.

She sighed as his mouth went to her shoulder, her neck, leaving a trail of fiery kisses that lingered for a while at the tender skin beneath her ear, making her shiver. Then down the trail went again, an inevitable path to her breast where he dallied longer still, teasing the tender buds with his lips and tongue and teeth until she was flushed and breathless. He knelt before her, staring up the line of her body.

"This is my favourite shade of pink," he said, his voice impossibly low and deep, the sound rumbling through her, his words stirring sensation deep in her belly. Cassius touched a finger to one taut nipple. "All the best and most wicked parts of you are pink. Deliciously, devilishly pink. Such an innocent colour everyone believes it, but it is dreadfully sinful."

Lottie's breathing hitched as he kissed her belly, his tongue swirling a circle around her belly button. She would have laughed, as it tickled, but the sensation was more than ticklish as his mouth moved lower. She knew what came next.

"Let's find somewhere else that perfect shade of wicked, shall we?" he murmured against her skin, and then he was nuzzling into the golden curls between her thighs, and then his tongue was there, and then....

She was dizzy, one hand flailing to grasp the bedpost as his tongue insinuated itself deeper and stroked and….

"Cass… Cassius…."

He continued, teasing and tormenting and though she had never swooned in her entire life, she felt very certain her knees would give out.

"C-Can't stand," she managed, breathing hard, her knuckles white as she clutched at the bed post. "Cass…."

He chuckled, warm breath gusting like a cool breath against her too hot skin. Goosebumps ran over her in response.

Cassius got to his feet and guided her to the bed. "Lie down then, love, before you fall down."

He looked horribly smug about that, the devil. Not that she cared. If he kept making her feel that way, he had every reason to look smug.

Lottie collapsed against the pillows, desperately impatient that he should join her but… but then she realised he was getting undressed, and *that* was worth watching.

She had seen him all but naked once before, when she had hidden his clothes after he'd swam in the lake. He'd still been wearing his small clothes, which had been so sodden they hid little, but he'd covered his most interesting parts with his hands, much to her consternation. This time he was hers, her husband, and she was free to look her fill.

He moved quickly, his coat and waistcoat slung on the nearest chair in a manner to ensure his poor valet would be in fits when he saw them, and then tugged the shirt over his head. Lottie's heart gave an erratic thud and it was hard to breathe. She took in the sight of powerful shoulders, that magnificent broad chest and the wiry hair there, that caught the late afternoon sun and shimmered copper and gold. Finally, she could touch him as she had longed to do. Her body ached to have him closer, to have the weight of him

upon her, inside her. That thought made the place between her legs
throb, a clamour of desire that only became more insistent as she
watched him disrobe. He was down to his small clothes now, and
then they too were gone, and he was striding for the bed.

Lottie was torn between demanding he keep still so she might
look at him properly and pleading with him to hurry. In the end,
she was too stunned to do either and then he was there, climbing
onto the mattress, his body moving over hers. The shock of his
skin upon hers was astonishing. Hot, he was so hot, and
surprisingly silky, yet so much harder, his flesh so much firmer,
muscle and sinew, the weight of him everything she had wanted
and needed. She gasped as his arousal glided over her sex, the
sensation so delicious she could only arch towards him, seeking
more.

"Lottie, oh, God, love. I thought I'd go mad wanting this,
wanting you."

"Hurry, then," she demanded, beside herself.

She knew what came next and she wanted it, her body
demanded it. Her hands clutched at him, her legs pulling him in
closer.

"I don't want to hurt you," he said, desperation in his voice as
he tried to calm her. "Perhaps we should—"

"No," she demanded, almost cross. "No, *now*. You won't hurt
me, just… please…."

He groaned, clearly aware it was pointless to remonstrate,
thank heavens. She held her breath as he found his place between
her legs and then he was pushing into her. Lottie gasped, panting
as the strange sense of fullness became uncomfortable and he
paused.

"Breathe," he said, nuzzling her neck with soft lips, before
finding her mouth and kissing her, deeply, slowly, until her
muscles unwound and her body relaxed, accepting him. He broke
the kiss and groaned. She might have relaxed, but his body sang

with tension, the muscles hard and taut beneath her hand until he moved again. He made a desperate sound that thrilled through her and thrust deeper.

There was a pinch of discomfort, but Lottie ignored it, too beguiled by the sight of Cassius, sweating and lost to passion, lost to the feel of being inside her. His pleasure was the greatest aphrodisiac in the world, and she loved the harsh, masculine sounds of effort and satisfaction he made, as his movements became harder, faster, and increasingly erratic. She stroked her hands over his shoulders, feeling the roll of muscle, the passion-damp slide of his skin under her palms. He moved then, hooking her leg over his arm, deepening the angle, and… she cried out, grabbing his biceps as if she needed anchoring to the earth as sensation rolled through her, building and building into a crescendo that she knew would overwhelm her. She welcomed it, chased it, closing her eyes and rushing towards it as he jerked and shuddered in her arms. The big bed shook with the force of it, his guttural cry loud and brutal and enough to send her tumbling after him. He stole her cry with a kiss, and she held onto him, breathless as she blinked up into his beautiful face.

"Lottie?" he said, breathing too hard to speak easily. "Lottie?"

"Marvellous," she replied, dazed but comprehending his question by the anxious look in his eyes. "Simply marvellous."

He gave a short laugh and collapsed on top of her, utterly spent.

The sky outside had long since grown dark by the time hunger drove them from the bed. Not for long, though. They carried the trays of food back with them and arranged a picnic on the mattress, sharing one glass of wine though the decanter sat on the bedside table.

"I'm famished," Lottie said, demolishing a dainty little pastry in one bite. She closed her eyes, chewing with an expression of bliss.

Cassius watched her with rapt attention, the chicken leg he'd taken suspended in mid-air.

"What?" Lottie asked licking the crumbs from her lips. "Are my manners appalling? Are you horrified?"

"Yes. You're disgraceful." His gaze fell to her mouth. "I shall be too ashamed to take you anywhere. I think I shall confine you to your bedroom and never let you out ever again."

Lottie lifted the glass of wine and took a large swallow, watching him thoughtfully. "Will you stay with me in my prison?"

"Always," he said. "Someone must keep you amused, and I am your husband. I spoke vows, remember."

She shrugged and picked up another pasty. "All right, then."

She popped the morsel into her mouth. Cassius watched as she licked each finger in turn.

"Are you going to eat that?" She gestured to the chicken leg and, when he failed to respond, plucked it from his fingers.

"You're terrible," he said reproachfully.

She made a snorting noise like a pig and he laughed, falling back against the pillows, too happy to make sense of his feelings, and really what was the point in analysing it? He loved her, she made him laugh, made his heart feel light, and made his mind race with possibilities for their future.

"God, I am a lucky devil," he said with a sigh.

"Yes," she agreed taking up another little pasty and holding it to his lips. "You are."

He took it from her, careful to ensure his lips touched her fingers. He held her hand until he'd finished chewing and then licked each finger in turn, watching her eyes darken as he did so.

"We'll make a dreadful mess," she warned him, her lips quirking.

She had that wicked glint in her eyes that he adored above anything, that made his chest want to burst with the force of happiness swelling inside him.

"Yes," he said. "Let's do that."

Epilogue

Dr Archambeau,

Despite your reassurances, Lady Elizabeth is still suffering headaches and megrims. She is pale and often has fainting fits. I think I do not need to remind you that ensuring her health is your priority, nor of the penalty you will incur if you fail to do so.

I suggest you do not delay in making your trip across the channel before the weather makes the journey impossible.

—Excerpt of a letter from Monsieur Nicolas Alexandre Demarteau to Dr Archambeau— translated from the French.

30th November 1838, Beverwyck.

"Lottie!" Cassius remonstrated as, before he could stop her, she leapt down from the carriage, hiked up her skirts and ran pell mell up the icy steps to the front door.

It opened, and the family butler, young Jenkins, ushered them in and closed the door upon the frigid November afternoon.

Cassius brushed snow from his hair as he handed his hat to a footman.

"Where is she?" Lottie demanded, ignoring the footman waiting to take her bonnet and cloak. "Is she well? Is she safe, what—?"

"Very well, Lady Charlotte," the butler said, his warm smile and calm demeanour going a long way to sooth Lottie's terror. "If you would like to wait for a few moments in the parlour, I will see if you can go in yet."

"Oh, but—" Lottie said, her beautiful face pale with worry.

"Love," Cassius said, taking her cloak from her and handing it over before tugging at the ribbons of her bonnet. "Jenkins said she's very well. Is he lying, do you think?"

"N-No," she said, wringing her hands together.

"No," Cassius repeated. "So do stop fretting."

He guided her up the stairs and through to the parlour, sat her by the fire and pressed a small glass of brandy into her hands. Once he had poured another for himself, he perched on the arm of the chair, and leaned down to kiss his wife.

"Better?" he asked.

"A little, though I shan't be happy until I've seen them both. I wonder if it is a boy or a girl?"

"Does it matter?"

"Oh, no," Lottie said with a wistful smile. "So long as they are both healthy."

"I don't know how your father has stood it. Eight children?" Cassius shook his head, his heart and stomach clenching at the idea of Lottie facing the perils of childbirth. Still, it was bound to happen, eventually.

She must have known what direction his thoughts had taken, for she reached out and clasped his hand.

"I want a big family, God willing," she said firmly. "And I'm fit and strong and healthy. There is nothing to worry about."

Cassius stared down at her, at the certainty in her eyes. He bent and kissed her, putting all the tenderness he felt into it.

"I love you," he murmured.

She smiled up at him and the tension in his chest eased, as it always did when she gifted him with such a look. "And I you. Always."

Cassius stood as the door opened and Eliza came in. She had put on a little weight since last he'd seen her, and there was a faint bloom of colour in her cheeks, but she was still not nearly as robust as she'd once been.

"Eliza," he said, moving to greet her before Lottie took his place and hugged her sister tightly.

"Are you well?" she said, giving Eliza a critical once over.

"Fighting fit," Eliza said, grinning and affecting a boxing stance, which was so unlike her Cassius laughed.

"Who taught you that?"

"Fred showed me," she said, putting up her chin with a defiant twinkle in her eyes. "Jules is teaching him the finer points of pugilism."

Cassius snorted and touched a finger to his jaw, to where the memory of a punch lingered. "Well, he knows a thing or two, I'll give him that."

"How's Mama?" Lottie said, taking her sister's arm.

Eliza's face softened. "She's well. Very tired, but happy. The doctor said she's doing marvellously and… and we have a new baby sister. Octavia."

Lottie gave a little squeal of delight and the two sisters hugged each other again.

"That's wonderful news," Cassius said, more than relieved to hear the duchess and the baby were well. Lottie had been fretting herself to death these past weeks as the duchess was so tired she had not even had the energy to write letters and, most shockingly of all, had put the writing of her latest novel to one side. "Why did she decide on coming back to town to have the baby at Beverwyck, though?"

"We were all born here," Eliza said fondly. "It's her favourite place to be. She's comfortable here, and her doctor is close at hand."

They all looked around at the soft knock, and a moment later young Jenkins opened the door.

"Her grace will see you now," he said, looking almost as proud as Cassius suspected the duke must be.

They made their way to the duchess's rooms and entered. The bedchamber was as lavish and opulent as befitted the Duchess of Bedwin, but the scene at the centre of it was intimate and quiet. The duke sat with his arm about his wife, and they both stared down at the little bundle in the duchess's arms, enchanted. They had not heard their daughters or Cassius enter, too lost in their own little world, and Cassius felt his breath catch at the look that passed between them. He understood that look, the depth of love and devotion between two people who had chosen to live their lives together. Lottie's hand slid into his. She had evidently seen what he had. Her big blue eyes were very bright, sparkling with happiness.

"Girls!" the duchess said, finally seeing them.

She carefully handed their new arrival to her husband and put out her arms. Eliza and Lottie ran to her, embracing and kissing her in turn.

"Well, done, Mama!" Lottie exclaimed as her father walked around the bed, looking very pleased with himself.

"What about me?" the duke said, affecting a look of indignation.

Lottie waved her hand. "Oh, you did the easy bit," she said dismissively. "Give me a cuddle with my new sister. I have so much to tell her."

The duke stared at the baby and gave a sad shake of his head. "Oh, I can feel the grey hairs growing already."

Reluctantly, he passed the baby to Lottie as Eliza peered over her shoulder.

"She's exquisite," Eliza said, one slender hand reaching out to touch the baby's downy head. "I wonder if she will be blonde like you, or dark like me?"

"Whichever she decides, she will be as beautiful as you both," Cassius said.

"Stop bewitching my daughters and trying to turn them up sweet, young man. You've got one, and believe me that's quite enough."

Cassius grinned at the duke. "Oh, I know it, sir. Believe me, I have the deepest admiration for everything you've been through."

"So I should think," the duke murmured.

He put his arm about Lottie, staring down at the babe in her arms before reaching for Eliza and pulling her close too.

"Eight, children," he said with a sigh, before adding with desperation, "and *five* girls. Five *beautiful* girls! It's a wonder I haven't run mad."

"Yes, and bearing in mind I did all the hard work, might I have my daughter back?" demanded their mama.

The duke laughed and took the baby from Lottie, who appeared loath to hand her back.

"Oh," she said, clutching her arms about herself. She turned to look at Cassius. "I want one."

Cassius blanched as Eliza gave a snort of laughter.

"Oh, stop it, Lottie. You're scaring him."

Lottie huffed.

"Well, there is no rush," she admitted. "Besides, I have a project this season. Mama is going to be busy with little Octavia, and so, now I am a respectable married lady, I shall take you to all the best events and get you a husband."

Cassius laughed as it was Eliza's turn to blanch, her mouth dropping open.

"Oh, no," Eliza said, shaking her head. "Indeed not. I know very well you are both desperate to go off on your adventures and I am not stopping you. I shall find my own husband in my own time."

"Stuff," Lottie replied. "You need my help for you have rotten taste."

"Oi!" Cassius glared at his wife, indignant.

"What? She didn't want *you*," Lottie replied.

Both sisters and the duke and duchess had a good laugh at that.

Well, Cassius thought wryly, you knew you were truly part of the family when they began making jokes at your expense.

Lottie drew closer to her sister and lowered her voice. "Did you ever hear any more from... you know who?"

To his astonishment, Eliza flushed scarlet.

"Who?" he demanded, instantly suspicious.

Eliza was his sister now, and therefore under his protection. If some fellow was taking an interest, he needed to know about it. After all, he might not be suitable.

Eliza glared at Lottie before turning back to him.

"No one," she said, her voice soothing. "You know how silly and romantic Lottie can be."

"Did we ever discover who sent all those flowers when you were ill?" he asked, not entirely convinced by this evasive answer.

"No," Eliza said with a shrug. "We never did. Whoever it was is clearly a shy soul and cannot bear to make himself known. So, he's obviously not the kind of man you need fret over."

"Hmph." Cassius remained unconvinced.

Eliza walked back to the bed to sit with her parents and coo over Octavia. Lottie moved to follow but Cassius put his hand out, stopping her.

"You were right," he said quietly. "We shall have to chaperone her carefully. If she's even strong enough to attend the season. I admit, I wish I knew who this secret admirer was."

Lottie nodded. "Yes. We will take the greatest care of her. For we cannot have my dear Eliza giving herself to some man who does not deserve her. That would break my heart."

"Mine too," Cassius said, raising her hand to his lips and kissing the fingers. "She deserves to be as happy as we are."

"Yes," Lottie agreed, a look in her eyes that made him wish he could take her back home that very moment. "Yes. She does, and we shall help to ensure that she is."

"Oh, do stop whispering over there," Eliza said, calling them over to the bed. "I just know you're plotting, and I won't have it. I am not going to agree to anything I don't want. Not ever again."

This was said with such defiance that her father looked at her in horror.

Eliza laughed and patted his hand. "Oh, don't fret so, Papa. I'm not about to start a revolution or run off to Gretna Green."

"I'm very glad to hear it," the duke said with obvious relief, but Cassius kept his attention on Eliza, long after everyone else had returned theirs to the baby.

There was something dangerous glinting in her green eyes, and he just hoped he and Lottie were up to the challenge.

Lottie watched Cassius as he tugged off the last of his clothes and then turned back to the bed. He paused when he noticed the way she watched him, and stood still, allowing her to look her fill.

"Like what you see?" he asked, lips quirking.

"Oh, yes," Lottie sighed happily, remembering the last time he'd asked that. "I like it very much. I'm so glad I married you."

Cassius gave a snort of laughter and then sighed. "You only want me for my body."

"Oh, that is simply not true," Lottie protested, pressing a hand to her heart with a theatrical flourish. "You are also a very fine artist and flatter me dreadfully. You know we goddesses need our egos attended to regularly."

"Is that so?" he asked, climbing onto the bed beside her and making the mattress bounce.

"It is."

He prowled towards her, lowering his voice to a deep rumble that made her heart skip with excitement. "Well, then. I had better attend to it right now, had I not?"

"I really think you ought."

Cassius bent and kissed her neck, finding the delicate place beneath her ear that made her giggle and squeal if he nuzzled it just right. He did it just right, as he always did, and she shrieked and wriggled beneath him, clutching at his big shoulders.

"Like this," he murmured, laughing against her skin.

Lottie sighed and stroked her palm down his spine. How marvellous it was to share her life with this man, this wonderful man who was her friend and her lover. "Just like that."

He stilled, pulling back to look down at her, his turquoise eyes full of adoration.

"No regrets?" he asked softly. "You don't wish you'd chosen someone else, someone you haven't known your whole life? I worry you'll get bored, knowing me as well as you do."

"Bored?" she exclaimed, staring at him in shock. "Cassius, you do say the most ridiculous things. How can I possibly get bored when we shall be off on our adventures soon?"

Cassius frowned. "We will?"

"Of course we will," she said, shaking her head at him."

"But Eliza—"

"Of course, Eliza, but I'm sure that won't take long. Everybody loves her, so she'll have her pick of all the men. I'm sure between us we can find her a nice fellow and she'll fall headlong into love in no time. Then as soon as she is settled and happy, we shall go away. We'll go to France first, and you can show me everything you discovered last time."

"Everything?" he asked, quirking one eyebrow.

Lottie remembered the nude painting of the lovely girl she had correctly assumed to have been one of his lovers.

She narrowed her eyes at him. "Yes, *everything*, providing I am the only lady you lavish your attentions on."

"How strict you are. Very well, then. An adventure it is. I shall pack my paints and a hat. What will you need?"

Lottie considered this, biting her lip as she considered, aware that his heated gaze was fixed upon her mouth.

"Just you," she said at length, grinning at him. "You are all I need."

"Good answer," he said with a smug smile. "And how long shall we stay away?"

"Until we miss home, or until you do your husbandly duty and we are forced to return, whichever comes first."

"My...." he began, and then remembered her demand that he give her a baby. "Oh. I thought you said there was no hurry?"

"Oh, there's not, we shall see the world, and you shall paint it, and then we will return home and begin another kind of adventure entirely."

"You have it all planned out, I see."

"Naturally," she replied, sliding her fingers into the silky warmth of his blond hair.

"Naturally."

"I have tonight all planned out too," she added, something mischievous twinkling in her eyes.

Cassius quirked an eyebrow. Lottie tugged at his head, pulling him close so she could whisper in his ear.

When he drew back, his eyes were very dark, the pupils blown wide against a thin turquoise rim.

"You wicked girl," he said, staring at her in shock, an intrigued smile curving about his lips. "I wonder you dare look me in the eye."

"Oh," Lottie said with a smile, twining herself about him. "I dare. I shall always dare to be wicked with you."

The stories of the **Peculiar Ladies Book Club** and their hatful of dares has become legend among their children. When the hat is rediscovered, dusty and forlorn, the remaining dares spark a series of events that will echo through all the families… and their

Daring Daughters

Next in the thrilling new series…

Dare to be Brazen
Daring Daughters Book Two

Their mothers dared all for love.
Just imagine what their daughters will do…

The perfect lady…

Lady Elizabeth Adolphus, eldest daughter of the Duke and Duchess of Bedwin is the most sought-after young lady of the ton.

Seen as the perfect debutante, beautiful, sweet-natured, and demure, she is besieged by offers from eligible gentlemen.

And she doesn't want any of them.

There is only one man she wishes to pursue, and he is far from eligible.

A dangerous man, with a dark past...

Monsieur Nicolas Alexandre Demarteau, owner of the infamous Parisian nightclub, Rouge et Noir, is the illegitimate half-brother of Louis César de Montluc, Comte de Villen. Having left Paris to escape a scandal, Nic is determined Louis César will marry the perfect English lady to secure his position among the ton, only to discover the woman Louis came to England to pursue is the embodiment of Nic's every dream. Keeping the promises he made Louis César will test his resolve when every instinct demands he keep Eliza for himself.

An English rose with a will of iron...

Now recovering from a near fatal accident, Eliza may appear more fragile than before, but her determination to make her own choices is stronger than ever. She is tired of always doing the right thing, of being polite instead of speaking her mind, of dancing with respectable men when the one she desires is the personification of wickedness... and he doesn't even seem to like her very much.

A passionate desire...

All Nic wants is for Eliza to be safe, but how can he protect her when all she wants is him. How can he resist her when she refuses to be the perfect lady a moment longer?

When she's decided... it's time to be brazen.

Prologue

N'écris pas. Je suis triste, et je
voudrais m'éteindre.
Les beaux étés sans toi, c'est la nuit
sans flambeau.
J'ai refermé mes bras qui ne peuvent
t'atteindre,
Et frapper à mon cœur, c'est frapper au
tombeau.
N'écris pas!

Do not write. I'm sad and pensive,
burning up my fire.
Bright summers without you are like a
darkened room.
My arms clasped tight again, but not
with their desire.
Beating at my heart is like beating at a
tomb.
Do not write!
—Marceline Desbordes-Valmore
1786 -1859

12ᵗʰ November 1825, Perigueux, France.

Nic curled his hands about his mouth and blew to
revive his numb fingers. The house had been quiet for at

least an hour, but that was no guarantee every occupant was asleep.

He looked up, muttering a filthy curse as soft white flakes tumbled from the inky skies above. The night was perishing cold as it was; all he needed was for every surface to be slick with ice. The weather did not care about the days he'd taken to get here, nor his carefully laid plans, and the snow fell with delicate insistence, forcing him to a decision. Either he acted now, or he must come back another night. Everything he'd discovered to date told him he could not wait. Whatever it was in his gut that had guided him out of more trouble than one twenty-year-old had a right to survive told him this was his only chance.

Nic stood, his limbs protesting the movement after crouching in the freezing temperatures, motionless for hours on the roof of the building opposite his target. It had been a grave disappointment that he could not find an easier way in, but the house was locked up tight, with a heavy front door, and the few windows were secured with shutters. In the middle of the small town of Perigueux in southwest France, and with houses on all sides, there was no way of breaking in without being seen. His best chance was to access the back of the house opposite, climb over the roof and then enter via the inner courtyard which was bound to be less well secured. There was just one problem. Nic padded to the edge, looking down at a drop which guaranteed broken limbs at best, and at worst a death sentence. Perhaps that ought to be the other way around, he mused, reaching for the thick coil of rope. What life for a man of his talents if his body was broken beyond repair? He'd not think of that. Nic had been taught from a very young age that fear was normal, but something he could ignore if he focused. If he was prepared, if he knew what he was doing and did it with a clear head, with absolute concentration, then fear simply... went away.

He took a deep breath, swung the grappling hook around and around, and flung it towards the building opposite. It hit with a crack that seemed to Nic to sound like gunfire in the still of the night. A dog barked somewhere down the street and a voice yelled to silence it. He crouched down again, waiting for someone to sound the alarm, to come out and investigate, but the snow kept drifting down and smoke from the chimneys kept coiling up. All was silent. Letting out a breath of relief, Nic secured the rope. He undid his heavy boots and tied the laces together, draping them over his neck, then pulled on the soft leather slippers, tying the laces firmly up around his ankles. It took longer than he liked to test and retest the tension and security of the rope, to convince himself the thing would hold, but he was no use to anyone with a broken neck. Usually the rope was secured on all sides to keep it still, but there were no such precautions here, and he would need all his skill to cross the gap before him.

Finally it was done, and he stood on the edge of the building, the rope stretched out before him. He steadied his breathing, emptying his mind of anything but the rope and his own body, sliding one foot out along the taut length, and then the other. It was child's play really, even with the disconcerting sway: a far shorter distance than he walked daily, delighting the crowds with what they considered an astonishing, death-defying talent. The tightrope creaked as he reached the middle, and Nic's heart gave a little jolt, but he kept moving forward. Movement was his friend, and any hesitation could see him fall. At last, the roof opposite was within reach. He stepped off and allowed himself a moment to breathe, then he grasped the grappling hook and threw it back to where he'd come from. He'd not be able to escape this way if he was successful, and he could not risk leaving evidence. Once again, the clatter as the hook hit the tiles seemed loud enough to wake the dead, but the fates were kind tonight, and a catfight in the street below was enough to make anyone believe the furious felines were responsible for anything that sounded like a crash.

Five minutes later and Nic, as sure-footed as the hissing creatures in the street below, had crossed the roof and climbed down into the inner courtyard. Cursing the snow that left his footprints visible, he crouched beside what he guessed might be the kitchen door and got out his lock picks. Too easy, he thought with a smirk, glad he'd taken the time to learn how before turning the well-oiled knob and silently easing inside the house. He closed the door and stood for a moment, accustoming himself to the sleeping house and listening for anything that might signal danger. The silence pressed down on him as he moved through the scullery and on to the kitchen. The fire was dying, the embers still glowing but devoid of flame, giving just enough light to see the slight figure curled on the floor in front of the hearth. Nic's heart contracted, pity and fury mingling together, but there was no time now, neither for sentiment nor explanations. He moved closer, crouched down, and put his hand firmly over the boy's mouth.

The body jerked awake, hands coming up to grasp at Nic's wrist, but he was skinny and weak and no match for a man of Nic's size.

"Quiet," Nic said, his voice stern. "I've come to help you. Do you want to get out of here?"

The boy stilled, and Nic moved around to face him, startled by eyes of such brilliant blue that there was no doubting the colour, even in the dim firelight.

279

"I'm not going to hurt you. If you come with me, I'll make sure no one ever hurts you again. *D'accord*?"

The boy stared at him, and then gave a sharp nod.

"I'm going to take my hand away now. If you shout for help, this will be your life, sleeping on a kitchen floor, working for that miserable bastard who treats you worse than a dog. Understand?"

The boy stared at him, unblinking, and nodded again. Nic took his hand away.

"Will you come with me?" he asked.

"Yes," the boy said at once.

Nic smiled. "Don't you care where we're going?"

"No."

"You trust me?" Nic said, unsure whether to be pleased or horrified by the nod that followed, that this boy should put himself into the care of a man he didn't know from Adam without a word of protest.

"Yes." The answer was fervent, determined.

Nic frowned, and despite their need to escape at once, he could not help but ask, "Why?"

"Because you're my brother."

Chapter 1

Dearest Eliza,

*I hope you are feeling better now. Mama told
me how ill you were last week, and that the
megrim did not subside for several days. Do you
not think that perhaps they are correct, and you
ought not attend the season this year? Perhaps
the south of France? The sunshine might do you
good. Cassius and I would happily accompany
you.*

**—Excerpt of a letter from of Lady Charlotte
Cadogan, Vicomtesse Oakley, to her sister,
Lady Elizabeth Adolphus – eldest daughter
of the Duke and Duchess of Bedwin.**

5th March 1839, Beverwyck, London.

Nic looked up from the book he was reading as his half-brother, Louis César, walked into the room. Louis strode to the cabinet that held a decanter of brandy, poured himself a large measure and came and stood by the fire, one arm on the mantel.

Nic withdrew his watch, frowning down at the timepiece. "You're back early."

"*Elle n'était pas là,*" Louis said irritably.

"English, Louis." Nic sighed at the glittering look Louis sent him. "We agreed. If we are to be accepted by the *ton* and make our lives here, it must be as natural as our mother tongue."

Louis rolled his eyes.

"She was not there," he repeated, enunciating each word with a precise, measured accent that illustrated his impatience. "Taken ill, I believe."

"What?" Nic sat up straighter, making a futile attempt to still the panic that made his heart knock about in his chest.

"A headache, I am told, and before you ask, yes, I said all the correct things, ensured I looked suitably bereft, and I will send flowers in the morning. What I would not do was endure the rest of the evening, bored out of my mind, when it was to no purpose."

Nic glowered at his brother but said nothing. Eliza was ill again, or at least suffering yet another headache, which was not merely a headache but a megrim that would leave her pale and wan for days after. He must get that idiot doctor back again. She ought not be suffering like this after all she'd been through. Guilt rose in his chest, so heavy and smothering it was hard to breathe around it. His fault. His bloody fault. He ought never have put himself in her way. What a bloody selfish fool he'd been. Well, that was done. Now he needed to stay away from her. Far, far away.

"I've been thinking," Nic said, the words as nonchalant as he could make them. "I ought to go back to Paris for a while, to check on things."

Eyes of shocking blue turned upon him, fierce with intelligence and burning with annoyance. "So, you try to think of a reason to abandon me, do you, brother?"

"I'm not abandoning you," Nic protested. "For the love of God, Louis, you're not a boy any longer."

"No, and I never was a fool. We both know Rouge et Noir is in good hands. Jacques does not need you breathing down his neck and acting like we don't trust him. You'll only put his back up. So, why don't you tell me why you have been acting so strangely of late?"

Nic's ground his teeth. The trouble was, Louis knew him too well. It was a miracle he'd not figured out what the problem was weeks ago. He knew it was only because it was so damned unlikely it would never occur to his brother that Nic had become infatuated with a woman he barely knew. A duke's daughter, no less. If it weren't so damned painful, it would be hysterical.

"I'm not acting anything," Nic replied, aware he sounded like a sulky boy.

Louis snorted.

"I think you are bored," his brother said, studying him critically. "In Paris you were occupied with the club at all hours of the day and night. The life of an idle gentleman does not agree with you."

Nic turned an incredulous look upon Louis. "And it does you?"

Louis waved an impatient if elegant hand. "I have always been better at dissembling than you. Besides, a fellow can find occupation enough if he puts his mind to it."

Nic made a disgruntled sound but said nothing.

"Why not go ahead with the new club you mentioned?"

"Because you said—" Nic began, but Louis silenced him.

"I know what I said, and I was correct."

"Naturally." The word dripped sarcasm, which Louis ignored.

"You cannot possibly be responsible for a club like Rouge et Noir here in England. It would damage us both. You could, however, try something different. Something exclusive and respectable."

"Respectable?" Nic regarded his brother's amused expression, aware he had exclaimed the word in the same way one might shriek '*plague!*'

"Is it really such a reprehensible idea? We have come here to be respectable, have we not?"

"*You* have," Nic grumbled.

He might be illegitimate, but his sire had recognised him for Louis's sake. If Louis married well and, if they avoided any scandal, Nic might... well, he *might* not cause his half-brother too much trouble by his continued association. Nic had tried to suggest he stay away completely on several occasions. The results had not been pretty. Louis believed he owed Nic his life, certainly his liberty, and he refused to accept any version of the future where Nic was not fully present in it. For some reason Nic could not fathom, Louis idolised him. Such love and loyalty touched Nic deeper than he cared to admit. Louis knew that, though.

Nic sighed, aware of his brother's continued scrutiny. "All right, all right. I'll look into it."

Louis smiled, an expression that made people catch their breath, for it was devastating to behold.

"Oh, stow it," Nic said, belligerent now.

"*Very* good, Nic. You sound like a native!"

Nic glowered. It was time for bed.

Two weeks later. Cheapside, London.

Eliza turned to look at her maid, Martha, who was standing, rigid with disgust, in one corner of the dingy room. A sensible, solid woman of perhaps thirty something years, Martha was not used to such distasteful surroundings, having been Eliza's lady's maid for almost a decade now. The woman's gaze darted from the door to the filthy window at increasingly short intervals.

Something scurried in the shadows on the opposite side of the room, and Martha flinched.

"Do relax, Martha dear. We have two burly footmen waiting outside the front door, and there is no other entrance… which I admit might not be a good thing, now I come to think of it. What if there were a fire?"

"A f-fire?"

Martha's eyes widened in alarm and Eliza sighed.

"Not at this second. Good heavens, but you do fret! Oh, bother. It's simply no good, and I had such hopeful expectations for this one."

"Oh, thank the lord," Martha said, letting out a heartfelt sigh. "Might we leave, then, my lady? His grace would have my hide if he were to discover—"

"Martha, I have told you over and again you will not be held responsible for my actions. I would not allow it, and my father would not act so unfairly. I forced you to accompany me, did I not?"

"Yes, my lady, but all the same, you ought not be here in this dirty, dangerous place. Not what with your health being—"

Eliza held up an impatient hand, having heard quite enough about her fragile health. Her own limitations made her wild with frustration, without having them thrown in her face at every opportunity. If she let them, those who loved her best would thwart her plans and keep her safe at home, tucked up by the fire and going out of her tiny mind with boredom.

Martha subsided, though Eliza was aware of the woman's desire to give her a good shake. To her intense annoyance, she felt a wave of fatigue roll over her, depressing her spirits and leaving her limbs heavy and cumbersome.

"Oh, let us go, Martha," she said, defeated, for today at least.

This must be the tenth building she'd looked at in as many weeks. Not one had been a suitable place to begin her school. She'd had high hopes for this one, as it had sounded so promising on paper. It was large enough and not in *such* a dreadful part of London, but it was dark and grim. There was little outside space and the one entrance in and out was not only impractical, but dangerous.

They made their way down the staircase. Eliza ignored the anxious glances Martha sent her and the way she hovered too close, just in case. Instead, she gripped the handrail tightly and concentrated on putting one foot in front of the other, moving slowly. Still, she was out of breath by the time they reached the bottom and emerged outside. The air was hardly sweeter in the darkened alley than the stale stench of rats and disuse inside, but still it was a relief. The footmen fell into step behind the ladies as they made their way back to the carriage.

Eliza grasped her skirts, holding the simple twilled cotton free of the filthy cobbles as they picked their way along the narrow side street and back out upon the main thoroughfare. She had dressed in her plainest gown, hoping not to draw too much attention to herself. As they stepped onto the main street, Eliza blinked at the sky, mole-like, relieved to feel the open heavens above her after the oppressive darkness of the unpleasantly close built red brick. No. It was certainly no good for her charitable school. Her girls would need air and space and light in which to grow, and she would dashed well find it.

She turned towards the carriage and then stopped in her tracks, arrested by the figure watching her on the opposite side of the road. His large, striking frame dominated those around him, rude as a bull in a spring meadow. Eliza's breath caught, stolen by the aggressively masculine sight of Monsieur Demarteau. The icy north wind that tugged at her skirts and fluttered the ribbons of her bonnet snatched away her little gasp of shock. The furious glint in his dark eyes did not help her composure as he stepped into the street, heading directly for her.

"What in the name of God are you doing here?" he demanded, before he was even halfway across the road, without so much as a good morning or an enquiry about her health—not that she would have welcomed that.

"Good morning, Mr Demarteau. How do you do?" she said politely, ignoring his dreadful manners.

"Never mind how I do," he said, practically vibrating with agitation. "How do you come to be in this wretched neighbourhood? Does your father know you are here?"

Eliza bristled, offended and annoyed. "My father does not need to be kept apprised of my every step outside the house. I am a woman grown, sir. I have my maid and two footmen for propriety and safety, and have no need of any further chaperonage."

"The devil you don't," he retorted. "I will see you home."

Eliza opened her mouth to rail at him for his high-handed manner and then stopped. What was she thinking? Though right at this moment she could not for the life of her fathom why, she had longed to see him for weeks and months, and now here he was, demanding to escort her home. It was too good an opportunity to miss. She remembered the last time she'd seen him, over six months ago. He had been as rude and surly as usual, and she had been hurt by it, but then his manner had changed, and he had spoken to her with such concern, such gentleness….

Are you well, Eliza? Truly?

Eliza had been so startled she'd turned quickly around to look and him and her wretched head had spun and she'd almost fainted, much to her dismay. Then he had swept her up in her arms. She recalled the way it had felt in that moment, the way he had lifted her into his arms as though she'd been made of lace and cobwebs, and her heart skittered about in her chest like a mouse pursued by a feline stalker.

Are you well, Eliza? Truly?

His words had been unguarded in that moment, filled with tenderness and anxiety. *That* man. She wanted to know that man, the one he hid behind a mask of rude indifference. She regarded him for a long moment, astonished when a faint tinge of colour touched the harsh planes of his face.

"Very well," she said quietly, acquiescing to his demand.

He did not look entirely pleased that she had done so, that she had not railed against his request, the tightening of his jawline belying his sanguine nod of approval. She placed her gloved hand upon his arm, though he had not offered it, immediately aware of the tension singing beneath her fingertips. She glanced up at him, but he looked ahead, guiding her to her carriage, his face unreadable. Martha's face, by contrast, was far from impenetrable. The maid was rigid with disapproval, her eyebrows drawn together in consternation, and she glared at Mr Demarteau as though he were a theatrical demon with horns and cloven hooves, sprung to life to walk among decent, God-fearing people.

Eliza shot her a look that demanded she stop at once, but Martha only huffed and folded her arms, turning her indignant glare upon the undefended streets of London beyond the carriage window. Once Eliza was settled in her place, Mr Demarteau ducked his head and climbed in, giving the carriage springs reason to sway and bounce as they accommodated his weight. He put his hat to one side, as his head near brushed the ceiling as it was. To her regret, he sat opposite her, beside Martha, who made a performance of shifting closer to the carriage door. If Mr Demarteau noticed, he did not comment or react to the slight. He sat at an angle, his legs too long to do otherwise without their knees touching. Still, Eliza was vibratingly aware of the way her skirts and petticoats brushed his trousers. Her lips twitched as she realised he mirrored her maid's disapproving posture, glaring out at the streets as though they had offended him. His arms were similarly crossed, except Martha's certainly did not bulge with muscles in that provoking manner which must cause his tailor as much distress as Eliza's own nerves, which were all a-flurry.

Stop it, you great ninny, she scolded herself, but to no avail. Eliza forced herself to look out at the streets too, but whatever her companions found so riveting eluded her, and her gaze soon drifted back to the vexing man opposite. Mr Demarteau's hair was thick and curling, utterly black, and the gossip surrounding him suggested his character matched the uncompromising shade. His eyebrows would have done Mephistopheles proud, and the hard line of his jaw was already shadowed with what would be a heavy beard if he allowed it to grow. She sighed over his formidable shoulders, which were wide and robust. Everything about him screamed strength and power. There was nothing soft about this man. He was all hard lines and sharp edges, honed by life to something that seemed to her sheltered mind, dangerous, civilised only by a thin veneer comprised of shiny boots and exquisite tailoring. What would he be without that veneer, she wondered? Unbidden, a tantalising image came to her of the man who sat so close, without the refinement of his elegant clothes, all hot skin and naked lust. Eliza felt heat climb up her throat and burn her cheeks. Naturally, the devil chose that moment to turn his attention back to her.

His eyes lit with some emotion Eliza could not decipher, but she had the unsettling notion he had read her like a blasted book and knew just what she'd been thinking. She swallowed, her mouth dry, her breath coming short, but she refused to look away from him. His eyes were such a dark brown there was little distinction between iris and pupil, but now they seemed a fathomless black, a bottomless sea containing all his darkest secrets, everything she wished to know. The temptation to dive in was so fierce Eliza curled her hands into fists, as though that might stop her from throwing herself at him. Thank God for Martha. If her loyal bulldog of a maid had not been there, Eliza was not certain she could have resisted. Good heavens, the man was a menace. Unsettled and nervous, she licked her lips and felt her heart thud harder as his gaze grew hot and sultry, fixed upon her mouth.

"Goodness, but John Coachman is taking his time. I'm sure this journey does not usually take this long, my lady. His grace will wonder where we've got to and be waiting at the door, no doubt, if he's not already sent out a search party."

Martha's rather desperate speech went some way to dissipating the crackling atmosphere in the carriage, for which Eliza was grateful. Well, she would have been if she'd had an ounce of sense, which she quite obviously did not, for she found herself instead rather irritated.

"Papa is out today, as you well know, Martha. He won't be back until dinner time."

Martha looked mutinous. "Yes, my lady. I had quite forgot."

Eliza turned away from her maid in time to see Mr Demarteau's lips twitch.

"What were you doing in Cheapside?" he asked, which was at least this time a civil enough question, even if it was none of his business.

"I am looking for premises," Eliza said, careful to keep her tone cool. It wouldn't do to let the man know how badly he ruffled her feathers, or how badly she wanted him to ruffle her beyond saving.

"You are going into business?" he asked with a quirk of one thick eyebrow.

She wondered what they would feel like if she smoothed them with a fingertip.

"My lady?"

Eliza dragged her attention back to the conversation.

"Yes. I am going to create a gin palace to rival that of Thompson and Fearon's on Holborn Hill. I hear on a good night they can make a guinea a minute," she said with a guileless expression.

He stared at her in shock for a long moment and then grinned. It transformed his face, turning him from something dark and forbidden into something far, far more dangerous, giving her a glimpse of the naughty child he must once have been. Her heart gave an awkward lurch, like a ship tossed about by an unforgiving sea. Mr Demarteau erupted with a bark of laughter that made her mouth curve irrepressibly up at the corners, no matter how she tried to stop it.

"*Petit diable*," he murmured, so low she barely caught the words.

She watched as he rubbed a hand over his face in what appeared to be frustration. Did she frustrate him as much as he did her? There *had* been something in his words that *could* have been mistaken for affection if one was completely unhinged. Well, that blow to the head she'd suffered when she'd fallen last year must have done more damage than anyone had guessed.

Little devil. It was hardly a compliment. If any lady of the *ton* had been addressed so by their beau they would have been affronted without a doubt, but to Eliza… something warm and happy unfurled in her chest for the first time in six months.

I have missed you.

Available April 2, 2021 - Pre-Order Here: Dare to be Brazen

The Peculiar Ladies who started it all...

Girls Who Dare – The exciting series from Emma V Leech, the multi-award-winning, Amazon Top 10 romance writer behind the Rogues & Gentlemen series.

Inside every wallflower is the beating heart of a lioness, a passionate individual willing to risk all for their dream, if only they can find the courage to begin. When these overlooked girls make a pact to change their lives, anything can happen.

Twelve girls – Twelve dares in a hat. Twelves stories of passion. Who will dare to risk it all?

To Dare a Duke
Girls Who Dare Book 1

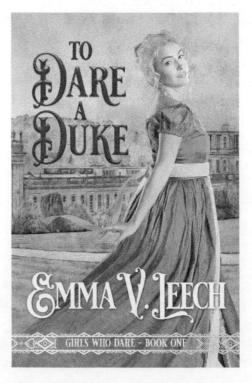

Dreams of true love and happy ever afters...

Dreams of love are all well and good, but all Prunella Chuffington-Smythe wants is to publish her novel. Marriage at the price of her independence is something she will not consider. Having tasted success writing under a false name in The Lady's Weekly Review, her alter ego is attaining notoriety and fame and Prue rather likes it.

A Duty that must be endured...

Robert Adolphus, The Duke of Bedwin, is in no hurry to marry, he's done it once and repeating that disaster is the last thing he desires. Yet, an heir is a necessary evil for a duke and one he cannot shirk. A dark reputation precedes him though, his first wife may have died young, but the scandals the beautiful, vivacious and spiteful creature supplied the ton have not. A wife must be found. A wife who is neither beautiful or vivacious but sweet and dull, and certain to stay out of trouble.

Dared to do something drastic...

The sudden interest of a certain dastardly duke is as bewildering as it is unwelcome. She'll not throw her ambitions aside to marry a scoundrel just as her plans for self-sufficiency and freedom are coming to fruition. Surely showing the man she's not actually the meek little wallflower he is looking for should be enough to put paid to his intentions? When Prue is dared by her friends to do something drastic, it seems the perfect opportunity to kill two birds.

However, Prue cannot help being intrigued by the rogue who has inspired so many of her romances. Ordinarily, he plays the part of handsome rake, set on destroying her plucky heroine. But is he really the villain of the piece this time, or could he be the hero?

Finding out will be dangerous, but it just might inspire her greatest story yet.

To Dare a Duke

Also check out Emma's regency romance series, Rogues & Gentlemen. Available now!

The Rogue

Rogues & Gentlemen Book 1

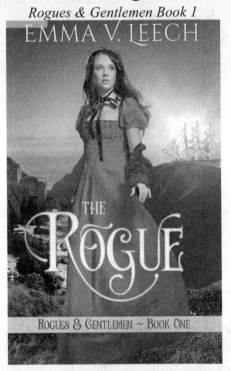

The notorious Rogue that began it all.

Set in Cornwall, 1815. Wild, untamed and isolated. Lawlessness is the order of the day and smuggling is rife.

Henrietta always felt most at home in the wilds of the outdoors but even she had no idea how the mysterious and untamed would sweep her away in a moment.

Bewitched by his wicked blue eyes.

Henrietta Morton knows to look the other way when the free trading 'gentlemen' are at work.
Yet when a notorious pirate bursts into her local village shop, she

can avert her eyes no more. Bewitched by his wicked blue eyes, a moment of insanity follows as Henrietta hides the handsome fugitive from the Militia.

Her reward is a kiss, lingering and unforgettable.

In his haste to flee, the handsome pirate drops a letter, a letter that lays bare a tale of betrayal. When Henrietta's father gives her hand in marriage to a wealthy and villainous nobleman in return for the payment of his debts, she becomes desperate.

Blackmailing a pirate may be her only hope for freedom.

Free to read on *Kindle Unlimited*: The Rogue.

Interested in a Regency Romance with a twist?

A Dog in a Doublet

The Regency Romance Mysteries Book 2

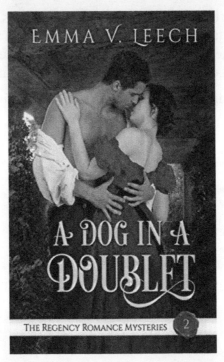

A man with a past

Harry Browning was a motherless guttersnipe, and the morning he came across the elderly Alexander Preston, The Viscount Stamford, clinging to a sheer rock face he didn't believe in fate. But the fates have plans for Harry whether he believes or not, and he's not entirely sure he likes them.

As a reward for his bravery, and in an unusual moment of charity, miserly Lord Stamford takes him on. He is taught to read, to manage the vast and crumbling estate, and to behave like a gentleman, but Harry knows that is something he will never truly be.

Already running from a dark past, his future is becoming increasingly complex as he finds himself caught in a tangled web of jealousy and revenge.

A feisty young maiden

Temptation, in the form of the lovely Lady Clarinda Bow, is a constant threat to his peace of mind, enticing him to be something he isn't. But when the old man dies his will makes a surprising demand, and the fates might just give Harry the chance to have everything he ever desired, including Clara, if only he dares.

And as those close to the Preston family begin to die, Harry may not have any choice.

A Dog in a Doublet

Lose yourself in Emma's paranormal world with The French Vampire Legend series…

The Key to Erebus

The French Vampire Legend Book 1

The truth can kill you.

Taken away as a small child, from a life where vampires, the Fae, and other mythical creatures are real and treacherous, the beautiful young witch, Jéhenne Corbeaux is totally unprepared when she returns to rural France to live with her eccentric Grandmother.

Thrown headlong into a world she knows nothing about she seeks to learn the truth about herself, uncovering secrets more shocking than anything she could ever have imagined and finding that she is by no means powerless to protect the ones she loves.

Despite her Gran's dire warnings, she is inexorably drawn to the dark and terrifying figure of Corvus, an ancient vampire and master of the vast Albinus family.

Jéhenne is about to find her answers and discover that, not only is Corvus far more dangerous than she could ever imagine, but that he holds much more than the key to her heart …

FREE to read on Kindle Unlimited The Key to Erebus

Check out Emma's exciting fantasy series with hailed by Kirkus Reviews as "An enchanting fantasy with a likable heroine, romantic intrigue, and clever narrative flourishes."

The Dark Prince

The French Fae Legend Book 1

Two Fae Princes
One Human Woman
And a world ready to tear them all apart.

Laen Braed is Prince of the Dark fae, with a temper and reputation to match his black eyes, and a heart that despises the human race. When he is sent back through the forbidden gates between realms to retrieve an ancient fae artefact, he returns home with far more than he bargained for.

Corin Albrecht, the most powerful Elven Prince ever born. His golden eyes are rumoured to be a gift from the gods, and destiny is calling him. With a love for the human world that runs deep, his friendship with Laen is being torn apart by his prejudices.

Océane De Beauvoir is an artist and bookbinder who has always relied on her lively imagination to get her through an unhappy and uneventful life. A jewelled dagger put on display at a nearby museum hits the headlines with speculation of another race, the Fae. But the discovery also inspires Océane to create an extraordinary piece of art that cannot be confined to the pages of a book.

With two powerful men vying for her attention and their friendship stretched to the breaking point, the only question that remains...who is truly The Dark Prince.

The man of your dreams is coming...or is it your nightmares he visits? Find out in Book One of The French Fae Legend.

Available now to read for FREE on Kindle Unlimited.

The Dark Prince

Want more Emma?

If you enjoyed this book, please support this indie author and take a moment to leave a few words in a review. *Thank you!*

To be kept informed of special offers and free deals (which I do regularly) follow me on *https://www.bookbub.com/authors/emma-v-leech*

To find out more and to get news and sneak peeks of the first chapter of upcoming works, go to my website and sign up for the newsletter.

http://www.emmavleech.com/

Come and join the fans in my Facebook group for news, info and exciting discussion...

Emma's Book Club

Or Follow me here......

http://viewauthor.at/EmmaVLeechAmazon

Emma's Twitter page

Can't get your fill of Historical Romance? Do you crave stories with passion and red hot chemistry?

If the answer is yes, have I got the group for you!

Come join myself and other awesome authors in our Facebook group

Historical Harlots

Be the first to know about exclusive giveaways, chat with amazing HistRom authors, lots of raunchy shenanigans and more!

Historical Harlots Facebook Group

Made in the USA
Las Vegas, NV
08 August 2024

93507058R00184